"*The Last Way Home* is a touching romance about making mistakes and starting over. Along with the cozy, small town setting and a cast of charming characters, the sparks between ex–hockey player Eli and the secretive, relationship-shy Violet will have you cheering for a happily ever after. Liz Johnson takes you on an uplifting, emotional journey that feels like coming home. I loved it!"

Kathryn Springer, *USA Today* bestselling author of *The Gathering Table*

"If you love sweet romance, second chances, and small-town charm, then this is the book for you!"

Jessica Kate, author of *Love and Other Mistakes*

Praise for *Beyond the Tides*

"Johnson kicks off her Prince Edward Island Shores series with this heartwarming romance. Johnson's fans will eagerly anticipate the next installment of this promising series."

Publishers Weekly, starred review

"Just when I think I'm getting over my obsession of visiting Prince Edward Island, Liz Johnson reels me back in. This novel has a depth and beauty that will make you want to dive into it."

Relz Reviews

The Last Way Home

Books by Liz Johnson

Prince Edward Island Dreams

The Red Door Inn

Where Two Hearts Meet

On Love's Gentle Shore

Georgia Coast Romance

A Sparkle of Silver

A Glitter of Gold

A Dazzle of Diamonds

Prince Edward Island Shores

Beyond the Tides

The Last Way Home

PRINCE EDWARD ISLAND SHORES • 2

The Last Way Home

LIZ JOHNSON

Revell
a division of Baker Publishing Group
Grand Rapids, Michigan

Published by Revell
a division of Baker Publishing Group
PO Box 6287, Grand Rapids, MI 49516-6287
www.revellbooks.com

Printed in the United States of America

Library of Congress Cataloging-in-Publication Data
Names: Johnson, Liz, 1981– author.
Title: The last way home / Liz Johnson.
Description: Grand Rapids, MI: Revell, a division of Baker Publishing Group, [2022] | Series: Prince Edward Island shores ; 2
Identifiers: LCCN 2021052178 | ISBN 9780800737382 (paperback) | ISBN 9780800741495 (casebound) | ISBN 9781493436224 (ebook)
Classification: LCC PS3610.O3633 L37 2022 | DDC 813/.6—dc23
LC record available at https://lccn.loc.gov/2021052178

Published in association with Books & Such Literary Management, www.booksandsuch.com.

Baker Publishing Group publications use paper produced from sustainable forestry practices and post-consumer waste whenever possible.

22 23 24 25 26 27 28 7 6 5 4 3 2 1

For Julia.
Go and chase your dreams.
You are always loved.
And you can always come home.

While he was still a long way off, his father saw him and was filled with compassion for him; he ran to his son, threw his arms around him and kissed him.

Luke 15:20

one

Eli Ross had a black eye, a fractured wrist, and nothing else to his name. It was not the way he'd planned to come home.

Then again, he hadn't planned to come home at all. He hadn't planned a lot of things. Didn't mean they hadn't happened. So here he was, standing in front of the little green house he'd called home until he was nineteen. It had been repainted—at least, the chipped paint on the side facing the bay had been scraped and replaced. The house nearly gleamed in the morning sun.

It still made him feel a little seasick, the memories from the other side of the white door just as fresh as they had been more than a decade before. His father's empty closet. His mom's pinched features. His brother's face twisted with rage.

He shouldn't be here. There was a reason he hadn't been back in nearly eleven years. A reason he'd kept his distance. A reason he'd never settled down and made a home of his own.

He didn't need a home. But at the moment, he needed a *place*. Somewhere to rest his head, to regroup, to be still.

If they would take him back.

He stabbed the fingers of his good hand through his short hair and flexed his other hand beneath the black wrist brace. The spring breeze off the bay carried the almost forgotten scent of salt water and sunshine, setting the clay wind chime on the house's white wooden porch singing. His mom had made that when he was seven or eight. She'd been inordinately proud of it, hanging it where all the neighbors could see it.

The other houses on the small block gleamed just as bright, the sunshine filtering through towering trees and dancing across two-story roofs. Lacy white curtains hung in kitchen windows, and bright welcome mats sat before front doors.

It would be better if he walked away. No uncovering of old sins or confessing new ones. No need for apologies and atonement. No fear that they might send him right back where he came from.

After all, Oliver had told him in no uncertain terms that he wouldn't be welcome back.

Leaving had been his choice. Returning, less so. He had nowhere else to go. And he'd spent his last loonie on the bus that had taken him over the Confederation Bridge and dropped him off along Route 1. He'd walked to Victoria by the Sea without the aid of a map, his feet sure of the way before his mind could be. They'd carried him past the white theater and Carrie's Café, both unchanged by time. They'd taken him down the old, paved street, the center line long faded.

He'd been standing in front of the old house for going on thirty minutes, and if he didn't make a move, one of his mom's neighbors was likely to report him for suspicious activity.

Although if the neighbor recognized him, he might be asked for an autograph—which would be much worse.

"They're not there."

Eli jumped, stumbling off the sidewalk and into the street, his gaze swinging toward a sprite of a woman who had snuck up on him. The top of her dark head didn't quite reach his shoulder, but the angle of her sharp chin and the power of her gaze made it seem like she took up more space than her slender frame actually did.

"Excuse me?" He glanced around. Surely she couldn't be speaking to him. But they were the only two people here.

"They're. Not. There." Her eyebrows rose higher on her forehead with each overly enunciated syllable.

"Who?" But his sinking stomach suggested he already knew. He just didn't know how she did.

He hadn't seen her before in his life. He was pretty sure. He squinted at her, studying the smooth lines of her fair cheeks, the button nose, and the plump pink lips set in a frown. But it was her eyes that convinced him. He'd have remembered that strange shade of brown—half intensity, half serenity, nearly amber.

"You're Eli Ross, aren't you?"

His entire body went rigid except for his hand, which ran down his face and over the early beard he'd hoped would mask his identity. "Have we met?"

She crossed her arms. "I know who you are."

Was he supposed to know her too? He scratched his chin and offered a fake smile, the one the team publicist had coached him to give until it was second nature. Maybe they'd gone to high school together. Truthfully, he hadn't paid much attention to anything beyond the ice. And the girls in the stands at every game.

"Good to see you again," he said.

Her frown turned into a smirk. "Again?"

He swallowed thickly. "For the first time?"

She nodded, quick and sure.

He turned to face her fully. "Then you seem to have the advantage. How do you know me?"

"Oh, I don't assume that I know you. I just recognize your face."

She was talking in riddles that made him want to shake some truth out of her. "But you assume that you know who—or what—I'm looking for." He nodded toward the house.

Her smirk turned sheepish, her nose flaring. "I suppose I do. Only because if I came home after eleven years, I'd probably be looking for my family too."

He nearly growled at her. "There you go again, making assumptions about my life. What makes you think I haven't been back in eleven years?"

"Because your mom misses you."

Her soft comment hit him harder than any opposing player checking him against the boards ever had, and he clenched his teeth, using everything inside him to keep from showing how much he hated those words.

And how much he'd longed for them.

Maybe he'd succeeded in keeping his face from reflecting his reaction. Or maybe he hadn't.

Her lips twitched, and then her whole face softened. "I guess it's really none of my business," she said and turned to walk away.

His hand shot out to catch her elbow, and she spun easily on the uneven sidewalk. "Who are you? How do you know so much about my family?"

Eyes turning serious, she glanced down to where his hand was wrapped around her arm. Her pointed glance back up at him made him drop his grip, and the intensity in her eyes dimmed a fraction. "I don't like seeing my friends hurt."

And he definitely wasn't one of her friends.

When she stepped away again, he didn't try to stop her. Instead, he watched her stroll past the deep purple house with the white porch at the end of the block. Mrs. Dunwitty used to live there—back when the house was brown and Oliver had mowed the old woman's lawn every other week.

She turned the corner and disappeared, and only then did he ask the question he should have from the start. "If my family isn't here, where are they?"

~

By the time Violet Donaghy returned to Mama Potts's Red Clay Shoppe from her midmorning walk, her pulse was racing, her head spinning. She slammed the front door and sank against the wall beside a two-meter wooden shelf. Rows of mugs made from the island's famous red clay rattled in their places, and she reached out to still them.

"Vi? Is that you?" Mama Potts's voice rang through the open door from the studio in the back. It carried a touch of worry, and Violet's heart pounded even harder.

Did Mama Potts know already? Maybe she'd heard the news. Maybe Victoria by the Sea's gossip mill had been hard at work spreading the word, ringing the church bells. Kill the fattened calf. Prepare the family signet ring. The prodigal son had returned.

Eli Ross was back in town.

"Yes." Violet's voice cracked, and she cleared her throat to try again. "It's me." She wanted to ask what Mama Potts had already heard, but she could manage only silence. Something Mama Potts knew well. After all, they'd heard exactly nothing from Eli in the more than seven months since every sports reporter on the continent had announced that he'd been released from his contract with the Rangers and ejected from the National Hockey League.

Not that silence was unusual from him. It was all that Mama Potts, Oliver, and Levi had experienced since Eli took off for his chance at a career in the pros. Therefore, it was all that Violet had ever known from him. Well, silence and the aftermath of heartbreak.

But he was every bit flesh and blood. And piercing blue eyes—despite an impressive shiner. And unruly black hair. And more than a five o'clock shadow at ten in the morning. And broad shoulders.

Not that she'd noticed. Much.

She scowled at herself.

Okay, so he was a broader, handsomer version of his brothers. He was also a selfish, thoughtless—

"I think there's something wrong." Mama Potts had rarely raised her voice in the ten years Violet had known her, but there was an edge to it now, an urgency that sent Violet pushing off the wall.

She weaved between the rows of waist-high wooden bookshelves that displayed countless pieces glazed in bright blues and greens and every other color of the rainbow. She whipped past a stack of purple platters, rattling them as her hip bumped the corner of the shelf. Pain shot toward her knee, but she didn't stop until she'd raced past the built-in counter and through the open door off to the left.

"Are you—" Violet's question and feet both stopped when she saw Mama Potts standing on the far side of their studio.

The older woman looked just fine, small but strong. Her fists were pressed against her hips, and her pretty features were pinched as she glared at the large round kiln in the corner.

Violet placed her hand over the thudding in her chest and tried for a smile. Whatever had made Mama Potts call out couldn't be that concerning. And most likely it did not involve any knowledge of Eli. She hoped.

Then again, that did leave her to share the news—the beans she was not eager to spill. These were family beans, and despite nearly a decade of mentorship and six years in business partnership, Mama Potts wasn't her mom, and Oliver and Levi weren't her brothers.

"What's wrong?" Violet finally asked.

Mama Potts shook her head and kicked the front of the metal kiln. "Something's off. It's—" She stopped at the exact moment the room filled with the acrid scent of burning rubber.

Violet twisted her neck, looking for the source, and shrieked as sparks jumped from the wall beside Mama Potts. Violet raced across the room and had nearly reached her side when the socket kicked out another round of fireworks and the white wall around the plastic plate turned black and charred.

"It's in the wall!" Mama Potts shrieked, grabbing Violet's arm and tugging her back.

But the fire didn't stay there. Flames suddenly burst from the electrical panel on the kiln and lit up the whole room. The morning sun shining through the open garage door made the flames disappear except for the blue at the center, which flickered in the wind.

Mama Potts's hand beat on Violet's shoulder. "Get the—get the—get the—"

Violet ran for the red fire extinguisher mounted below the wooden steps that led to her apartment on the second floor. She fumbled with the release, and when she finally got it open, she spun around just in time to see the flames jump to the wooden shelves that held pieces waiting for their turn to be fired.

Right beside the shelves sat a pile of rags atop a small pallet holding metal cans of glaze mixed with solvents. All with plastic lids.

Her stomach hit the cement slab floor. She tried to scream, but her throat closed.

The wind whipped the fire across the pallet, igniting the rags and melting the lids.

The explosion wasn't like in the movies. Shrapnel didn't go flying. The roof stayed firmly in place.

And the fire was manageable. Until it wasn't. The blaze went from blue to towering orange flames in an instant, consuming everything in its path. Wooden racks filled with months of work burned and then tilted, mugs and plates crashing to the floor. An entire summer's worth of inventory destroyed.

The shock weighed on Violet's shoulders, dozens of kilos pressing her arms to her sides. She couldn't even lift the extinguisher in her hands. Not that it would have helped.

Mama Potts scrambled back from the flames, her heel catching on a worktable and sending her sprawling on the ground. She cried out in pain, cradling her arm against her stomach.

Violet screamed, trying to check on Mama Potts, but her words were lost. She glanced at the extinguisher again but threw it down without any real consideration. The spray it held wouldn't stop the inferno devouring their studio. But at least she could get Mama Potts out safely.

Rushing toward the heat, she squinted into the light as sweat poured down her back. When she reached Mama Potts, she squatted next to her, bracing an arm behind her back. "Here. Get up. Come on."

But when the older woman, her arm still protected in front of her body, braced her foot against the floor and began to push herself upright, she cried out again.

Violet gasped, immediately choking on the smoke and chemicals filling the air. Her lungs burned, and tears rushed to her eyes. "Come on. You have to help me."

Mama Potts coughed, doing her best to scoot across the floor. She cringed with each centimeter, and Violet turned to see how far they had to go to reach the sunshine-covered yard.

Please, let us make it.

She didn't pray as often as she had as a child, but if ever there was an occasion, this was it. She hoped God heard even the desperate cries of those who had almost forgotten how to pray.

Then there wasn't time to think about it. There was only a massive black silhouette in the open door, his arms pumping and his feet swallowing up the ground.

"Oliver!" Violet couldn't help the tremor in her voice as relief rushed through her. His dark head bowed over his mom, and he scooped her into his strong arms. Mama Potts rested her head against his shoulder, coughing into his shirt.

Free of the building and the suffocating smoke, Violet pressed her hands to her knees, savoring the salty tang of the fresh air. The wind dried her tears to her cheeks as she looked back at the building, half of their studio already consumed.

The metal cans glimmered among the flames near the kiln. Right where she knew better than to leave flammable solvents. Right where she'd left them anyway.

This was her fault.

Her stomach heaved, and she gasped for oxygen as sirens split the air. They were still a kilometer or more away, but they were coming. She hadn't called. Neither had Mama Potts. They hadn't had time.

Oliver. He must have called for the firefighters. When she turned to thank him, her insides twisted again. This time she really was going to be sick.

The man gently setting his mom on the ground wasn't Oliver Ross. Or even his little brother, Levi.

In the sunlight and free of the shadows, there was no denying the way his mom cupped his cheek and whispered his name with pure love.

"Eli."

two

Eli had fully forgotten the tenderness in his mom's embrace until this moment, her arms wrapped tightly around his shoulders. Maybe he'd never truly appreciated how sweet it was, how gentle and comforting the words she whispered over him. Like rain after a drought, they seeped into the cracks of his heart.

Perhaps returning to the island had been a good choice. It was his only choice, but maybe it was the right one too.

"My sweet boy. I've missed you. *We've* missed you."

He tried to tell Mama Potts that he'd missed them too. Maybe not right away. He'd been far too foolish as a young man. Far too filled with his own desire to make a name for himself.

Before he could say anything, the wind shifted, covering them with a cloud of black smoke. A deep cough tore from his chest at the same time that a shelf in the studio crashed, and the other woman cried out, stumbling back.

Even beneath the layer of soot covering her face, he immediately recognized her as the one who had given him a tongue-lashing in front of his childhood home. But there wasn't time to ask for an introduction as a fire engine—sirens blaring—pulled into the yard, Victoria's volunteer fire department piling out of the cab. They tapped into the water line and ran meter after meter of hose until their spray covered the flames, tamping down the thick smoke.

The woman beside his mom groaned, wrapping her arms around her narrow waist and folding herself in half. Her chestnut-brown hair hung over her shoulders, cutting off his view of her face. But her muttered pain was clear enough.

"Oh, Vi." Mama Potts let go of him, turning to her friend and seeming to swallow the other woman in her embrace.

Eli stared at the brace around his wrist, their shared moment almost too personal to watch—even if he didn't know why. He coughed again as the smoke billowed away from the flickering flames, turning his back to the blackened studio just as a shiny black truck flew off the highway and skidded to a stop parallel to the fire engine in the little parking lot.

A pretty blonde—all long legs and vaguely familiar—launched herself from the passenger seat. Not even bothering to close the door, she raced toward the women and wrapped her arms around them without giving him a second glance. Mama Potts gasped in pain, which launched a whole new titter of concern.

"What happened? Are you all right?"

When the driver's side door opened, Eli could hear only the ringing in his ears, feel only the flip of his stomach.

Before the driver stepped out, Eli knew—he *knew*—who it was.

He'd also known this day would come. No amount of dreading it or wishing it could be under different circumstances had changed the facts.

His left hand squeezed into a fist, and the motion shot sparks all the way up to his elbow. With a quick shake, he tried to release the tension, but the pain lingered.

Just because he'd known this moment was coming didn't mean he hadn't avoided it for as long as possible. And he sure hadn't anticipated an audience of three chattering women and a half dozen bustling firemen swiftly putting out the flames of what the gas station attendant had told him was Mama Potts's shop.

Still, he couldn't look away from the man leaning out of the truck. His shoulders were broader, his hair longer. But the set of his chin hadn't changed, or the crook of his nose. Eli still remembered breaking it in a backyard wrestling match.

This was his little brother Oliver, nothing between them—except one warning to never return and eleven years of silence.

Oliver didn't see him at first. Or he didn't recognize him. Eli was certain of it.

Oliver was halfway to them before his eyes—the same blue Eli saw every morning in the mirror—flicked up, and he stumbled. He stopped, the features of his face telling a tale. A muscle in his jaw jumped, and his nostrils flared. His black brows pulled into a single line, but he never blinked.

Eli snuck a quick breath, steeling his shoulders and preparing for what was certainly to come.

Oliver opened his mouth but quickly snapped it closed. His gaze darted in the direction of the women, then back to Eli, a battle clearly in play. He could make a scene in front of Mama Potts, or he could wait until they were alone to escort Eli out of town.

Pain shot through Eli's jaw, and only then did he realize he'd clenched his teeth.

Maybe homeless on the streets of New York had been a better choice. He had a feeling the guys serving chicken noodle at the soup kitchens would at least have had a smile to go with it. But they probably would have recognized him too.

How did someone go from the front page of the sports section to taking handouts? From a brownstone in Brooklyn to begging for bread? From dating the latest socialite to hiding under cardboard to keep out of the rain?

He hadn't thought he had a choice, but the look in Oliver's narrowing eyes made him reconsider. He should go back.

Before Eli could take one step, a short man in full turnouts huffed and puffed over to them. His boots clomped on the ground, and he rested his hands on his hips when he stopped. "I'm sorry, Mama Potts."

She looked up, keeping an arm around her younger friend and holding her other arm across her chest. "How bad is it?"

"Not as bad as it could be." He waved a yellow-gloved hand toward the man holding the end of the hose.

Eli hadn't even noticed the water had been turned off.

"Jimmy kept the fire from getting into the shop, and the roof is good. But the studio is in bad shape."

The woman he'd met that morning let out a low squeak before clapping her hand over her mouth. Tears turned her eyes to glass, and she blinked furiously but remained still other than that.

Eli glanced toward the scene. The old garage's frame still

held its shape, but more than half of the interior had been painted with char and ash. The bitter scent drifted with the wind, mocking and pungent.

“It all ” Mama Potts shook her head. “It all happened so fast.”

“We observed what looks to be an accelerant of some kind near the eastern wall.”

The woman let out a terrible sob from behind her hand. “It’s my fault!”

Violet couldn’t stop her hands from trembling and her shoulders from shaking, even when Mama Potts held her close.

“It’s not your fault, hon.”

“Yes, it is.” She couldn’t help the quick glance in Eli’s direction and then in Oliver’s. This was their mom’s love, and Violet had ruined it. Had nearly killed them both. “I’m so, so sorry.”

“It was an accident,” Mama Potts said, adding an extra squeeze to her hug.

Meg, who had arrived with Oliver, patted her shoulder. “You can’t blame yourself.”

Ha. They had no idea. She was a pro—an absolute pro. Blame was her game, and she’d have been called up to the majors at sixteen if there had been a big leaue for such things.

Just watch me.

She almost said the words aloud. And she would have if there hadn’t been a few extra sets of eyes on her—including those of the guy she’d just met that morning, who was staring at her with barely restrained disgust.

She wanted to glare back at Eli—to go toe to toe with him over who had broken his mama's heart more. Sure, Violet had just nearly burned down Mama Potts's Red Clay Shoppe—and her own apartment in the process. But at least she'd stuck around to try to help. She hadn't bolted. And she wouldn't.

Wrapping her arms around Mama Potts's waist, she held on with all of her regrets.

Eli, on the other hand, had the nerve to look at her like he was the good son. Like he hadn't run out on his family when they needed him the most. He'd probably never even felt bad about it.

Okay, that wasn't entirely fair. She didn't know the guy. Between cover stories in *Sports Illustrated* and the gorgeous socialites hanging off his arm in the New York City gossip pages, maybe he'd felt a pang of remorse.

Eli blinked at her, his icy blue eyes still flashing intensely, and this time she met his gaze full-on. He wasn't going to win.

But the truth was, they'd all lost—maybe everything. That punched her in the gut, and she let out a low wheeze, finally looking at the others in her vicinity.

Oliver relaxed the glower he'd settled on his brother to check on her. "Vi? You all right?"

She nodded, then shook her head before the words tumbled out. "We don't have enough inventory for the season now. We don't have enough to keep the store open, and if it closes . . ." She couldn't bring herself to even whisper the words, but they echoed in the corners of her mind. *If it closes, we might never reopen. And it's all my fault.*

Mama Potts squeezed her shoulders again. "It's going to

be okay." But the tremor in her voice bared the truth. She was thinking the same thing.

Tourist season wasn't just their busy season. It was their only season. It was the one thing keeping their little shop afloat. June, July, and August were the only months bringing in income to pay the mortgage on the property for the other nine months of the year.

"Won't your insurance cover rebuilding?" Meg asked. Her teeth clamped down on her bottom lip.

Mama Potts nodded. "Most of it. I hope."

As she spoke, Zeb Gleeson, the volunteer firefighter still standing nearby, looked like he wanted to bolt. Violet had met him at a lobster cook-off the year before, and he'd always waved across the church lawn at her and smiled when they passed in the grocery store aisles. Even after a disastrous date where they'd remained silent for 95 percent of it, he'd been friendly.

The tense line of his lips wasn't as cordial now. The round shape of his usually jovial face held no joy and made her stomach drop.

"Honestly, Zeb, what are we looking at here?" Oliver asked, his hand squeezing Meg's.

Zeb shook his head. "It's not good. It took out most of the east wall. And maybe part of Violet's apartment."

She didn't know why she glanced at Eli just then, but his eyes had narrowed and were filled with something other than ice. Her gaze darted back to Zeb before she could decide what it was. "How . . . is . . . ?"

She wanted to know how much of her stuff had survived. She just couldn't ask the question.

Instead, she went a different direction. "I was using flammable solvents, and I left them out—right next to the kiln. There were rags, and then the fire. And they just went up."

Zeb sighed. "That'd just about do it, I guess. Looks like it did in your shelves too."

Pain gripped her middle, scorching everything in its wake, and she had to work to catch her breath. They barely had a month's worth of inventory in the shop. Even if the insurance came through with a new kiln quickly, they no longer had any pieces ready to fire in it. No pieces, no profit. And that equaled one big problem. One that just kept getting worse.

"Jimmy's going to tape off the building," Zeb said, apparently oblivious to her entire train of thought. "No one in or out until someone from the fire marshal's office signs off."

"How long is that going to be?" Oliver asked.

Zeb shrugged. "They have to come over from Charlottetown. Could be a few days. Or more."

"More?" Meg's voice rose in indignation. "At least let Violet into her apartment to get her things."

"Sorry," Zeb said, his voice laced with regret. "The stairs were hit hard. They're pretty charred. They'll probably be okay, but I don't have the authority to release the scene. You'll have to wait until the inspector takes a look."

Violet opened her mouth to say there had to be some alternative, some way to work around the situation. If the stairs were probably okay, she'd risk it—just to have her own pillow and her toothbrush and maybe a change of clothes. And the pictures tucked carefully under her mattress.

But she couldn't seem to form the words. She was still trying to when a deep voice interrupted her thoughts.

"I'll go in. I'll get her things." Every eye shot to Eli, who held up the brace around his left wrist and shrugged off the attention. "I'm already damaged goods."

Oliver scowled, but Mama Potts turned to Eli and threw an arm around his waist with a hiccupped sob. "Still so sweet."

Oliver muttered an unintelligible word or two under his breath while Meg reached for his hand again and latched on. Which left Violet wholly and undeniably untethered. For a split second she feared a stiff breeze would knock her over. Perhaps it would have once.

It wouldn't any longer.

"If anyone is going in there, it's me," Violet said.

Mama Potts's gaze settled on her. But she could physically feel Eli's, making every bit of her exposed skin tingle.

"What?" She bit out the word a little more sharply than she'd meant to, but something about Eli just wormed its way under her skin. She couldn't exactly be held responsible for her reaction when he insisted on looking at her like that.

"Well, it could be . . ." Mama Potts started, her voice fading off.

With a quick breath and a tight smile, Violet tried again. "I'm perfectly healthy, which is more than I can say for either of you."

Zeb stepped toward Mama Potts, apparently only then noticing the way she favored her right hand. "Were you hurt?"

Mama Potts took on the persona of someone half her age, rolling her eyes clear to the sky. "I just scraped it on the floor. I'll be fine."

"You should check her ankle too. I had to carry her out." There was no bravado in Eli's tone, and what he said was true. Violet never would have gotten Mama Potts out of the fire without him.

Oliver's face flinched, and Violet wanted to pull out her big-sister routine—even if she was younger than Oliver by a year—but this wasn't the place to dig into what he was feeling. Not in front of Zeb and a handful of other firemen stowing their hoses and replacing their gear. And not in front of Eli.

It didn't take a Mountie to figure out the bad blood between the brothers. After all, she already disliked Eli profusely, and all she really knew about him was that he'd broken Mama Potts's heart.

"Ma'am, can you rotate your wrist for me and show me your hand?"

Mama Potts's gaze shot hotter than fire, and her eyebrows nearly reached the hairline of her once-black curls. They had turned gray at some point along the way, but not because of age—she was still young. Probably because of stress. Because of Eli.

Zeb stumbled to correct himself. "Sorry. I mean Mama Potts—not ma'am."

Her face relaxed slowly, then she turned her arm, and all pretense vanished. Her face turned red, a terrible hiss escaping through tight lips. "I'm all right," she managed.

No, she wasn't.

"Let's get you over to the rescue so we can take a better look." Zeb tucked himself into Mama Potts's side and practically carried her forward. Eli looked like he was going to take his mom's other side, but Oliver beat him to it, Meg hurrying after. That left Violet and Eli, alone for the first time. Well, the first time since he knew who she was, anyway.

Perfect timing to tell him she didn't need his help.

Zeb turned around from across the yard, his eyes hard and even his round face unrelenting. "Remember, no one inside the studio until it's cleared."

Eli crossed his arms, the scowl falling back into place. The one that looked a little bit too much like his brother's. "I guess that's that," he mumbled.

Well, it was something. But some things were more important than rules.

three

Eli slid out of the back seat of Oliver's crew-cab truck, his feet hitting the solid red clay—a single patch between the gray gravel driveway and the green grass. A two-story white cottage cast a long shadow to the base of the detached garage, and Eli squinted toward the setting sun.

So this was their new home, the place they'd settled when they were free of his dad. Free of him.

The blue shutters seemed to wave a welcome in the breeze, warm yellow lights glowing in every first-floor window. Quaint. Cozy.

Home.

Something he hadn't had in more than a decade. Something he'd never have again. But his mom deserved it.

Oliver stepped out beside him, his gaze still hard, his tongue still silent.

This reunion was going about as well as his first pro game. All he needed to re-create it was a bloody nose and a loose tooth. Given the look on his brother's face, Oliver would be all too happy to give him both.

His brother disappeared around the front of the cab, quickly joined by Mama Potts and Meg.

Meg Whitaker, Oliver's fiancée.

His brother was engaged. He hadn't stayed the same angry seventeen-year-old kid.

Eli hadn't thought he would. Neither had he pictured his skinny brother bulking up. "Fishing'll do that," Meg had whispered when she caught him staring at his brother in the hospital waiting room while Mama Potts got her arm and leg x-rayed.

Oliver's new bulk would put a lot of the guys in the pros to shame. Even more of them during the off-season when they let themselves go a little. And if Oliver had been anyone else, Eli might have been proud of him. Or maybe if Eli were a better man, he would be.

He scowled to himself as the door on the side of the house flew open and a blur of black hair and blue flannel raced across the grass and scooped Mama Potts into a hug. She kept her casted right arm elevated, but her face relaxed into the shoulder of the tall man.

"I'm fine," she said, her voice muffled against the embrace. "I'm not going anywhere. Just a hairline fracture in my wrist and a sprained ankle. I don't even need surgery."

The dark head nodded above her shoulder, his arms holding tight as the toes of her gray walking boot skimmed the ground.

It wasn't until the other man looked up and their matching blue eyes locked that Eli recognized him. Levi. His kid brother. Who wasn't a kid any longer.

Levi had been barely fifteen the last time Eli saw him. Not

anymore. His lanky frame was still lean, but the angles of his face had turned pronounced, fixed. His shoulders were no longer skinny and slumped. His eyes were hard, as though he'd faced things that no one could possibly know.

Before Eli could formulate even the simplest greeting, Mama Potts turned around. "Look who's home."

Levi nodded once. Nothing warm or welcoming in his features.

The only silver lining—he wasn't obnoxiously glaring as Oliver had been doing for the last few hours.

Eli returned the nod. "Levi." His voice nearly cracked, and he cleared his throat even though he had nothing more to say, nothing else to offer.

Levi didn't seem to feel the need to fill the silence. Instead he looked down at their mom still holding on to his arm with her good hand. With a tilt of his head toward the house, he helped her in that direction, practically carrying her so she didn't have to put any weight on her injured foot.

Before she got more than a step, she paused. "You're staying with us, right, Eli?"

He froze, the weight of Oliver's disgust paralyzing.

"Mom, I think—"

Mama Potts cut Oliver off with a flick of her wrist. "He's staying with us. No arguments." Her gaze swung to all three of her sons. "From any of you."

Eli managed a slight nod. Yes, he'd stay with them. Where else was he going to go? He was as homeless in Victoria as he had been in New York.

"Come on in," she said.

Eli had a feeling he was the only person there who needed

such an invitation, but Oliver's hand clamped on his shoulder and stopped him from following her.

"We'll be right behind you," Oliver said.

Meg raised her eyebrows in a way that seemed to ask if Oliver was going to be okay. That didn't seem fair. Eli was the one with the fractured wrist. Plus he hadn't been in the gym in months. Oliver looked like he could bench-press his own fishing boat. He gave Meg a gentle smile—a hint of the boy he'd been—and she disappeared behind the others.

"What are you doing here?" Oliver didn't even wait for the ref to drop the puck.

Eli held up both hands, brace and all, taking a quick step back.

Oliver's hands dropped to his hips before he locked his fingers behind his neck and stared at the ground. "I didn't think Mama Potts was ever going to see you again."

"What about you?" Oh, man. He was a glutton for punishment.

Oliver looked up, squinting toward the point where the sun met the sea. "I wasn't sure I needed to."

"I guess you said just about everything you needed to the last time we spoke."

Oliver's tongue poked at his bottom lip, his gaze still far off. "Listen . . ."

Eli didn't want to hear whatever Oliver had to say, so he waved him off. He remembered everything his brother had said to him more than a decade before. Even if he had forgotten the words, no number of hits on the ice could erase the memory of the fire in Oliver's eyes or the snarl of his lip.

Eli had been nineteen, Oliver a couple years younger. But

they'd been evenly matched—the same height, the same build, the same stubbornness. Their dad had left, and then a few days later the call came. The chance of a lifetime. It wasn't the Show. Yet. But it was his chance to get there. Maybe his only chance.

They'd met on the lawn of their home—their old house. Toe to toe, eye to eye.

"I'm going. I leave tomorrow." Eli hadn't known how to make the blow any softer. Sure, he knew it would be hard on the family, but they would be all right. Honesty was the best he could offer them. "I won't make much at first, but . . . I have to try."

Oliver's eyes, usually so cool and collected, flamed with something Eli hadn't seen there before. When he spoke, his lip curled with menace, with hatred. "Fine. Go. We don't need you. Don't bother coming back. You're going to break Mom's heart, and it'll be easier if she never sees you again."

Eli had nearly doubled over at the truth of those words. Pride had kept him standing, and it still did now. Almost eleven years, and the tension between them only pulled tighter.

"Oliver, I know what you're going to say."

"Doubt it."

His gaze whipped to meet Oliver's at the muttered words. "What's that supposed to mean? You planning to kill the fattened calf for me or something?"

Oliver scrubbed his face with his whole hand and sucked in a loud breath. "Probably not."

"Figured as much." Something boiled in his stomach. Anger. Regret. Maybe even fear. Eli wanted to analyze it about as much as he wanted to have another run-in with Tony Moynahan. His wrist throbbed, and the cut at the corner of his eye that had only just healed stung.

Coming back to this island had been a foolish idea. Not quite the stupidest thing he'd ever done, but it was right up there.

Dropping his hand, Oliver squared his shoulders, his gaze unwavering. Eli had no choice but to meet and hold it. It took everything inside him not to squirm.

A muscle in Oliver's jaw twitched, but when he opened his mouth, nothing came out. He closed it, and the silence between them could have sunk a ship.

"Go ahead," Eli said. "Say whatever it is you want to get off your chest. Tell me I'm a rotten brother. Tell me to stay away from Mama Potts and your pretty fiancée."

Oliver's head swung toward the closed door, and a smile flirted at the corner of his mouth. "She is pretty, isn't she?"

It was probably a rhetorical question, but Eli nodded anyway. "Can't believe she actually picked you." He wanted to swallow those words right back to where they came from. They belonged to a different relationship, to teenage brothers who ragged on each other. They had no business being thrown about by a prodigal son who showed up without warning.

A full-fledged grin split Oliver's face. "Me neither."

For a moment Eli thought Oliver might have forgotten why he'd held Eli back from going inside, but the light in his eyes when he'd talked about Meg slowly dimmed.

"It's been a long time."

Eli nodded.

"I should have . . ." Oliver clapped a hand to the back of his neck but never looked down. "The thing is . . . Mama Potts has missed you. She was—that is, we were—worried when you didn't come home. After the story broke."

With another nod, Eli steeled himself for the inevitable question. What *had* he done to get kicked out of the NHL?

Only, Oliver didn't ask it. "I think she was worried that if you didn't come home after that, you might never come home. So, why now?"

Eli shrugged. Wishing he had a better response.

The truth. That was probably how he should respond. But admitting he didn't have any other place to go . . . well, that was hard to admit to himself and near impossible to confess to the tight-knit remnants of the Ross family. Especially when it would require revealing his own stupidity.

Oliver didn't fill the silence that followed his question, clearly willing to wait.

The shivers that raced down Eli's arms didn't give him the same option. "It seemed like time."

"Uh-huh. And what are you going to do on the island?"

Eli looked around. He'd almost forgotten he was back on the shore, the gentle clapping of the waves against the red sand beach a familiar evening soundtrack. Yet it felt foreign too, without honking cars and rumbling subways beneath city streets.

The billowing trees and knee-high grass waving in the breeze didn't hold any answers. Neither did the purples and oranges painted across the sky where it met the western horizon. He didn't have a clue what he was going to do.

Except stay as far away from Tony as he could.

"I don't have a plan just yet."

Oliver crossed his arms over his chest. "Well, I guess Mama Potts and Violet could probably use a hand right about now."

"Yeah, Violet . . . What's her story?"

Gaze narrowing, Oliver shook his head. Hard. "Don't even think about it."

"What?" Eli held up his hands in surrender. "I'm not thinking anything."

"That's not what the tabloids said."

"And you trust what's printed on the same page as an article about Elvis's alien love child?"

Oliver didn't bother answering the question. Apparently he did believe those stories. That knowledge stung more than Eli wanted to admit.

"Vi is part of the family," Oliver said. "She filled a hole . . ."

That Eli had left.

Oliver didn't need to say it. The words were as clear as if they'd been written across the sky.

Eli wanted to say he was sorry. He wanted to tell Oliver that he wished he'd never hurt Mama Potts. Any of them. But he couldn't apologize without saying he wished he'd made a different choice. He regretted a lot of things, but playing in the NHL wasn't one of them. It was the best thing that had ever happened to him.

And you'd still be there if you weren't so stupid.

Well, *that* he would apologize for. He already had, more than once. It hadn't made a difference. The commissioner had said he had a zero-tolerance policy. His coach had said they were going to make an example of him.

The league was right to do so.

Shaking off the memories of that last meeting in the commissioner's office and the knot in his chest that always accompanied it, Eli sighed. "Message received. I won't even think about Violet."

"Good." Oliver's eyes narrowed again. "You hurt a lot of people when you took off."

Oliver's words—though softly spoken—hit like the Red Wings' lead defender.

"Even Mama Potts wouldn't forgive you if you ever hurt Violet. She's the daughter Mom always wanted, and she made the Red Clay Shoppe a reality." Oliver dipped his chin, his gaze somehow more direct. "We lost everything—Dad, the house . . . you. Mama Potts weathered it all. And it was mostly because of that woman."

Violet sounded like some kind of superhero. But maybe she was the key to getting back into the whole family's good graces too.

Not that Oliver had been harsh. Not nearly as much as he could have been—had threatened he'd be. But as far as welcomes went, this one hadn't exactly been warm. Sure, his mom had hugged him with all the considerable strength in her little frame. But forgiveness wasn't that easy. One hug, one night under her roof, wouldn't be enough to atone for his sins.

Especially not for Oliver. Levi too, probably.

But the Rosses of Victoria by the Sea had a soft spot. A soft spot with ice and fire in her eyes, porcelain skin, and chestnut hair that shimmered in the sun.

After a long moment of observation, Oliver seemed to decide that Eli could be trusted with Violet and offered a curt tilt of his chin. Then he nodded toward the house. "Come on. Mama Potts will want to grill you about everything. And Levi will want to ignore you."

Eli stubbed his toe—again—and swallowed the sharp cry on his tongue. A flashlight would have been helpful right about now. Or a switch on the wall that wouldn't threaten to burn the whole place down again. But he wasn't an electrician, and he wasn't about to risk another fire, even if it meant putting a toe or two in peril as he weaved his way toward Violet's apartment.

He reached out to feel his way along the top of the wooden table whose leg had just connected with his big toe. While his feelings for the hunk of wood were less than fond, he kept his touch gentle. The tabletop had picked up a fine coat of silt, maybe ash or soot or residue from the island's famous red clay. Rubbing his finger and thumb together, he couldn't tell which it was, so he brought his fingers to his nose. A quick sniff didn't reveal anything more. There was no scent. At least nothing distinguishable beyond the heavy essence of smoke that covered the whole studio.

Glancing over his shoulder, he tried to catch a glimmer of moonlight, but he'd closed the door behind him after ducking under the caution tape. Only a hint of the muted light snuck through the bay door's windows, leaving the furniture mere outlines.

Outlines solid enough to break a toe.

He grumbled under his breath as he gave the corner a wide berth. And immediately tripped over something that didn't budge.

Pain shot up his injured arm as he landed hard on his hands and knees, the cement floor unforgiving. Immediately he cradled his wrist against his chest, hissing against the sparks setting off where both his ulna and radius had been fractured.

Tony Moynahan.

Eli could see his sneering face even now, weeks after Tony had informed him that his payment was past due. He hadn't been able to pay then. Not much had changed except his location.

Pushing himself up with his good hand on his knee, he groaned.

"Who's there?" The hushed cry came from above him, and he looked up into the darkness.

"Who's asking?" He kept his voice low, not wanting to draw attention from beyond the building. Clearly he wasn't the only one with the idea to break in.

"I live here."

"Violet?"

She sucked in a sharp breath, and her silhouette stepped onto a landing at the top of the stairs, their charred outline making them disappear into the darkness even more. "Eli?"

Light erupted, hitting him square in the face and making him recoil. He nearly tripped over the same piece of furniture again. Holding his good arm in front of his eyes, he blinked at the spots that danced there. "You want to put that thing down before I'm injured *and* blind?"

"Not really."

He'd give her points for honesty. He wasn't used to that level of frankness. Nearly everyone else in his life wanted something from him—and they were happy to say whatever it took to get it. He didn't think he'd have to worry about that with Violet.

"How about before someone realizes we broke into a fire scene?"

The light on her phone immediately turned off, plunging them back into darkness. Or maybe that was just his eyes trying to adjust to the change.

"What are you doing here?" she demanded.

"I could ask you the same thing." He took a step forward toward the foot of the stairs, then shot a glare back at the outline of whatever had tripped him. A low table with a flat top. A pottery wheel. Of course.

"I live here. I'm supposed to be here."

"Um . . ." He scratched at his chin, fighting a smile that he'd almost forgotten he had. "I think firefighter Zeb would have something else to say about that."

"Yeah, well, this is where my stuff is. And it's mine." Her voice rose an octave as she spoke. "And—and—you have no business being here."

He climbed the stairs slowly, a hand on the rail and a flat palm against the cinder-block wall. Just in case Zeb's worst fears were realized and the steps gave way. "I figured I could help."

Even in the dim light, he could see her eyes narrow. Or maybe he just imagined it because of the snark in her voice. "Help who?"

"You." Okay, not entirely true. But he didn't know what else to say. Nothing else made sense. Nothing else could possibly explain the ludicrous idea that he hadn't been able to let go of.

"No."

He'd almost reached the top of the stairs, only three below where she stood on the small landing, her glare nearly palpable. He looked her directly in the eyes as he challenged her response. "No, what?"

"Just no. Just . . ." Her hand waved toward the door he'd snuck through. "Just . . . you don't even know me. I don't know why you're here, but it's not to help me. It probably isn't to help anyone but yourself."

He wasn't sure what they were talking about anymore. Was "here" the fire scene? Or was it the island? Or back in his family's life?

Worse, she was right. The whys behind his return and all those questions were at least partially selfish.

But what was a guy supposed to do when he had nowhere else to go? And if he hoped that by helping the brown-eyed girl pick up a few of her things, he'd begin building a bridge between him and his brothers . . .

It was a stupid idea on the surface. It was probably a stupid one deep down too. But so far it was the only idea he had.

His family all seemed to love Violet—a whole lot more than they loved him. Well, Mama Potts and Oliver at least. He'd barely seen Levi, who had said exactly zero words in his presence. But if Eli had to wager on it, he'd guess that Levi's feelings would land in the near vicinity of their mom's.

Hence, a late-night trip to the scene of the fire. A chance to start winning them all over again.

Eli lifted his foot and rested it on the next step up, leaning toward her. "I only thought I could help. Since I'm here . . ." He shrugged one shoulder. "Might as well let me."

"And just what did you think you were going to do when you got here? Rifle through my underwear drawer or something?"

All right, his plan might have lacked any real forethought when he'd snuck off the couch and out of the house after Mama Potts turned off her light. Clothes had not made it on his list. "Of course not. I was just going to grab a few essentials—your pillow, your electronics, your pictures."

Her shoulders jerked taut, her head snapping up. "My what?"

"Pillow," he said softly. "But now that you're here, you can do all the rifling, and I can do all the hauling. Just consider me your packhorse."

Her eyes darted in the direction of his wrist. "An injured pack mule."

"Horse. I believe I called myself a *horse*."

"I know what you said, and I meant what *I* said."

He snorted an unexpected laugh. "Whatever you need me to be."

If he'd thought she was going to roll out the red carpet, thank him profusely for his assistance, and invite him into the smoke-tinged haze of her room, he was sorely mistaken. Instead, she did her best Superman impression, hands on her hips, angled elbows filling the space between him and her apartment.

Eli straightened his bent knee, fully rising to the second step. Violet glared at him. He didn't need any light to recognize the tension coming off her in waves.

He moved one foot back down a step. Her glare didn't decrease.

"I get the feeling you don't like me very well," he said.

"I get the feeling you're not used to people not liking you."

True. Up until several months before, he couldn't have named a single person who didn't like him. Save his brothers and maybe his mom. And it was a lot easier to forget that they hated him when he didn't see them.

Avoided them.

Semantics.

Everyone else in his world—his coaches, his teammates, his girlfriends—all loved him. Well . . . *love* was a strong word. Maybe not quite *love*. But they sure liked it when he splurged for a round of drinks and hosted poker nights at his townhouse. They liked him.

Violet did not.

That made his skin crawl. It made his scalp itch and his throat burn. It made him feel like he was wearing pads three sizes too small.

He was not a bad guy. Despite a very loud and irrational phone call from his ex, Lauren. Despite the rumors in the locker room. Despite that look on his coach's face when he'd learned the truth.

He hadn't set out to hurt anyone. This was a step in showing them that. Including surly Violet.

"Just let me help you." He tried for a dazzling smile. "I promise I won't drop anything."

She was pure ice. Colder than a rink. "I don't need your help. You can go home."

He nearly coughed on her use of the word. Home was a bit of an ethereal concept at the moment, even if his mom had offered him a place to crash on her couch.

"Or I could help you?"

She marched down the stairs that separated them, stopping right in front of him. She carried with her the scent of soap, subtle and clean and just powerful enough to break through the charred memories that haunted the building.

"Why are you being so stubborn?" she asked. "I know who you are, and I know what you did."

He nearly fell down the stairs, because for a split second he thought she might really know it all. All the stupidity. All the arrogance. All the darkness.

He wanted to clarify, to ask the depths of her knowledge, but the words couldn't make it past the lump in his throat. So he turned and did what he did best. He left.

four

When Eli's form finally disappeared through the doorframe and into the yard, Violet ducked back into her once sanctuary. The wooden walls of the single room, painted white, shone even in the darkness. They had always reminded her of an old farmhouse. Even though she'd never lived in one, she'd liked the idea. She'd liked the possibilities. Secluded. Remote. Hidden. The clean walls had felt like a reprieve from the messiness of her art. The messiness of life.

Now all she could smell in her little studio apartment was the scent of her mistakes. And all she could hear were Eli's sweet-talking pleas to help.

Sinking onto the edge of her bed, she held her face in her hands. She'd been too hard on him. Maybe he really did just want to help.

Or maybe he was trying to worm his way back into his family's good graces. Sure, technically they were *his* family, not hers. But wasn't ownership something like nine-tenths of the law? She'd staked her claim. She'd put in the hours. She'd been there for them when he hadn't.

Yes, she'd needed Mama Potts's well of kindness. She'd needed little brothers to tease. She'd needed to belong. But they'd needed her too.

Eli Ross had no business waltzing back into their lives like he belonged. Like he had a right to show up at her apartment without even asking.

She jumped up when the phone in her pocket rang, and quickly answered it. "Meg?"

"Vi." Meg sighed her name with all the empathy and sorrow that family could. Well, nearly family. Two months and three days to go. Meg would be a Ross then.

"Hi." It was all she could manage to get out, and she was afraid it sounded like that too. But anything more and her bottom lip would start to quiver. Unacceptable.

"Where are you? Do you need a place to stay? Oliver said that Mama Potts has a place for you, but I don't know where, especially with Eli staying there. And I know Eli isn't staying with Oliver."

Violet nearly laughed at the mental image of Eli bunking with Oliver in his tiny apartment over the garage at Mama Potts's place. The way Oliver had been glaring at his brother—well, they were liable to do more damage than a fire if someone forced them to share a room.

"No, Eli is sleeping on the couch." And the fact that his tall frame wouldn't fit on the short sofa made her smile.

"Oh my! That's going to be . . . interesting." They shared a laugh, but when Meg spoke again, her voice had turned serious. "Where are you staying?"

"I'm . . ." Violet stood and turned around the room, the sinking truth settling into her stomach. She'd hoped to stay here. But even if she managed to stick around without being caught by the fire marshal, she couldn't fall asleep beneath blankets that smelled of her own failure.

"Great. You'll stay with me. I have a very comfortable pull-out couch. Okay, it's pretty comfortable. Fine, it's a little lumpy. But it's clean."

"I can't tell if you're trying to talk me into staying with you or out of it."

Meg scoffed. "I'm not trying to talk you into anything. I've already decided."

Violet tossed a suitcase on top of her made bed. "Isn't this usually my role?" She had been playing the part of big sister—and all the bossiness that went with it—for years. When Meg joined the family—permanently attached to Oliver's hip—she'd fallen into step with the younger Ross brothers. Until now.

"Well, it is when you're making good choices."

With a low chuckle, Violet tossed a handful of T-shirts and several pairs of jeans from the distressed green dresser into her bag. "I'm going to take that to mean that I'm not making good choices at the moment."

"Only if you decide to argue with me." Meg paused for a long second. "Besides, I don't even know what decisions you're currently making. What are you doing right now?"

Violet tried to come up with something that wasn't exactly a lie but also wasn't entirely the truth. But there was no way around the whole truth. "I'm packing up a few things."

"At your apartment?" Meg's voice rose in disbelief.

"Yes."

"All by yourself?"

Violet glanced around the dimly lit room, trying not to

think about how Eli's presence lingered long after he was gone. "I am now."

"What does that mean?"

"Um . . ." Her tongue stuck to the roof of her mouth. It shouldn't matter that Eli, who she'd known for exactly twelve hours, had been to her apartment. He hadn't even made it inside. So why was it so hard to say his name?

"Was Mama Potts over there?"

"No." She bolstered herself with a deep breath. "Eli."

"*Eli*, Eli?" Meg's voice went comically high, and Violet could picture her eyebrows raised all the way to the hairline of her blond ponytail. "As in, the prodigal son extraordinaire?"

"He's the only Eli I know."

"What was he doing there?"

She had absolutely no idea. Sure, he'd said he was there to help her out, but there was something deeper. Something he hadn't confessed. Something she had a feeling he desperately wanted to.

He was up to something, and she wasn't going to fall for it. Whatever it was.

"Oh, something about picking up some of my stuff for me."

Meg let out a surprised pop of breath. "Did you know he was going to be there?"

"Nope."

"And he was just going to throw your underclothes in a bag and bring it to you?"

Violet snorted as she dug through the very drawer of unmentionables and tossed handfuls on top of her T-shirts. "That's what I said. Weird, right?"

"So weird. What is he up to?"

"I have no idea, but I sent him on his way before he could touch any of my things." Even if he'd said he only wanted to get her pillow and her electronics—and her photos.

The backs of her eyes burned. He'd meant the framed ones of Aunt Tracy on her walls. He didn't know about the others. No one did.

After collecting the pictures, she tossed her e-reader into her purse. When she pulled the charger free of its socket beside the three-legged stool that served as a nightstand, sparks shot from the plug.

Maybe Zeb had a point.

Meg must have heard her zipping the bag closed. "I'll be right there to pick you up."

"No." The single word was far too fast for the kind offer, and Violet scrambled to cover her mistake. "I'm fine. I'd like to walk tonight. It'll be nice to breathe air that doesn't smell like glaze fumes and smoke."

"If you're sure."

Violet mumbled an agreement before assuring Meg she'd see her soon and hanging up.

Pillow, blanket, and purse piled on top of the upright suitcase, she took another quick look around to make sure she hadn't forgotten anything. And to make sure she was still alone. The corners of the room only held shadows. Putting her shoulder against the mattress, she slid it away from the box spring, easily finding the small tear she'd made there. She slipped her hand inside. Her fingertips immediately bumped against the metal box before she wiggled it free. It had been months since she'd looked at the tokens inside, years since she'd begun collecting them.

In the darkness, in the aftermath of another mistake that could still cost her everything she loved, Violet couldn't bring herself to open the lid, its tiny hinges as rusted as the day she'd found it in Aunt Tracy's attic. Her hand gliding across the rounded corners, she closed her eyes and tried with everything inside her not to see the faces on the pictures inside.

Still the smiles flashed across her mind's eye, the memories so vivid of a time filled with joy and life. Before the accident. Before the darkness.

She didn't need to keep the pictures. But she couldn't bring herself to throw them away. Neither could she answer the questions they would surely bring if anyone found them.

Her little would-be farmhouse haven wasn't hers anymore. At least it wouldn't be as long as the fire marshal was still investigating. As long as they weren't sure the studio was safe.

Clutching the box to her chest, she wheeled her suitcase through the tiny kitchen and past a small round table with only one chair, through the door, and onto the charred stairs. The wheels clicked and clacked down each step, nearly bouncing her pillow over the railing to the floor below.

It was darker when she reached the bottom, but she had long ago memorized the maze of furniture, and she made her way toward the shelves of tools near the sink under the stairs. Mama Potts had taught her how to clean them after every use, how to take good care of her tools so they took good care of her. But at the moment, she needed a tool not to shape the island's red clay into a mug or vase but to create a hiding place.

With a practiced motion, she brushed her fingertips along the tops of the tools until she found the right wooden forming tool. It was flat but sturdy, its end coming to a sharp angled point. It would do just fine.

Outside, the air smelled of sea salt and wind, grass and moonlight, and she sucked in a deep breath as though she'd forgotten what freshness was. Tall trees left shadows across the yard, and she kept to the darkness. Not that anyone was watching her. She checked again to make sure.

Picking the biggest tree in the yard, its roots weaving a map through the ground at the base of its trunk, she knelt. Between two large roots, she found an empty place, the soil moist and rich, and she dug into it with her little tool, scraping and clawing at the earth until the hole was wider than her hand, her fingernails caked with the reddish dirt. Then she wrapped her little treasure in a plastic bag and tucked it into the hole. She wasn't entirely sure the box qualified as a treasure. It wasn't anything extraordinary or special, except to her. And she'd rather forget what it reminded her of anyway.

But she couldn't afford for someone to find it, for anyone to ask questions about the family in the pictures inside the box. They would expect answers that she couldn't—wouldn't—provide.

After filling in the hole and packing down the dirt, she pushed herself up and went back inside to wash her tool and her hands. Then she pulled her suitcase down the gravel drive toward the road and ambled in the direction of Meg's place in town, the church's white steeple peeking out above the treetops.

If only the memories could be so easy to walk away from.

Eli held out his elbow for his mom, who clasped it like she never intended to let go and led him toward the crowd of curious gazes at the big wooden door to the church.

But it was the gaze behind him that he could feel boring into the back of his skull. Violet wasn't particularly large, but she had built up a full-size loathing for him in what had to be record-breaking time. They'd met exactly seventy-two hours before, and she'd done a pretty great job of ignoring him for about seventy of those hours.

Not that he was trying to get her attention. He had more important things to think about. Like trying to figure out what on earth he was going to do now.

Shaking off the tangible weight of Violet's glare, he plastered a smile into place and focused on the familiar old building. The outside of the church looked just the same as it had when he was young. White wooden walls tapered toward the steeple, broken up only by the big windows on the east and west sides, framed with wooden grids. The lush green lawn at the front and side of the building hadn't changed much either, save for more shade from the birch trees that had doubled in size in his absence.

It was the inside that had changed. Or rather the faces of the people in the pews. Once-little children had become young adults. Mature faces had gained a few more wrinkles, eyes turning a little paler, hair a little whiter.

Then there was the sound. As a kid, he'd sat in these pews every week, the silence nearly deafening. So eager for the scrape of blades on the ice, the crash of pads against the boards, and the roar of the crowd, he'd closed his eyes and gone there in his mind. But now a low buzz filled every corner of the sanctuary, reaching to the tallest point of the vaulted beams. Whispers spun and slid from pew to pew, hands ineffectively raised to cover them. Gazes not even attempting to be coy.

Eli felt the weight of every single pair of eyes and knew the questions the people asked even without meeting their stares. They wanted to know why he was back after so long. They wanted to know if he intended to stay this time. And they wanted to know what he'd done to be expelled from the NHL. Those were the same questions in his mom's eyes.

He just didn't want to answer them.

"Eli Ross."

A big hand clapped on his arm, and Eli jerked to a halt in the aisle between the ends of two wooden pews. He snapped his head around to look into the face of Walt Whitaker. Oliver's soon-to-be father-in-law.

"Mr. Whitaker," he said with a quick nod, already braced for the questions to hit.

"Ah, now, it's just Whitaker to everyone who knows me. We're about to be family." He winked at Meg, who strolled up to him and rolled her eyes at her dad.

Eli offered her a silent dip of his chin, and she smiled in return. But it never turned soft or inviting. Her lips were tense, her eyes narrowed.

Maybe Oliver had told her about Eli's last night on the island. About how Oliver had begged him to stay or to forget the way home. About how Eli had left anyway.

Or, worse, what if she'd figured out why he'd had to leave New York?

His stomach cramped like he'd taken a stick to the gut.

What if Oliver and Mama Potts knew the truth too? He risked a glance in his mom's direction, but her hand hooked into his elbow hadn't budged. Neither had the radiant smile on her face.

He let out a quick breath just as the piano player banged out an opening chord.

Whitaker patted his arm again and said, "It's good to have you back," as he slipped into the row in front of them. Meg scooted to her dad's side. Oliver sailed in, bypassing the Ross family row in favor of sitting beside his fiancée, barely looking in Eli's direction.

Eli sat beside Mama Potts. Well, she pulled him down next to her anyway. Levi was on her other side, Violet on Eli's.

As the music began in earnest and a thin man at the front of the room began singing, Violet reached for the hymnal tucked into the pew before them. When Eli leaned over to read the words he didn't remember, she put a stiff shoulder between them and tilted the pages away.

He leaned closer. She scooted farther.

He closed the gap between them, and if a scowl could make a noise, he heard hers. Her eyes were lasers. Message received.

He pressed in even more, surrounded by the smell of soap and something sharp and tangy.

"Get your own," she whispered between clenched teeth, nearly burying her nose between the yellowed pages. Her lips moved to the lyrics, but her melody was lost among the others singing.

Tempted to push just a little harder, he closed the distance between them a fraction of an inch, only then catching the gaze of a wide-eyed, freckle-faced kid in the row behind them. He wasn't even pretending to sing along with the song in the book his mom held before them. Because Eli was disrupting him.

Maybe he didn't deserve to be back in this place, but he sure wasn't going to distract an innocent child. Shifting back and turning to the front, Eli tried to pay attention to the words of the hymn. Until Violet took a deep breath. Then he could think of nothing else but what he could possibly have done to make her hate him so.

There were plenty of girls back in New York who had reasons—good reasons—to hate his guts. But none of them had started off that way. No girl had ever seen his smile, seen his sweater, seen his Stanley Cup ring, and scowled in return.

All he had left was his smile—and maybe it wasn't enough to earn him one in return. Maybe he wasn't enough.

He glanced at Violet again, her back straight and chin lifted. She didn't deign to look in his direction.

Eli hadn't planned to spend the entire service thinking about Violet, but when the pastor closed his Bible and bowed his head, he realized he'd missed the whole sermon. He'd also missed his only chance for peace. While the pastor had preached, no one whispered about Eli, no one speculated about what had happened.

The second the pastor's prayer ended, so did the reprieve. Before he could duck toward the exit, two women hustled in his direction, effectively blocking Violet's escape. She glared over her shoulder at him to let him know just who she blamed for that, and he shot her an unapologetic smirk.

"Eli Ross?"

He hadn't even opened his mouth to respond to what he assumed was a question from the taller of the two women when the other dived in.

"We can't believe you're back, and it's such perfect timing. The team is just falling apart without a coach, and it's so sad. I mean, they weren't ever going to win provincials, but shouldn't they get to win at least one game? And—"

Eli held up his hand to stop the rush of words spilling out of the woman's mouth. "What?"

The woman, who had dark hair and even darker eyes, smiled as though he hadn't interrupted her, and he had an immediate desire to rewind time. Or run as far as he could.

"Our team, the Stars. Their coach. The timing is just perfect. I mean, it couldn't be better. You just have to."

He blinked, still not sure what it was exactly that he *had* to do.

"Hush, Ellen. Don't scare him off." Her friend elbowed her in the side before turning her gaze to him and employing what she clearly thought to be a convincing smile. It wasn't.

Eli risked a glance at Violet, who didn't even try to cover her smug grin. "Yeah, Eli. The timing couldn't be better."

Holding up his hands, he began to shake his head, but Ellen's friend grabbed his arm. "You probably don't remember me. I'm Mable Jean Huxley. You went to school with my boy Branden."

A faint outline of a skinny boy with a blond mullet took shape in his memory, and he nodded, forcing a polite smile. "Of course. So nice to see you." He patted her hand on his arm. "If you'll just ex—"

Mrs. Huxley's grip only grew tighter. It wasn't going to be that easy to escape. "Please. Just hear us out. We need you."

The glee in Violet's eyes deepened with every passing second. Even when Ellen stepped back, unblocking the row's exit, Violet didn't move, her eyes dancing with delight as they bounced back and forth between him and the older ladies.

Mama Potts was still at his back but in an animated conversation with Whitaker. Which meant he was left on his own in the middle of a power play he didn't fully understand.

"Mrs. Huxley, I'm sorry. I don't think I can be—"

"Yes! Yes, you can. We *need* you." She batted her lashes at him. "And call me Mable Jean. Really. Everyone does."

His stomach sank, his grin faltering. Maybe he should at least hear them out. What could it hurt? Except he already knew his answer. Whatever they were looking for him to do, he couldn't do it. He wouldn't do it. He'd given up on hockey.

Or maybe hockey had given up on him.

It was his own fault. His own stupidity. His own arrogance. And he wasn't about to open that door again.

With a slow shake of his head and a regretful frown, he said, "I'm sorry, ladies. I'm not your guy."

"But it won't take that much time," Ellen rushed to say. "The spring season is half over anyway, and sure, they're not the best bantam team in the Maritimes. But they try hard. It's just for six more weeks, and the Stars deserve a coach like you."

He snorted at that, drawing frowns from the older ladies and a smirk from Violet, whose brown eyes glowed nearly gold.

Of course they wanted a coach. But he definitely wasn't their guy. If they'd had a clue about his past, there was no way they'd put him in charge of some impressionable teenagers.

"I'm flattered. Really." He pressed a hand over the buttons of his borrowed shirt and stretched his shoulders against the confines of the cotton, wishing Levi was just a little broader. "I'm sure you have a great team, and I wish them all the luck, but I'm not a coach. I'm a—"

He nearly swallowed his tongue. He *had been* a player. He wasn't anymore.

Gaze dropping to the brace on his wrist, he lifted his arm. "I'm still healing."

Mrs. Huxley's eyes went wide as though she'd only just noticed his injury. "What happened?"

A well-placed boot. And the weight of the man standing in it.

He wasn't ready to be that honest. He wanted to blame it on the game. But even in Victoria—maybe especially in Victoria—they would have heard that he hadn't played in more than seven months. "An accident."

"Well, New York is a dangerous place." Ellen patted his good arm. "But what better place to recover than here at home, and to help out the local team? Remember when you were playing for the home crowd?"

"Yeah, Eli. Remember?" The smooth line of Violet's jaw twitched as her voice danced up an octave.

It was like she wanted him to coach those boys. But he couldn't come up with any reason why she would. More likely she didn't care one whit. She just liked watching him squirm.

Catching and holding her gaze, he squared his shoulders and forced himself to be absolutely still, despite two pairs of scrutinizing eyes on him. "There's got to be a dad or uncle or someone better qualified."

"Hardly." Mrs. Huxley ran a hand over her graying hair. "Just think what you can teach them."

"I never was very good at school." He tried for a chuckle that fell flat.

"It's not like you have to teach them to skate. Most of them have been on the ice their whole lives." Mrs. Huxley's folded hands were nearly at her chin, her pleading reaching orphan-Oliver levels.

Bantam minor hockey. That was for thirteen- and fourteen-year-olds.

"They know the game," she continued. "But without some real leadership, some strategy, they don't have any hope." She took a deep breath. "We just don't want them to be discouraged—you know, if they don't win any games this season. Maybe you could help the ones who have a future."

He felt the gut punch. He remembered how important those years, those coaches had been for him. Traveling teams. Scholarships. The pros. These boys had big dreams. Every kid growing up on skates did.

But he wasn't a coach, and he couldn't help them. He was no one's idea of a role model, and he sure couldn't teach them how to make the right decisions.

Ellen leaned closer and glanced around as though to make sure no one else was listening. "Do you have another job lined up? Are you going to be playing again?"

His throat burned, and the backs of his eyelids felt like sandpaper as he blinked. No. He was not going to play. And he'd repeat those words to himself a million times until they didn't feel like he was losing a limb.

"You must have had so many offers," Mrs. Huxley said,

clearly not concerned about being as subtle as her friend. "We know we're only local, but this is your hometown team."

"I'm sorry. I'm sure you'll find someone—"

Suddenly his mom's hand slipped around his elbow. "Ellen and Mable Jean, you're not trying to guilt my son into coaching your team, are you?"

"Of course not, Debi." Ellen rolled her eyes just enough to let Mama Potts know how much she didn't appreciate being called out on exactly what she was doing.

His mom's interruption was precisely the excuse he needed. "I'm sorry, ladies. I'm not available. I'll be helping Mama Potts rebuild the studio for the next several weeks."

"You will?" Joy threaded through Mama Potts's words.

"You will?" Violet repeated with significantly less enthusiasm.

Eli couldn't hold back a smug grin in Violet's direction. "Where else would I be?"

five

From the exterior, Mama Potts's Red Clay Shoppe didn't look like much had changed. The blue paint on the wooden-shingle siding practically glowed in the morning sun, a near reflection of the cloudless sky. The red sign hanging from the eaves swung with the playful breeze. White shutters framed the matching cheerful windows on opposite sides of the white door. Even the view through the window in the top of the door beckoned, an invitation to come inside for a visit, to take home a custom piece, a memory of a sweet island visit.

Except the sign in the window had been flipped to CLOSED.

"Fire marshal's office, this is Bigsby."

Violet fumbled her cell when the gruff voice interrupted the repetitive hold music she'd been listening to for several minutes. Nearly dropping the phone, she screeched as she shoved it back against her ear.

"You all right?"

"Hi. Yes. Hello." She panted the words, sounding about

as put together as the charred insides of the building before her. "This is Violet Donaghy. I'm calling about the—"

"The Red Clay place." His words came out clipped, wedged together to fill as little space as possible.

"Yes, I—"

"I haven't done my inspection yet."

"Right. Yes. I know." A gust of wind blew her hair into her face, and she wrestled it out of the way. "Do you know when you *will* be out for the inspection?"

Some papers rustled on his end of the line for only a split second. "Looks like it'll be at least a few days."

Days before she could move back in. Days before she could begin rebuilding the studio and replacing the inventory lost to the fire. Days before she'd even be able to evaluate how much she had to do. On her own.

Mama Potts was in no condition to pitch in. Not with her sprained ankle and broken wrist. And they couldn't afford to wait. Every day was lost inventory. Lost revenue.

And every day without the work of the studio left Violet's mind with far too much time to wander back to another mistake, another regret.

"Is there any way to get us on your schedule sooner? I mean, we really need to get the insurance agent out here, and the—"

"You and every other person who's experienced fire damage."

Violet snapped her mouth closed, swallowing quickly against a suddenly dry mouth. "You're right. I'm sorry. I just—is there anyone else in your office who might be available sooner?"

"No."

Give this guy an award for most succinct.

She shoved her fingers across her scalp, her eyes darting toward the cloudless blue sky. "Well, is there anything you can tell me?"

More rustling papers and a thunk of what sounded like a coffee mug against a wooden table. She knew that sound well.

"The report is pretty straightforward. Electrical fire. Damage to interior walls and wooden structures. Unlikely there's damage to the cement foundation. Accelerant on the premises."

Her stomach heaved, and she wrapped her arms around her middle.

Mr. Bigsby tapped an impatient rhythm on the other end of the line. "If there's nothing else, Miss Donaghy . . ."

She didn't want to ask the question, but sometimes it was better to step into the light. "That accelerant . . . How much worse was the fire because of it?"

"What do you mean?"

"Would the fire have been that bad if there had been no accelerant?"

The tapping stopped, and for the first time, he let silence linger. "Ma'am, it's fire. It's always bad. Did the accelerant help the situation? No, definitely not. Did it make it worse? No one can know for sure. But here's what I do know for sure." A smile rang through his words. "Everyone got out safely. There were no critical injuries. And after twenty-seven years in this office, I can assure you—buildings can be rebuilt. Things can be replaced. People can't."

That was a lesson she'd learned long ago, but the reminder still paralyzed her tongue. She managed only a mute nod as he assured her he'd be out to make his inspection as soon as he could.

Her phone had been silent for several long seconds before she fully realized it. She finally shoved it into the back pocket of her jeans and blinked away old memories and fresh accusations.

"What are you thinking about so hard there?"

Violet jumped, her skin immediately crawling at the deep voice in her ear. She swung at Eli, mostly out of surprise. Maybe a little bit to wipe that smug grin off his face.

"Good morning to you too," Eli said as he dodged her arm. "Didn't sleep well?"

She narrowed her eyes and ignored his question. "What are you doing here?"

"I told you yesterday. I'm going to help you get the shop back up and running."

"I don't recall saying I needed your help."

He looked around exaggeratedly, his eyes scanning the horizon past their nearest neighbors. "I don't see anyone else here." He paused his survey and crossed his arms, head tilting side to side. "Where's your car?"

She bit back the threatening scowl. "I don't have one."

"Why not?"

She swallowed the memories, debating if she should steer the conversation elsewhere. But if Eli had proven to be anything, it was stubborn. "I don't drive."

He snorted—part chuckle, wholly disbelief.

"It's not like you have a car," she said.

"Yeah, but I live—I lived—in the city. I had a driver when I needed one."

"Oooh. A driver." She singsonged the words, but she couldn't quite cover the punch this revelation brought.

He didn't pick up the bait, only dropping his hands to his hips and leaning a little bit closer. "So, why don't you drive?"

"I just don't." She had nothing more to say on that topic, so she marched toward the shop, rounded the side, and headed toward the studio. The smell of smoke and the remnants of fire stung her nostrils. But the blue wall remained unscarred, its only wounds internal.

She forced herself not to dive into that thought, to analyze how similar her own injuries were or how the fire seemed to bring them to light.

Eli's steps were quick behind her. "I'm going to get you to spill the story."

She stopped, and he bumped into her back, his body too big, too firm, too warm. Spinning so she was right under his chin, she glared up. "You think you're something else, don't you? Well, you're not fooling me, Eli Ross. I'm not one of those girls from the city, hanging on your every word. So you can go back to—to—wherever you call home and leave me be."

His smile dimmed, and for a fleeting moment, she thought her words might have hurt him.

Before she could apologize, his grin returned.

With a sigh, she turned her back on him, opened the studio door, and ducked under the caution tape. Eli followed her like a shadow.

Inside, in the light of day, the damage was worse than she'd remembered. Dark dust motes danced in the beam of light through the garage door's upper windows, a spotlight on the charred remains of half the building. Tears jumped to her eyes, and she sniffed them back.

"Aren't we supposed to wait for the fire marshal?" Eli asked.

Violet shrugged. "Supposed to and going to are two different things. He's not going to be here for a few days, and I can't afford to wait."

He raised his eyebrows in a sincere—if silent—question, his grin gone.

"I just can't." She walked toward the blackened shelves on the wall beside the kiln. Broken ceramics littered the ground, pieces that had been nearly complete reduced to rubbish. "There's so much to do, and the tourist season isn't going to wait."

That was the truth—but not all of it. The whole truth involved a mortgage and a business that had been thriving. Just not well enough to sustain an entire summer of lost sales.

Yes, buildings could be rebuilt, but sometimes, when a dream was stolen, relationships were lost too. There was no way she was going to let Mama Potts lose this dream.

"Where are we going to start?"

She just shook her head—at both Eli and the situation. He couldn't seem to understand that there was no *we* in this scenario. And she had no idea where *she* was going to begin.

"If we do much today, the fire marshal will know we were here."

Violet shrugged, trying to decide if she cared. But if her being in the studio somehow delayed its official release, she'd never forgive herself.

"I guess, maybe . . ." She took a slow stroll around a

blackened table. "Maybe I should take inventory. See what's been damaged, what can be salvaged."

"Sounds good." Pulling out his phone, Eli swiped with his thumb like a pro. "You call them out. I'll make the list."

The minutes flowed into hours, piles growing on the two worktables that had escaped the fire unscathed. She didn't go near the pallet or the metal cans strewn about near the charred kiln. But blocks of red clay lined the back wall, so she inspected and stacked them, sorting out the ones that had been hardened and ruined by the heat of the fire.

True to his word, Eli marked down everything while giving her distance. Until she tried to stack a fifth unsalvageable block of clay on the appropriate pile. She pressed onto her tiptoes but still couldn't quite reach the top. Suddenly he was by her side, easily removing the heavy brick from her hands and placing it on top of the pile.

"Maybe we should get you a forklift," he said.

"Not all of us can be giants." She hadn't meant to make him smile, but he did—a genuine smile, not the smirk she was so used to. It caught her off guard, all those straight white teeth. No wonder he'd made the cover of more than one tabloid over the years. He was far too attractive for his own good. Worse, he knew it.

Violet turned away and picked up another brick. The protective plastic had melted around the front half of the clay, but the back part of it might be saved, so she set it on a new pile.

"What are you labeling that?"

She pursed her lips, resting her hands on her hips for a long moment. "Cautiously optimistic."

He nodded, his thumbs quickly typing the words.

"How do you do that?"

Glancing up from the screen, he raised his eyebrows.

"Type so fast," she said. "With your giant thumbs."

He snorted again. Then an actual, real laugh filled the air, rising to the second-story ceiling. His chuckle was cut short for a moment, his smile faltering then beaming again. Almost like he'd surprised himself. Like he'd forgotten how to laugh—or at least forgotten how much he enjoyed it.

"I'm not just good at getting a puck in the net," he said.

Maybe she'd imagined it, but Violet could have sworn that the joy in his eyes died at that moment. He tried to keep up the smile, but thin lines formed around his mouth, tension he couldn't hide.

She wanted to ask—everything inside her wanted to know—why he'd given up the thing that he'd lived for, the thing that had been worth abandoning his family for. But she couldn't, not without caring a little bit. And the Lord knew she didn't want to care. Not after what he'd done.

She turned back to the clay bricks, already imagining what might take shape from them. Coffee mugs and coasters, plates and platters. In blues and purples and greens. Stamped with an outline of Prince Edward Island. Made from the island's very foundation.

They worked in silence for another half hour, sorting and noting until the two tables were covered in supplies. Then the sound of gravel crunching on the other side of the garage door made them both freeze. Violet's heart fluttered in the back of her throat, and she stared at Eli without blinking.

"Are you expecting anyone?" he whispered.

She shook her head. "Wasn't even expecting you. And Mama Potts can't drive, between her sprained ankle and broken wrist."

"Oliver or Levi?"

"I don't think so."

Beneath the black whiskers on his face, his jaw twitched. "Fire marshal?"

Violet cringed. "He said it would be several days, but I don't know who else it would be."

Shoving his phone into the pocket of his jeans, Eli waved her toward the door at the far wall. "Hide in the shop. I'll deal with it."

"Come with me." The words slipped out before she could really consider them, and his grin almost made her take them back. But there was no sense in either of them getting caught.

With a wave of his hand toward the table, Eli said, "I think he'll know someone was here." He turned and strolled toward the door, and she raced to the entrance of the shop and slipped silently between the display cases. Sidling up to the rear window, she peeked outside.

~

When Eli stepped into the late morning sun, he was prepared to take a hit. He froze instead. Where he'd expected to see an official truck, there sat a red convertible, top down. The passenger looked like he'd had to shoehorn himself into the seat, his chair reclined as far as it would go. The driver had stepped out, taking a slow spin around the gravel parking lot.

Eli recognized them immediately. And the familiar rock in the bottom of his stomach.

"Pretty place. Big trees. The ocean is nice here. I see why you came back."

He swallowed the lump in his throat and glanced over his shoulder to make sure Violet hadn't followed him. Then he turned back to Tony Moynahan, who was wholly out of place in his black leather jacket. "What are you doing here?"

"What kind of welcome is that for an old friend?" Tony's smile was more of a sneer, showing off yellow teeth and chapped lips.

"Is this how friends treat each other?" Eli waved his wrist brace in the general direction of his right eye, which he knew still bore a purple shadow.

Tony pressed his hand over his heart, leaning back and shaking his head. "Elijah. Elijah. We've known each other too long to focus on the past."

"It was two weeks ago." Sweat rolling down his back despite the cool breeze, Eli forced himself to stand perfectly still.

"Yes, it's been two weeks. And you made me a promise. Then you went and left town, without even a forwarding address." Tony looked back at the car behind him and the man still reclining in the passenger seat. "My brother Bobby was a little worried you might not have meant what you said."

Eli's stomach rolled. "It's not like I had an address to give you. I didn't even have one in the city." And maybe he'd thought Tony wouldn't track him down so quickly.

That had been a foolish hope. Tony worked for a crime family whose racket ran most of the Eastern Seaboard, their connections extending far across the Canadian border. He probably hadn't even had to use them. Every sports reporter in New York had been fascinated by him, a rookie from Rinkydink, Canada.

Tony clicked his tongue, his toothy grin dimming. "And whose fault is that?"

His. Eli had owned it. Was still owning it.

He squeezed his eyes closed against the memory of first meeting Tony, against the regret. He'd thought he could handle the thug, could take care of the threats. He'd been wrong.

Eli scrubbed his hands against his face before opening his eyes to see that Tony's faux smile had returned.

"Bobby thought you might be trying to make us look bad—you know, with the family. But I said there was no way. Not Eli Ross. We had a deal, didn't we?"

"We still do," Eli said. It took everything inside him to keep his fists at his sides and the fight bubbling inside from reaching his face.

Tony stepped forward, ignoring common boundaries of personal space. The scent of his spicy cologne hung over him like a cloud, overpowering that of the salty sea and the grass. "Elijah, we agreed on two months. You said you'd be ready to pay in full. I think that was more than generous."

It was. After all, he had already been two months late when Tony and Bobby last paid him a visit and gave a little reminder that everyone paid up.

His wrist throbbed at just the memory of Tony's foot pressing against his arm. Eli had been on the alley floor, laid low by Bobby's single blow to his eye, which was already swelling closed. Lying in a puddle that wasn't water in the shadow of a dumpster that hadn't been emptied in ages, he'd heard the crack of his bones. Dogs barking, cars flying by, sirens wailing—all disappeared into that single snap.

That had been his lowest point, the moment he'd known he needed a fresh start. The problem with fresh starts was that they only happened in the movies. There was no such thing when his history insisted on following him.

Tony put a paw on Eli's shoulder and squeezed like the grizzly he hid beneath a relaxed exterior. "You have seven weeks left. And if the rumors are true, you don't have a job. How are you going to get me my money? Your mother going to pay it for you?"

Eli swallowed, his throat thick and coated with sand. "She's not part of this. You don't need to get within a hundred feet of her."

"Eli, Eli." Tony almost sounded like a father—well, like *his* father—as he leaned in another foot. There was no space between them, no mistaking the threat in his tone. "I don't want to get your sweet mother involved. Especially after her recent injuries."

Eli's head snapped up, and he glared at Tony. "How do you know about her accident?"

Tony cocked his head to the side and scoffed. "Come on now. How long have we known each other? You think I don't keep tabs on my favorite associates?"

"I'll get you the money." The words came out between clenched teeth. Fifty grand wasn't likely to wash up on shore. Even if it did, with his luck, he'd be the last person to find it.

Once, he'd blown that much on a night at a club after the Rangers made the playoffs. Private room. Bottles of Scotch, whiskey, and Dom Pérignon. Maybe the only redeeming moment of that night had been the moment their waitress had seen the tip. Probably enough to pay her rent for the month.

But that was a different life. That man didn't exist anymore.

All that was left was the debt.

"We're agreed, then. Seven weeks. Not a day longer."

Eli nodded. "I'll be in touch."

Tony laughed again. "Oh, now, you don't have to worry about keeping track of the calendar. Me or Bobby"—Bobby raised two fingers from where his hands were folded over his round girth, not even bothering to open his eyes—"will be around. Count on it."

Eli's stomach churned, and he pinched his eyes closed again as Tony got back in his car, slammed the door, and drove off, spitting gravel in their wake.

"Who was that?"

Eli sighed at the quiet voice behind him. Perfect. Now he had to explain to Violet how he knew one of New York's biggest bookies. How he owed money to a family that was almost certainly on the FBI watch list.

"No one for you to worry about."

"I don't think that's a decision you get to make for me. He seemed like someone you shouldn't mess with. Are you in trouble?" She crossed her arms, and he couldn't tell if the line between her eyebrows might actually be genuine concern for him.

He shook his head. "Of course not." The lie slipped out easily.

"Who was he then?"

"Someone I owe a favor to."

"Was he coming to collect?" Violet nibbled on the corner of her lip.

He scratched at the back of his neck, staring over her shoulder, well beyond the shop and into the gently sloping hayfields. "Not exactly. More like a warning." He snapped his mouth closed. He hadn't meant to say that. He *shouldn't* have said that.

Violet grabbed his bare forearm, and it was like being slammed against the boards. He could feel her touch in every inch of his body.

Her face twisted, and she jerked her hand away. But she got right into his face. "What kind of warning?"

He shrugged her off, turning back to the studio, but her clamped hand on his shoulder stopped him. Maybe he'd been prepared after her first touch. Or perhaps the cotton of Oliver's T-shirt was enough of a barrier to her electricity. Either way, she only stunned him that time. The rounded tips of her long fingers were stained red, striking against his black shirt, and he couldn't look away from where they dug into his shoulder.

"Eli, what did you bring home with you?"

"I told you. You don't need to worry about it."

"You keep saying that like it's your decision to make. If it affects Mama Potts or the Red Clay Shoppe, I'm going to worry about it."

Because she was family, just like Oliver had said. Violet loved Mama Potts more than Eli had. Or at least she'd shown her love. Eli had packed his up, put it on a bus, and tried to forget it. Remembering a love he'd walked out on was too hard. It was a lot easier to fill that hole with pretty girls and big parties.

He couldn't change those wasted years. But there was one thing he could do.

Eli looked up from his shoulder, meeting her gaze and holding it. "I swear, I won't ever let it hurt Mama Potts or this shop."

six

Eli stared at the list in his hand for the fourth time, then back at the aisle of breakfast cereals. He had a feeling the Lucky Charms weren't for Mama Potts. Levi had loved them when they were kids too.

He threw an extra box in his cart, just because he could. After all, Mama Potts had shoved a handful of colorful twenties into his fist when he'd volunteered to do the shopping. He hated that he couldn't offer to pay for the food—or the roof over his head, for that matter. But he was as broke now as he'd been when Tony paid him a visit three days before.

Leaning his arms on the handle, he pushed the cart into the next aisle.

"Eli Ross, you look like someone stole your last lollipop."

He blinked as he looked up from the tan tiled floor. The face of the woman standing behind her own cart was familiar, but it took him three long seconds to put a name with it. "Mrs. Huxley."

"It's Mable Jean, please." The pink of her lipstick seeped

into the wrinkles around her lips, her smile wide and warm. "Imagine running into you here."

He glanced around the small grocery store, then back at her. "Not many other options, are there?"

She giggled like a schoolgirl. "Oh, you do beat all. So funny."

He frowned. He wasn't trying to be funny or charming. He knew when to turn it on, but he didn't need anything from Mable Jean. Besides, the general store was literally the only place that sold groceries within five miles of Victoria. To get to a real grocery store, he'd have had to drive all the way to Summerside.

Mable Jean either didn't notice that he wasn't playing along or didn't care. "And you're so talented too."

His stomach dropped. This was headed in the same direction it had at church. "Well, it was good to—"

"I know it's not couth to talk of such things in public." Her voice dropped. "But did you turn us down because of the salary?"

"Of course n—"

"I know we can't pay you anything near what you were making in the NHL, but I've talked with the other boosters, and we're willing to offer you . . ." She glanced around them. Then she pushed her cart closer to his. "We'll make it worth your while."

"I'm sorry, it's not about the money." Well, that wasn't entirely true. He hadn't been thinking about the money on Sunday. But thanks to Tony, now he was. And there was no way they would offer him what he owed. Still, he asked, "How much are you talking?"

Mable Jean's eyes flashed with hope. "How much would you need to make it worth your time?"

A lot.

He shook his head. "You first."

"Good boy." She crept forward until they were close enough that she could pat his arm. "Always make the other person give the first number. Can you give me a range?"

With another hard shake of his head, he asked, "How far into the spring season are they?"

"We have six weeks left. Four games and a tournament."

There was no way they were going to pay him ten thousand American dollars a week. He scrubbed a hand down his face. He had no business even considering this. He wasn't a coach. And he sure wasn't a role model. He could only tell them how to ruin a career. He was an expert at that.

"I think you'll love the team. They're all strong skaters and eager players."

"I'm sure they are. But as I said on Sunday, I'm just not—"

"Do you have something else lined up?"

She couldn't have known how hard that hit. Like he needed another reminder that his debts were due and the only thing he had going on was helping a woman who pretty openly loathed him.

Closing his eyes until all he heard were the scrape of blades against the ice, the buzzer of a goal, cheer of the crowd, Eli forced himself to breathe. "Can you do twenty-five?"

Mable Jean sucked in a sharp breath, her voice nearly dancing. "Hundred?"

He opened his eyes to find her face filled with joy and cringed when he corrected her. "Thousand."

Her smile faltered, the lines around her eyes sagging and the loose skin of her neck quivering. "Oh my, I never thought we'd be so far apart. We're not the NHL, but maybe . . ."

She kept saying they weren't the Show, like he had a choice about going back. "How much are you paying?"

"Well, we had talked about maybe seven or eight thousand. It's not full-time. It's only a couple of hours a day. But I bet we could get you ten—yes, I'll talk the boosters into it. We'll find you the money."

Ten thousand Canadian dollars. It was a start. He could find a way to multiply that times five. His current account balance times a thousand was still zero.

"All right. I'll do it."

Violet forced her shoulders back and her chin up and tried not to look guilty as Michael Bigsby, the fire inspector, surveyed her. Looking down at his clipboard, he scribbled something on the form there. "Are you the registered property owner?"

"No, sir."

His eyes darted toward the caution tape still blocking the studio door, and her stomach twisted. He had to know that she'd snuck back in. More than once. But what could he expect when it had taken him *days* to come out for the inspection?

"It's in the name of my business partner, Debi Ross."

He frowned. "Which one of you is Mama Potts?"

If she looked old enough for anyone to call her Mama *anything*, she'd go jump in the bay. "The business is named after

Debi." The name was strange on her tongue. Before she'd known her as Mama Potts, she'd been simply Mrs. Ross, a friend of Aunt Tracy's. There had been no middle ground.

"Who makes the pottery?"

Violet was pretty sure that the last couple questions weren't on his form. "We both do."

"Got my wife a set of coffee mugs from you last year."

She froze, not sure from his tone if his wife had enjoyed them or thrown them against the wall.

He continued scraping his pen against the form. "She won't let anyone else use them."

Violet still wasn't sure what that meant. "Oh?"

Finally he glanced up with the barest hint of a smile on his lips. "She's afraid we'll break one."

"I'm—I'm glad she likes them." Despite his compliment, Violet kept her arms wrapped around her middle, praying he wouldn't realize that things inside had been moved, that she'd sorted and even begun trashing more than a few pieces.

"Sorry I'm late."

She didn't bother turning around at the nearly out-of-breath greeting. She was coming to know that voice. Maybe a little too well. But before she could ask Eli why he had apparently run across town to join her, Mr. Bigsby dropped his clipboard.

"You're Eli Ross." He reached out to shake Eli's hand, grabbing it before Eli had even extended his arm. "I watched all your games. Wagered on a few too."

Violet didn't dare look away from Eli's response, which was a subtle grimace and a mumbled, "I hope we won them for you."

"Oh, you betcha. My kid loved watching you play. Always said he was gonna be just as good as you." Mr. Bigsby looked over his shoulder, then leaned in even closer. "So what happened?"

Oh, the gall of this guy. Violet had wanted to ask the same question since she'd learned about Eli's expulsion from the NHL. But as far as she knew, even Oliver hadn't asked for an explanation. And she wasn't entirely sure Mama Potts cared about the reason for her son's return.

But Eli cared a great deal, if the deepening lines of his forehead were any indication. He bit his lips together and closed his eyes. Maybe he didn't have a ready-made response, although he should have. This was Victoria, and not much had changed in a decade.

"I mean, it must have been bad."

Violet's stomach dropped. Mr. Bigsby had absolutely no tact. And suddenly her hand fisted at her side, like . . .

Like she was going to defend Eli Ross. Ha. Not likely. He didn't deserve—or need—her defense. Still, the silence was awkward.

Eli rubbed his big hand across the back of his neck, his shoulders hunching beneath an unseen weight. "I guess my time was just up."

"Well, sure, but I mean, it wasn't like you—"

Bending over, Violet snatched the dropped clipboard from the gravel parking lot and shoved it into Mr. Bigsby's hands. "I think you were just about to take a look around inside to make sure it's safe for us to get to work cleaning it up so we can reopen our store." She wasn't going to stand by and watch this guy dig into a big bowl of none of his business.

"Um . . ." He glanced between her and Eli, then down at the documents. "Sure. I'll be back."

He ducked under the tape and disappeared into the cavernous studio, leaving her and Eli alone in their silence. Except it was never silent on the island. There were always birds chirping and the rustling of leaves in the wind, the clap of the waves against the shore.

After many long moments, Eli said, "Thank you." He was still facing the studio and the back of the store, and he hadn't even looked in her direction. "I guess I should have been more prepared. It's what everyone wants to know, isn't it?"

She nodded—not that he saw her. She wanted to know. But she also wanted to know who the men in the red sports car were. And if Eli would really keep his word to not hurt Mama Potts again. And if he could be trusted or if he was the same man who had walked away all those years ago.

When it was clear Eli wasn't going to give her any more answers than he'd given the inspector, she asked, "Why are you here?"

"That seems to be everyone's favorite question lately—well, maybe their second favorite."

She let out a soft sigh. "Well?"

He shrugged. "Do you mean back on PEI?"

"Right here. Right this minute. Why are you standing next to me? Why did you sound like you ran all the way here, like you were in a hurry to see . . . something?" She'd almost said "me." But that was ludicrous. He wasn't there to see her. He didn't know her.

He finally faced her, hands shoved into the pockets of

shorts she was pretty sure she'd seen Oliver wearing on more than one occasion. "Because I did."

"What?"

"I ran here. I didn't want to be late. I went to the general store for Mama Potts, then I ran into Mable Jean Huxley, and I didn't get the message that the inspection was happening, and . . . well, I ran."

"But *why*?"

Eli pushed the toe of his shoe into the ground, lifting a shoulder in a dismissive shrug. "Because it's an important day, and I didn't figure you'd want to be alone. Because I said I'd be here."

There was something more to what he said. Something deeper. Like he was trying to prove not only to her but also to himself that he was a man of his word.

The problem was that she'd have to see it to believe it, which required spending more time with him.

She'd never planned on coming face-to-face with him. But he'd shown up with no word of warning and no explanation. Maybe Mama Potts could overlook that, but Violet didn't have to.

"What did you expect when you came home? I mean, you haven't spoken to your family in so long."

He closed one eye, squinting the other, his tongue poking at the corner of his mouth. "Honestly?"

She nodded.

"I don't know. But I was homeless and hungry, and I figured I could be just as homeless and just as hungry here. We had lean years when I was a kid, but even then, we had each other. I guess I was looking for that *each other*."

"You were homeless?" She couldn't help the hitch in her voice. "Why didn't you stay with a friend?"

He looked at her hard, as though he could make her understand the real world.

"I mean, you had friends, right? Teammates?"

"Funny how fast you learn just what kind of friends you have." He frowned, his gaze wandering to somewhere in the past. "So long as I was buying the booze and paying for the parties, they were quick to show up. When the money disappeared, so did they."

"You haven't heard from any of them?"

He shook his head.

"But your teammates? They had to—"

"I messed them over. Bad. Getting kicked off the team, out of the league, didn't just hurt me. It hurt them too. It was too soon for forgiveness."

"Is that what you were hoping for when you came back—forgiveness?"

Eli gave a bark of a laugh. "Some things are beyond hope." He scraped his nails down his face, his beard hissing beneath the motion. "No, I'm not looking for forgiveness. I don't deserve it. I was just hoping for a dry place to sleep and a fresh— No, I can't start over. But maybe I could begin to make up for at least some of the pain I've caused."

She rubbed her fist over a pinch in the center of her chest. Ugh. She did not feel sorry for this guy. She wouldn't. But how genuinely sad to not have a single actual friend. He'd spent his whole adult life focused on a game, focused on himself. And he'd missed the whole point of life.

No, she didn't feel sorry for him exactly. His situation was entirely a consequence of his own actions, at least as far as she knew. But she did pity the fool he'd been. And she was beginning to wonder if he was still the same guy or if something had changed.

"Where do you plan to start?" she asked.

"Here, I guess. And at the rink. With the Stars."

She couldn't help the bubble of laughter that broke free. "You decided to coach them?"

He shrugged. "Mrs. Huxley cornered me at the general store and made a convincing argument."

Oh, this was going to be something else. Eli Ross back on the ice—sort of.

Before she could dive any deeper into that thought, Mr. Bigsby raised the garage door, its springs creaking. He waved them in, and when they got closer, he said, "It looks like someone's been moving things around in here." With a watchful eye on her and Eli, he asked, "Either of you know anything about that?"

Violet had to bite her tongue to keep from spilling out a lie—or worse, the truth. Eli followed suit with a casual shrug.

Pursing his lips and tapping his pen against his clipboard, the inspector stared hard. Finally, he turned back to the damage, pointing out what she already knew. "The fire started in the electrical outlet on the far wall, and an accelerant made it shoot across the wooden shelves there." He pointed to row after row of ruined mugs that had been ready to be fired. "The structure itself is stable—the walls and steps up to the apartment."

"So I can move back in?" The eagerness in her voice made *her* sound like the homeless one.

His eyebrows pulled together. "Well, technically, I guess."

Perfect. She'd call Meg and pick up her stuff.

"But you won't have electricity until the whole place is rewired and up to code."

Right. Electricity. That was a bit of a necessity.

"We're going to have to hire an electrician," she said. There was no question about that. But there were plenty of questions about who to hire and how they were going to afford it, especially with no income.

Then another question jumped to her mind. "Wait—but just the studio, right? We can open the store."

With a quick shake of his head, he dashed her hopes—and any possibility of a future for the store. No electricity meant no air-conditioning, no lights, and no cash register. And most importantly, no way to power a kiln and replace the precious inventory they'd lost. Which all added up to no sales. And no sales equaled no future. That was an equation even she could work out.

This wasn't the first time she'd had a hand in ruining a dream.

Her stomach heaved, the back of her throat burning.

Some things couldn't be fixed. She'd learned that ten years before. Some mistakes couldn't be undone. But this was fixable. It had to be.

The inspector tore off the pink copy of his report and handed it to her. "Good luck, Ms. Donaghy." Then he got in his truck and kicked up gravel as he left the parking lot.

Eli crossed his arms over his chest and surveyed the room. "Well, where do we start?"

"I'm not sure." Violet dropped onto one of the stools at the closest charred table, letting her forehead fall against her arm in an epic mope. She just needed a moment to let the regret simmer. Then she'd figure out her next step.

"All right." He took several steps, his shoes slapping against the cement, and she heard him rummaging around. "Let's chuck everything you've already labeled a loss. Decluttering always helps me think better."

She looked up at him out of one squinted eye. "Decluttering? You're into the minimalist lifestyle?"

He chuckled. "I am now. I don't even own anything I'm wearing."

"I'm sorry, I shouldn't have—"

Waving her off, he rolled an empty plastic garbage bin across the floor. "It wasn't always like this. And it's not so bad. Doing laundry is a snap."

She chuckled, pushing herself up and joining him next to a table stacked with ruined vases. "Mama Potts said she'd like to keep any of the broken pottery. Let's put it in a box for her."

He threw an empty cardboard box at her feet, and they began filling it. She tried not to cringe with the crack of the pieces as they shattered against each other.

"I'm sorry about this," Eli said, gingerly setting a stack of platters broken in half into the box.

"I can make new pieces. But without a kiln, I can't fire them, so I can't sell them."

"So, we'll get you a new kiln." He said it so nonchalantly that she almost believed it could be that easy to solve her problem. Almost.

"Well, without a storefront, we can't afford to buy one—and even if we could, we don't have a place to plug it in."

Eli paused, the pieces in his arms heavy enough to make the muscles and veins in his forearms pop. It was hard to miss that the man was built like the Confederation Bridge. His wingspan was probably nearly as wide. But somehow he was still gentle with the broken pieces of her studio.

"Okay, so we have two problems—well, three, really." He dumped his haul into the bin before ticking off the problems on the fingers of his good hand. "Storefront, kiln, and electricity. We can solve those."

"We?" He seemed to suggest that every time he showed up, every time he insisted on helping. Even though Mama Potts considered her one of the family, Violet had been on her own for a lot longer than she wanted to remember.

"Sure."

"Don't you have a job now?"

He smirked. "You trying to get rid of me again?"

"Maybe."

"Your technique needs some work."

Rolling her eyes, she tossed the last of the ruined mugs before grabbing the edge of the box. When she tugged, it didn't budge. She pulled again. Same result.

Eli grabbed the other side, giving it a push while she pulled. Cardboard scraped against concrete as they shimmied kilos of clay toward the yard.

"One thing I learned in the game, it's always better to have a teammate," he said. "It makes the load a little lighter."

"I wish you wouldn't do that." She shot him a half scowl, half smile as they stepped into the fresh air.

His face was all innocence. "What?"

"Make valid points."

seven

Eli slipped through the side door of the rink, walking a path he'd taken a thousand times as a teenage player. The old block walls still needed a paint job, and the tunnel toward the locker rooms had lost a few more light bulbs.

He moved to hoist his bag, only there wasn't one. No gear. Barely a stick and skates. And those only because his mom hadn't thrown his high school ones away. Even his clothes were borrowed, sweats from Oliver.

He couldn't even get a kit together, and they wanted him to coach their team. Worse, he'd agreed to it. And he'd beaten himself up over it a dozen times in the four days since. He had no business getting back out there.

Still, the ice called to him, a siren whispering any number of promises.

A man in a blue jumpsuit with his name sewn above his heart pushed a yellow mop bucket in his direction. The man looked up, his eyes suddenly wide. "It's true then. They actually got you."

Eli shrugged. "I guess so."

"Can't believe you're back."

Eli glanced at the map of deep crevices splitting the man's face before dropping his gaze to his name badge. Peter. Eli squinted hard, trying to match the name with the man he'd known. "Carson?"

"Just the same." Peter Carson held out his hand, and Eli adjusted his stick so he could shake it vigorously.

"I can't believe you're still here."

It was Carson's turn to shrug. "Never left. No better place to be."

Maybe this was where all the washouts ended up. The man had been a legend—the first local to make it out of Victoria based on his skill with a stick. He'd come back a few months later. As far as Eli knew, Carson had never talked about his failure, but he was always the best player on every county team.

"You still playing?" Eli asked.

"Not so much. Arthritis in my knees."

Eli tapped his own knee, empathetic pressure building there. "I'm sorry, man."

"It's not so bad. They still let me manage the place. Drive the Zamboni. Watch the kids learning. It's enough."

Eli wasn't entirely sure Carson was talking only about himself, and he hoped it was true that coaching could be enough. Otherwise it would be torture.

Carson wheeled the mop bucket toward a closed door. "You have everything you need?"

"I have no clue. Never coached before."

Carson laughed. "You got a whistle?"

Eli shook his head.

"Man, you weren't kidding. Come on." Carson led him toward the rink, the smell of the ice holding Eli in a warm embrace.

After Carson showed him the surprisingly well-stocked supply closet, he pointed Eli toward the ice. "The team is already in the locker room. Better get out there."

Eli nodded and stumbled toward the bench, its wooden edges made smooth by years of young hopefuls. He fell to the seat, trying to remember the last time he'd sat in this same spot. The last time he'd played on this ice. The scoreboard at the far end of the ice was dark, but it still drew his eye. It had flashed and lit up with his final goal of the game. His team had been up by a dozen heading into the third period. And if it had been any other game but his last with the team, his coach would have made him sit the bench.

Funny how the smell of popcorn and the burn of sweat in his eyes was sharper a dozen years later than his last game in the Show. He hadn't won that game. He'd been too focused on himself.

He'd left one team with pride, the other in defeat. And he was about to pick up a brand-new team that was looking to him to save their season.

Heaving a sigh, he pulled off his sneaker and shoved his toe into the end of his skate. It was snug and stiff, barely enough room for him to wiggle his toes.

It felt like home.

With both skates on and laced up, he leaned forward and pressed his hands to the bench, drawing a deep breath of the cool air through his nose. The cold made his cheeks feel alive. He risked closing his eyes. A terrible mistake.

In an instant he was back on another bench. Twenty thousand spectators cheered until they drowned out even the crash of his teammates against the boards. They waved bright foam fingers and banners, jeering at the refs. And then the line change. They chanted his name as he swung his leg over the wall and his blades hit the ice, and he could fly.

His eyes flew open, and he jumped to his feet. This had been a terrible idea. It wasn't worth it. These kids would find another coach.

The clanging metal of the rink door broke through his thoughts, and he looked up as a line of kids in black and red skated into a large circle around center ice, helmet shields pulled low, blades scraping the telltale song of the game. With bent knees and swinging arms, they picked up speed with each turn.

If he was going to turn back, this was the moment.

He stepped on the ice.

Mama Potts had clearly gotten his blades sharpened because they slid across the surface like a hot knife over butter. Making a mental note to thank her later, he approached the team as they slowed to a halt, some more steady than others, every head turned in his direction.

He blinked at them, his tongue stuck to the roof of his mouth. He should have brought a bottle of water. His swallow was thick and echoed in the cavern.

Great first impression, 23.

Nobody had called him that in months, but something about the ice beneath his blades had his number on repeat in the corners of his mind.

Clearing his throat, he tapped his stick against the toe of his skate. "I'm Coach Ross."

"Duh."

He nearly jumped back, the voice much higher than he'd expected. Poor kid probably hadn't hit puberty yet.

"Madison," hissed the kid behind, shoving him with a solid elbow shot.

Good. They were a physical team. Even if the kid who pushed Madison nearly fell over at the effort.

"Well . . ." The prepubescent Madison swung his arm in a wild gesture. "We know who he is." It wasn't until Madison turned around to push his teammate in kind that Eli noticed the long hair whipping behind him.

He couldn't look away from the tawny-colored braid. Until he noticed the blond one on another kid and the black one on the kid beside him. And the strange row of intertwined ponytails on yet another.

His stomach sank, and he couldn't blink. Skating backward, he put some distance between them. "I'm sorry. I'm looking for the Victoria Stars."

Nearly in one motion, they pulled off their helmets, big, bright eyes staring at him from decidedly feminine faces. Soft jaws, long hair, and more eye makeup than any hockey players he'd ever seen.

Nope. Nope. Nope. This was not what he'd signed up for. Bantam hockey. Spring league hockey. *Boys'* hockey.

"We *are* the Stars." Madison. No nonsense.

They were girls.

Of course they're girls, stupid.

His brain couldn't make sense of it. He glanced over his

shoulder toward the bench and saw Carson there, leaning on his mop handle, a smug grin pulling at his craggy features. Then he glanced at the cluster of hockey moms in the metal stands, all focused on him.

They all knew. They had to have known.

And they'd tricked him.

"Practice is over," he said.

Madison's jaw dropped, and she skated forward. "What?" She looked at her teammates. "You're kidding, right? We haven't even started."

He skated away anyway.

"You knew!"

Violet nearly dropped the box she was carrying as she pushed her way through Mama Potts's kitchen entry. Eli was ticked about something.

Oliver's laugh suggested he didn't feel the same. "Of course I knew. The whole town does."

Eli tossed his hands into the air, stomping a short path to the sink and then back to the table, where Oliver and Levi exchanged loaded glances and knowing smirks.

"And I suppose you knew too," Eli said, spinning on her.

Setting the box on an empty wooden chair, Violet raised her eyebrows. She had a pretty good guess what she'd walked in on, and even if she didn't, she would have faked it just to annoy him a little more. "I am part of the town. The big question is, how did you *not* know? Haven't they been around for a while?"

Eli waved his hand dismissively. "They weren't . . . on my radar back then."

"Yeah," Oliver said. "Eli only paid attention to the cute girls in the stands when he was that age."

Violet could just imagine teenage Eli giving his mom fits while he ran around town with some cutesy hockey bunny, and it made her blood simmer.

"Not true," Eli said, turning on his brother. "I was too busy playing in every league on the island to have time for girls."

"So you made up for it when you got to the pros?"

Three pairs of matching eyes turned at Violet's question, all wide and unblinking.

"What? I know what a newspaper is."

Levi winked at her, a half smile playing across his lips, as Oliver let out a full-on roar of laughter.

Eli looked away, muttering, "Don't believe everything you read." He stabbed his fingers through his hair and marched a few more steps. "What am I going to do with a bunch of teenage girls? What do I know about them?"

By some miracle, Violet managed to keep her mouth shut. Oliver wasn't afflicted with the same.

"About as much as you know about women of any age, which—given your current situation—probably couldn't fill a teaspoon."

Eli shot him a glare while Levi's shoulders shook silently, his fist pressed against his lips and his eyes glowing.

The truth rushed through her. This was family. These brothers had missed out on so many years of teasing and roughhousing and all the ways brothers showed they loved each other.

She wondered if she'd have teased her brother in the same way. Would the difference in their ages have made it harder or easier? More than ten years, and just the memory of Garrett made her chest ache and her lungs refuse to breathe. Strange how the memories were so much closer to the surface since the fire.

This was her family now. The home she'd chosen. The gift she'd never expected. One she absolutely didn't deserve.

"So what did you do when you met the girls?" Oliver asked Eli.

Eli ducked his head and seemed to scowl at himself. "I ended practice."

Violet couldn't hold her tongue a moment longer. "You walked out on them?"

He peeked at her out of the corner of his eye, his hand rubbing the back of his neck.

"Eli!" Oliver beat her to the reprimand. "What were you thinking?"

"That—that—that I don't know a thing about how to coach a bunch of girls, and I'm only going to mess them up."

Oliver blinked slowly, and Levi looked up from the doorstop of a book in his hands.

Something churned deep in her gut. "I'm going to assume that your hesitation to coach isn't because you think girls are lesser players or don't deserve to play the ga—"

"Are you kidding me right now?" Eli said. "I was literally sitting in the front row when the Canadian women's team won the gold in Sochi. No one cheered louder. Women players are tough and talented."

"Then what's the problem?" she asked. "It's the same game, right? How much different can it be?"

Eli stomped a few more steps around the kitchen, which

felt infinitely smaller than normal with all three of the Ross brothers in it. "I don't know how to relate to girls. I grew up with these miscreants." He gestured toward his brothers, who both shrugged off the jab. "What if I get loud and I hurt their feelings?"

Violet fell into the kitchen chair beside Oliver with a giggle, resting her hand on his shoulder. "You're right. You know nothing about teenage girls. Thirteen-year-old girls can eviscerate you with one look." Turning to Oliver, she said, "I'm more worried they'll hurt *his* feelings."

Eli stopped pacing, his shoulders squaring. "I can handle myself."

"They're playing the same game you love. It's not that complicated."

"Why do you care so much?" he asked.

"I—I'm not—I mean, the Stars are my team too. And those girls have worked really hard." But the question still bounced around inside her, seeking a true answer. Why *did* she care?

She didn't know.

Yes, you do.

The truth whispered deep in her heart, even if she didn't want to accept it. Truth was funny like that.

Somewhere deep in her spirit, she wanted Eli to be the man his mother saw, the one she'd missed all those years. Mama Potts saw him as the man he could be—not as his bad choices. And a small part of Violet was grateful that his coaching duties would keep him from spending as much time at the studio.

"She's right, you know," Oliver said.

Eli slumped against the white counter, resting his head

against an upper cabinet. "I know. But I can't even go into their locker room."

"Get a team mom." When Levi spoke, everyone listened. And his suggestion made a lot of sense.

Oliver nodded quickly. "That's what they've done before. Just have one of the boosters in the locker room with you."

Eli's lips twitched. "A booster? That won't work. They all have agendas and would want me to play their kid. Parents always do."

With a shrug, Levi went back to his book, clearly no longer interested.

Oliver chuckled. "What about Violet?"

She bumped his shoulder. "What did I ever do to you?"

But Eli had perked up, his eyes narrowing on her. Goose bumps broke out across her arms, and she had to restrain herself from rubbing them.

"I'm too busy getting the shop back up and running and the studio repaired. See?" She gestured to the almost forgotten cardboard box filled with tools that needed to be cleaned. To prove her point, she pushed herself up and looked around for Mama Potts, who hadn't made an appearance since Violet arrived. "Where's Mama Potts? I came to see her, not to get wrapped up in whatever Eli is doing."

"She's resting." Oliver pointed toward the stairs that led to the bedrooms on the second floor.

"Okay, I'll call her later."

"Wait!" Eli grabbed her arm, his fingers warm and gentle. "Is it such a terrible idea?"

"Looking for Mama Potts?" She was purposely obtuse as she tried to tug her arm free.

He didn't release it, cocking his head to the side as his eyebrows pinched together. Her skin tingled under his evaluation, and she wanted to flee. She basically wanted to pull an Eli Ross. But something in his eyes wouldn't let her.

"I need some help with these girls."

Violet shook her head. "There are plenty of other women in town. I'm sure someone would be available."

"But I don't know that I can trust them."

A muscle in her neck jumped at the simple implication.

Even Levi looked up from his book, his eyes glowing brighter than before.

She pulled at her arm again, and Eli's grip loosened, sliding from her elbow to her wrist. His long fingers wrapped all the way around, callused yet tender. The contact made her insides take a slow flip.

Violet looked up into his eyes, catching her breath at the strange intimacy of how close they were. He'd nicked himself shaving that morning. She could see the red mark on his neck just below the line of his well-trimmed beard. She couldn't help but wonder if it had stung when he'd applied the spicy aftershave that lingered.

She didn't like this man, and she shouldn't enjoy being this close to him. She definitely shouldn't have to remind herself of that.

"I don't know very much about hockey," she said.

The corner of his lips twitched. "That makes you perfect for the job."

She raised an eyebrow. "Oh, is this a paid position?"

Something close to sadness flickered in his eyes as he shook his head.

"I'm not interested. Besides, like I said, I'm busy with the studio."

Eli nodded slowly. "And I'm still going to help you get it reopened."

She tried for a flippant laugh but failed. "That's all right. I don't need your help." But she wasn't entirely certain that was true. Meg and Oliver were busy finishing up the school year and launching their new fishing tours during the early summer. Levi's job at the school never seemed to end—walls to be painted and pipes to be fixed. She'd even heard rumors that he was looking to buy a home of his own and move out. And Mama Potts needed to rest if her ankle and arm were ever going to heal.

"It's nonnegotiable." There was a firmness in Eli's tone that invited no argument. "I will help you."

She glanced at Oliver, looking for his support. He offered only a useless shrug and a barely suppressed smile.

"Seriously, focus on your team," she said. "Let me worry about the shop. I'll be fine."

Eli nodded. "You will be. I'll make sure of it." He gave her wrist a gentle squeeze. "And I could use your help."

She wasn't sure if it was the pleading in his eyes or the certainty in his tone, but she wanted to say yes. Or maybe she wanted to accept his help. More likely, she just wanted to keep an eye on him. To make sure he didn't have another opportunity to hurt his mom. To make sure he didn't walk out on those girls again.

The man basically needed a babysitter.

"I . . . um . . ." She glanced at Oliver one more time. He just looked smugly pleased.

Eli's grip tightened for a moment before he let her go, let her make the decision if she'd walk away from helping him. "You can make sure those girls don't eat me alive. Or the boosters. They're going to track me down after this afternoon's debacle."

"Well, I suppose someone has to."

eight

Violet stopped at the locker room door, questioning again why she'd agreed to such absurdity. She had no business helping Eli when she needed to get her shop and storefront fixed. She snuck a glance at him out of the corner of her eye. His mouth was a tight line, eyebrows serious, eyes squinting.

That had to be his pregame face.

But these girls weren't his opponents. They were looking to him for direction and help. She was here to make sure he didn't let them down. And to make sure the livid boosters buzzing around the rink didn't make him walk out for good.

Stupid. Stupid.

Eli scratched at his chin, freshly shaved.

"What happened to your beard?"

He didn't look in her direction or give any indication that he'd heard her until he responded. "I figured there's no hiding behind it now. The whole town knows I'm back, and no amount of facial hair is going to keep them from recognizing me when I'm on the bench with the team."

"I don't know." She motioned to her collarbone. "One of those grizzly-bear, full-neck beards, long mustache—you could hide behind one of those, probably."

His scowl told her exactly what he thought of that idea. "It itched."

She shrugged. That was a valid point. "Are you going to hold this team meeting from the hallway?"

"No." But he didn't make a move to open the door.

She crossed and uncrossed her arms, glancing at her non-existent watch. "Are you waiting for an invitation?"

"No."

"Did you wake up on the wrong side of the bed?"

He turned his head toward her, his shoulders still squarely pointed straight ahead. "I sleep on the couch."

Well, that would explain his surly mood. The guy probably hung off both ends of that sofa.

"So what's the problem? Let's get going."

"I'm visualizing the g—the meeting."

Ah, right. He'd probably had a sports psychologist helping him visualize every play of every game. This was as close to the ice as he was going to get, and old habits were hard to break.

She left him in peace for another long moment. Then he nodded and knocked on the door. Violet didn't suffer the same need, pushing the door open and calling in, "Everyone decent? There's a man coming in."

A low murmur of voices echoed off metal lockers, but there was no scramble to cover up. Violet led the way in, peeking around the corner into the square room. Every seat on the three benches was taken by a young woman in full gear, save helmet. Even the goalie sat in the pads that nearly swallowed her whole.

Violet tucked herself into the far corner of the room, a row of black lockers on her left and a shiny whiteboard taking up half the wall to her right.

Eli stalked in, took a deep breath through his nose, and turned to face the girls. He'd left his skates and stick at the bench beside the ice, but he looked like he belonged. He was hockey. And everyone in the room knew it.

"I owe you all an apology."

Violet choked on her own tongue and tried to cover her cough with her hands. Whatever she'd expected him to say, that was not it. The girls appeared to be equally stunned. The one on the end of the bench closest to Violet almost fell off. Eyes throughout the room grew round. But not a single person spoke, riveted by Eli's deep voice.

He didn't twitch or simper. He simply spoke clearly and concisely. "I shouldn't have walked out on you yesterday. It won't happen again."

Their silence filled his pause. Perhaps they were waiting for a slew of excuses. If so, they were disappointed.

Violet couldn't look away from him. His presence permeated the whole room, and she wondered if he visualized that too. He had basically perfected the art of drawing every milligram of attention to himself.

"All right. Let's move forward. As you know, I'm Eli Ross. You can call me Coach or Coach Ross. I'm not Eli, Buddy, Dude, or Hey You. I'll be on time to practice. I expect you to be too. If something keeps you from practice, expect something to keep you from playing in the game."

Eli waved her over, and Violet stumbled toward him, both drawn to him and appalled by that very fact. She stopped just shy of his shoulder and turned to face the girls, offering what she hoped was a genuine smile.

Most of the faces she knew from church and her short-lived stint as a Sunday school teacher. Some of them had been in the Red Clay Shoppe. But for a moment all of them looked foreign. No, that wasn't quite right. She was the foreigner, the one from away. She felt every bit of that awkwardness standing in front of them.

Two heads in the back row leaned toward each other. "Who's that?" one of the girls whispered.

"Isn't she the one from Charlottetown whose parents were rich? They died." She didn't try very hard to keep her voice from carrying.

From the bench on the left, another girl chimed in as though Violet wasn't even in the room. "No, her dad sent her away when he got remarried. Her stepmom didn't want her around."

Violet nearly snorted. That was a new one. Very Disney princess. And about as true as the fairy tales.

Eli cleared his throat with an authority that left zero space for continued whispers and snapped every gaze to him. "Enough."

She was supposed to be keeping Eli from getting eaten alive. Somehow he'd flipped the script on her.

"If you haven't met her, this is Violet Donaghy. She's our team . . ." He gave her a quick once-over, his gaze like a branding iron. "She's our . . ." He came up short again. Apparently he hadn't visualized this part of the meeting.

"Well, if you have any issues with anything not related to hockey, take it up with Miss Donaghy." He spoke her name like she was a spinster librarian, and she had a sudden urge to pull out her ponytail and touch up her makeup. She was neither a spinster—not that there was anything wrong with being unmarried at twenty-seven or any age—nor a librarian. Even if she did enjoy a paperback before bed most nights.

A girl in the back corner slowly raised her hand. Eli nodded at her, and she grimaced. "What *kind* of issues?"

"You know . . ." His motion to encompass the whole of female existence fell flat, and he dropped his hand back to his side. "Makeup, hair, or clothes."

Violet tilted her chin down and gave him her best childhood librarian look. "You think that's all girls think about?"

"No," he said quickly. "Of course not. Friendship, parents, school, dreams . . . all of that is Miss Donaghy's realm."

The girl who had almost fallen off the bench earlier flipped her long brown braid over her shoulder, uncovering the number 17 on her jersey. "So she's responsible for all that—and what is it you're here for, exactly?"

"Hockey. I'm here for the game. I'm here for stick drills and footwork. I'm here for strategy. I'm here to help you win games. If you want to talk about your feelings, I'm not your guy. But if you want to win, then let's make it happen."

Number 17 grunted, seemingly satisfied with his response, but Violet wanted him to fess up to more. More depth. More emotion. Just more. There was no way he'd lost the biggest thing in his life and not learned how to deal with it. Unless he was the king of suppressing pain and grief.

But she was the queen of suppressing pain, and she didn't

recognize herself in him. No, he wasn't consumed by the loss, but neither was he whole. Maybe he was just in the process of dealing with it.

And the counselor she'd seen in Montreal had said it was a process.

A few muttered words from the peanut gallery drew her attention from Eli, and she whipped around in time to see a girl with a blond ponytail say, "She's probably a bender."

"I am *not* a bender." Violet spat out the retort so quickly that she didn't even have time to consider the insult. At least, she was pretty sure it had been an insult, given the girl's tone. Staring down the girl, she leaned into Eli's warmth and whispered, "What's a bender?"

His straight face broke into a broad grin. "It's someone who skates with their ankles bent."

She pushed her nose up into the air. "Oh, I know how to skate."

The girls laughed. "Sure."

"Seriously. I'm a good skater." Not nearly as good as anyone else in the room, probably, but her dad had taught her. And he'd been the star of his local league. Though she hadn't been on the ice in more than a decade, it had to be like riding a bike, right?

Eli fought to rein in his smile, the twitching corners of his lips on clear display without his beard in the way. "I think you'll have to prove that. But not today." Turning back to the team, his voice fell even deeper. "Today you're going to show me what you can do. No scrimmaging. Just drills."

Groans echoed, but when Eli tilted his head toward the door, they stood up and filed out of the locker room, skates clicking against the floor, sticks waving in the air. The ice was covered with orange cones in straight lines when they reached the rink. Eli didn't say anything about it but gave a small salute to Carson, who was wiping fingerprints from the outside of the glass.

"Number 17, lead the stretch, then single-file slalom through the cones. Work your edges."

The girls did as Eli instructed, and Violet followed him to the bench.

One of the hockey moms called out to him, her arms crossed and her eyes angry. He nodded to acknowledge her. "I'll be happy to talk after practice," he said. Whether it was due to his dimples or his experience, the mom nodded and stepped away slowly.

He sat and pulled off his shoes before shoving his floppy white socks into his skates. "Thank you, Violet."

Her gaze jerked from where she'd been watching the team move in synchronized stretches. "For what?"

"For this. For being here."

Plopping down next to him on the hard wooden bench, she frowned. "I haven't done anything though."

"Hey, if the girls are eating you alive"—he cracked a crooked grin—"maybe they'll be too busy to turn on me."

She elbowed his ribs, his faded jacket probably enough padding to keep it from hurting. But his exaggerated moan made her smile. She looked up into the stands where the hockey moms stared in their direction, whispers evident. "What else do you need me to do today?"

He shook his head as he tugged on the laces of his skates, his fingers moving like the motion was imprinted on his very

DNA. "Just be here, I guess. Or . . . I mean, you can go if you need to."

"All right." She fully intended to get up. But when he stood and slipped over the boards and onto the ice, she couldn't look away from him. He moved like a tiger, powerful, long strokes eating up the ice. His blades scraped in a music all their own as he flew around the girls, who had started weaving between the cones.

She barely noticed them. Eli commanded her attention as he circled and cut. His blades flew over the ice, both making the melody and dancing to it all at once.

She wasn't the only one transfixed. Number 24—Chloe Baker—stared at Eli too. When she clipped one of the cones, she lost her balance and careened to the ice.

Violet jumped up, ready to help the girl. But Eli only gave Chloe a look that seemed to ask if she was going to get up. She did, grabbing her stick and finishing the line of cones without giving him another look.

Because he wasn't here for feelings. He wasn't here because he cared about the kids or the community. He'd have come back a long time ago if that was the case. He wasn't even here because he loved hockey, though he did. She didn't have to be a mind reader to know that. It was in every line he carved on the ice, the way he handled his skates, the light inside that made his eyes glow.

But he wasn't on the ice for the girls or the game.

Perhaps it was a good thing she couldn't keep her eyes off him. Then maybe she could figure out what he was really up to.

Eli kept his gait as easy as he could, strolling up the gentle hill to the Red Clay Shoppe the next morning. He didn't need another car to roll by, its driver wondering what was wrong with the Stars' new coach. Even if he was thinking the same thing.

He'd been skating for so many years that it hadn't even occurred to him that a two-hour practice would leave him nearly as lame as Mama Potts with her sprained ankle. She had laughed at him as he kissed her forehead and hobbled out of the house ten minutes before. She had not, however, offered him any of her miracle muscle cream.

Not that he'd have accepted. The stuff was so pungent that half the town would have known he was wearing it the minute he stepped outside. His thighs and calves may have ached like he was on his first traveling team, but he wasn't interested in advertising that. Or thinking about how long he'd been off the ice to make it true.

As he reached the T intersection, he glanced to his left to check for cars. The figure ambling his direction stopped him. When she was within earshot, he said, "Good morning, Violet."

"Eli—or should I call you Coach?"

"Yeah, Eli is fine." He winked at her as they fell into step side by side. "When it's just the two of us." She was on the outside, so he made a quick move behind her, putting himself closer to the traffic and letting her walk along the gravel beside the swaying grass.

She gave him a strange look and asked, "So if we're with your mom or brothers, then . . . Coach?"

"Absolutely. Nothing less. I'm thinking about getting a jacket embroidered with it, just so no one forgets."

"Or get one with your title and number across the back, like your jersey."

"Sweater."

"What?"

"We call them sweaters."

She stopped, and he was a few paces ahead of her before he noticed. When he turned back, she said, "We?"

"Hockey players. Hockey . . . people. You're a hockey person now. You should sound like it."

Her eyes narrowed, and he missed even the fraction of vibrant amber that had disappeared. But the intensity there made up for it, settling deep in his chest, warming him in places that the sun couldn't touch.

"What if I don't want to be a hockey person?"

He shrugged, moving toward the studio again. "Too late now."

"I think I should get to make that decision."

"You already did."

She scrambled to catch up with him. "I think I'd remember something like that."

"When you agreed to help with the team."

"I didn't know I was signing up for an entire shift in my identity. Seems like there should have been a warning label or something. As I recall, all I agreed to was making sure you didn't end up as prey for a middle school wolf pack."

He laughed at the mental picture, rediscovering the rumble in his chest like a long-lost friend. Pressing a hand over his heart, he tried to remember the last time he'd felt happy. He'd never have guessed when he met her two weeks before that Violet would be the one to make him feel that again.

Maybe that was what his family all found in her too.

It was a lot of pressure to put on one person, expecting her to make an entire family happy. And he didn't want to crush her—even if she seemed strong enough to hold back the sea.

She lifted her face toward the sun, her eyes closed, the breeze toying with the dark strands of her ponytail. The lines of her face were smooth and symmetrical. She wasn't a showy beauty like the girls who'd hovered around the locker room door. They were primped and powdered, sporting dresses that left every single curve on full display. Violet wore loose jeans with large stains of red clay and bright glazes down both legs, remnants from weeks and months before. Her green T-shirt was clean but baggy, the sleeves rolled up nearly to her shoulders, showing off her lean arms. Eli wasn't sure she was wearing any makeup, but her skin glowed in the sun, which shimmered off golden strands in her hair.

"What's your story?"

She blinked like she'd forgotten he was even there. "What do you mean?"

She knew what he meant. He was sure of it. But he offered her an explanation anyway. "How'd you end up in Victoria? It seems like there are a lot of rumors but not a lot of fact."

"I took a bus."

He laughed, reminded again that they were both without wheels—Violet by choice and him by bad choices. "No, I mean, what brought you to such a tiny map dot? When did you get here? You weren't in school when I was."

"How do you know? Maybe I was a wallflower."

"I'd have remembered you—or at least your eyes." He hadn't meant to say that out loud.

The radiant eyes in question opened wide for a split second before she ducked her head and stared at the ground, her white shoes rolling across the dirt.

"It's been more than ten years since I left. You weren't here then, were you?"

She shook her head. "I started at the high school the year after you graduated."

"The same class as Oliver?"

"I'm a year younger."

His foot slipped off the pavement and across a patch of gravel. She seemed like everyone's big sister—or at least Oliver and Levi's. But she was probably just a few months older than Levi.

"So what brought you to Victoria?"

She stared at him. Hard. "Why'd you leave the Rangers?"

He gave a shake of his head, his only real response a mirthless chuckle.

There was no hemming and hawing around her question. It was too blunt to ignore—and maybe the most direct version he'd heard yet.

But he still wasn't going to answer it.

Confessing his sins wasn't part of his plan. Especially not to Princess Violet, who would probably be far too happy to share them with his family.

But she seemed to have some secrets of her own. He'd never known a woman who didn't like talking about herself. Then again, he didn't know anything about Violet that hadn't come from his brother or Mama Potts. Except that she said she could skate, and she seemed pretty proud of that fact. He would have to make her prove it.

She couldn't answer an innocuous question like what had brought her to town, which meant it wasn't innocuous. If keeping secrets had taught him anything, it was how to spot others hiding their own.

As they crested the small hill, still strolling in silence, he pointed toward the single building a few hundred yards beyond the gray shingles of the Red Clay Shoppe. Its bright yellow siding refused to fade into the sky, the long porch inviting a lazy afternoon in one of the Adirondacks. "Whose place is that?"

"Jenny and Dylan's. She owns a specialty soap and body scrub shop. He runs a red-dye T-shirt store and a confectionery."

"There's a candy store within a puck shot, and you're only now telling me about it?"

She snorted. "You couldn't shoot a puck that far."

"Yes, I could. I just need a rink that big." He motioned between the buildings. "And get me some ice."

Her scowl wasn't entirely authentic, and he could see the smile she was fighting when she grumbled, "Get your own ice."

"All right, I will. Just you wait until December."

"Are you going to be here in eight months?"

He tried to shake off the honesty in her question, this one blunt as well. The trouble was he didn't know the answer. He hadn't thought much beyond Tony's deadline. And after that . . . well, it all depended on if he could scrape together what he owed.

"Do either of them sell pottery?" He waved his hand toward Jenny and Dylan's building.

She squinted across the grass in need of mowing. "I don't think so."

"Would they?"

nine

Eli rubbed his hands together, already looking forward to the last practice of the week. The girls were going to hate him.

Good.

A quick rap on the locker room door had brought the girls filing out.

"What's the plan today, Coach?" 17 asked as she stepped onto the ice, her eyes darting toward parallel lines of cones at one end of the rink. The other girls followed her out, making a big circle around where he stood at center ice.

He checked the bench for Violet, but she hadn't arrived yet. She'd said she might be late. He'd given her a pass since she was still trying to track down the electrician to give her a quote on the studio. He just hoped she'd make it, since he had some plans for after practice. Violet had a reputation to defend.

In the meantime, he was going to run these girls ragged.

"Go ahead and stretch. 24, you lead."

Half the girls looked down at their sweaters, and he ran his gloved hand over his face. Thankfully 24 wasn't one of the girls confused about her number, and she skated to the middle, calling out stretches for their hamstrings and quads, calves, and arms.

Eli took the time to make a slow circle around the group, analyzing each girl, watching the way she held her stick and how comfortable she was on the ice. Some looked like they'd been born in a rink, but one poor girl, 7, still looked like she was afraid the ice would jump up and bite her. They needed to fix that. Fast.

"Take a couple laps," he said to the girls as they wrapped up their stretching.

They took off, 17 at the front, her long brown braid flapping. 24 and 11 weren't far behind, with the rest of the team trying to keep up. Then 7. And finally the goalies, fighting their oversized gear for every inch.

"Hustle, hustle!" His voice echoed, and several of the moms in the stands stared at him. One waved and smiled, and Mable Jean watched over it all like a mother hen, Ellen right by her side.

Turning his back on them, he focused on the girls. This wasn't about the parents or the town. This was about what these girls needed in order to succeed. He'd figure it out for them.

Just as he was about to call out the first drill, a movement at the bench caught his attention. Violet.

She smiled, and he put his hand to his ear like it was a phone. She laughed—because clearly he looked like an idiot. But she nodded.

Good. She'd finally gotten an appointment with the electrician. They were going to get the store open. Hopefully before the summer tourists flooded the island.

"Um, Coach?" One of the girls had skated up to his elbow, a hand on her padded hip, the other balancing her stick. He looked up to see all the other girls staring at him. Right. They were in the middle of practice, not an update on the Red Clay Shoppe situation.

"Okay, split up in the four corners. This is corner one, two, three, and four." He pointed at each. "One and two line up and pass back and forth. Three and four do the same."

The girls split up, and he skated from group to group, watching them work in silence. "This is a passing drill, but it's also a communication drill," he called. "Talk to each other."

The chatter started softly but grew as the girls called to take the puck. 7 held back as though she'd only just realized she was holding a stick, her eyes wide. The other girls were fighting for a chance, calling for the pass to come to them. But 7 looked like she'd rather be on the bench with Violet.

Eli skated up behind her and leaned onto his knees. "You're looking at that stick like it dropped off a UFO. It should be your best friend."

She looked up at him, slapping her stick a few times before losing control. It swung toward him, and he ducked and bobbed just in time to save himself a knot on the side of his head.

Her eyes filled with horror. "I'm sorry, Coach. I just can't seem to use it."

He pulled it from her loose fingers, holding it up next to his own. It was only an inch or two shorter. "That's because it's too long for you. Where'd you get this?"

"It was my brother's."

He grinned, leaning in even farther until it was like they were the only two on the rink. He tugged on the collar of his sweater. "I'm the oldest, and I'm still wearing my brother's clothes."

"Really?"

"You bet. But you can't play with a stick you don't trust." He looked around, hunting for a familiar face. "I think I saw some extra sticks in the storeroom. Why don't you go ask Carson if he has one that's more your size?"

As if he knew when someone was talking about him, Carson waved from the entrance, where he'd been watching practice. 7 took off, dragging her stick behind her.

One problem solved. But the rest of the girls still had too much energy. So Eli blew his whistle and gave them another drill. Then another.

With fifteen minutes left of practice, all of them were dragging. Including Eli. He called for them to scrimmage anyway.

He dropped the puck and watched 17 face off against 24. The girls kept going. And they kept fighting. All the way up until he blew his whistle one last time to end practice.

The girls dragged themselves toward the locker room. He'd been expecting them to be too worn out to chirp and chatter, but their hushed whispers still carried as they disappeared through the weathered yellow door.

"Did you see his eyes?"

"And his dimples."

"What dimples? He scowled at us the whole practice."

That had to be number 17. What was her name again? Madeline? No, Madison.

"Oh, he has dimples. I've seen them at church."

The first voice piped up again. "Well, he could scowl at me all day with those blue eyes, as long as they come with that jawline and those shoulders. I bet he doesn't even need pads to fill out that sweater."

Eli nearly spat out a laugh until the second girl chimed in again.

"That man is stupid hot."

Eli's ears burned, and he was pretty sure his neck was on its way to a matching red hue when another teenage voice broke through.

"Forget his dimples. Coach can flat-out play." Madison again.

Thank God for girls who loved the game.

"Besides, he's old."

Perhaps his gratitude had been premature.

He chuckled. He sure felt old these days. He'd turned thirty on his last birthday, even though there'd been no party and no presents. And after a lifetime of taking hits and a fair share of concussions, he couldn't expect to feel differently. Didn't mean he needed the reminder though.

Before the girls could continue, a warm breath blew in his ear. "Are they still talking about how cute you are?"

"What?" His voice jumped to a range he hadn't used since before puberty. Immediately he dropped it as he spun to face Violet. "No." He swallowed thickly. "Wait. You think I'm cute?"

"I did not say that." She was pretty cute herself, with a half scowl and her hands on her hips.

He couldn't help himself. Or a grin he was sure was too smug. "Yes, you did."

She shook her head, crossing her arms. "I most certainly did not."

"Oh, so you think I'm 'stupid hot' then?"

If she'd been drinking anything, she would have sprayed it all over him. He enjoyed the wild flash of her eyes as they combed over him from his hair to his blades. If she even half agreed with the girls—and a chunk of the female population in New York—she hid it well behind firmly set lips and rebar shoulders.

He tried not to notice. Or care.

"Well, I think you're at least one of those things," she said.

He doubled over, leaning on his stick and letting the humor flow through him.

"Where did you even hear a phrase like 'stupid hot'?" she asked.

With a tilt of his head toward the closed locker room door, he said, "They don't just think I'm cute."

She rolled her eyes and uncrossed her arms long enough to push him out of the way, swing the door open, and march into the locker room. "Ladies," she announced. "Eli—I mean, Coach—is on his way in."

He could hear the chatter even as he paused by the open entrance. Out of habit, he leaned away, knowing the ripe scent of a teenage locker room. Only . . . it wasn't there. That couldn't be right. He'd pushed them hard during practice.

He took a test sniff, then another. Then he leaned his whole head into the entry, closed his eyes, and breathed deeply through his nose. It smelled like, well, not exactly dryer sheets, but relatively clean laundry, with a hint of something earthy.

There was the smell of ice and cold and even sticks. And beneath all that there was the smell of hard work.

But there was no underlying fragrance of dirty socks and unwashed teenage armpits. No stench of forgotten sandwiches molding in the bottom of gear bags.

"Good work out there today, ladies."

Madison beamed. The rest might have too if they'd had anything left in their tanks.

"I know you worked hard, but I'd like to invite you to stick around for a little while longer."

Their ears seemed to perk up.

"For the public skate."

All the girls groaned.

"Come on, Coach," Madison said. "It's madness out there—all those kids who don't know how to skate running into you. Mrs. Halverson even had her kid in a stroller on the ice one time."

"Well, you can consider it another drill—avoid running into everyone else." He shrugged. "Plus we have a guest skater." He bent over and picked up a pair of black-and-white hockey skates from under the nearest bench. When he held them up, the room went quiet. He looked at Violet, whose mouth dropped open as her eyes went wide. "I think it's about time we find out if we have a bender in our midst."

The room exploded.

"No." Violet waved her hands in front of her, trying to calm the girls down. "I don't think that's—"

"Come on now, you told us you knew how to skate. You

weren't exaggerating the truth there, were you?" Eli's eyebrows pumped twice. "Prove it."

"I haven't been on the ice in a while, and I'm not exactly prepared."

"What do you need to do to prepare?" Chloe asked. "It's just skating."

Maybe when you were fourteen. Maybe when a fall didn't also risk a broken bone or more. Violet had more than a decade on these girls, and they were on the ice five afternoons a week.

"I don't think so. If I break my arm or my hand, I can't do my job." Mama Potts had already proven there was no way to throw a pot one-handed.

"I promise, I won't let you fall," Eli said.

Promises, promises. He'd been making a lot of those lately. But he still hadn't convinced her he knew how to follow through.

Eli held out the skates as an offering. "I've already cleared it with Carson. The whole team can skate for free—but just today." He tilted his head and gave her what had to be his most convincing smile.

The rat.

She was supposed to be the advice giver, the everything-but-hockey support for the team. He'd set her up. She couldn't very well say no now. Even if she was bound to look like an absolute fool in front of her semi-charges.

She glared at him but reached for the skates. The girls cheered, and Eli told them to get comfortable. The rink opened back up in fifteen minutes.

Violet followed him out of the locker room, mumbling

under her breath, imagining just how much she'd enjoy plucking out each and every one of his eyebrows.

When they reached the bench, she yanked off her shoe and nearly chucked it at him. "That was low."

"What?" He tried to use his innocent face.

It wouldn't work on her. "You knew I couldn't say no to the girls. And now you're putting me on skates in front of the whole town when you know I haven't been on the ice since I was a kid."

"I knew no such thing. How could I?" He put his hand to his throat in mock horror at her accusation. "Besides, you told us all that you knew how to skate."

She jammed her stockinged foot into the skate and wiggled her toes. A perfect fit. "How do you know what size I wear?"

"Mama Potts may have let it slip."

Violet jerked on the laces, and Eli cringed. Getting down on his knees before her, he looked up into her face. "Let me."

She wanted to swat his hands away, but they moved with such assurance that she couldn't deny him. Especially since the skates felt like a forgotten friend. Like she wasn't sure where their last conversation had ended or where to begin again.

"Put your heel all the way back." Eli wrapped his hand around her ankle, then adjusted the skate, tucking the hem of her jeans inside. When he seemed satisfied, he pulled on the laces until the skate was snug and tied them off with a flourish. Then he slid her other shoe off and set it on the floor.

His bent head gave her a moment to really look at him, to watch the bunching and shifting of his shoulders and the precision of his fingers. She couldn't remember the last time someone had put her shoes—or skates—on for her. It was oddly personal, the way his blunt fingertips squeezed the instep of her foot as he slid it into place. More tender than she could have imagined. His hand slipped up to cradle her heel, and she felt it all the way in her spirit—protected, treasured.

Sparks fizzled up toward her knee, and she wanted to yank her foot out of his grasp. But then he might think she was refusing to skate. He'd think he'd won. Because somewhere along the line this had become a competition. She didn't have a clue what they were competing for—but they were definitely competing.

He glanced up. "Does that feel okay?"

Better than. Not that she would ever give him the satisfaction. "It's fine."

With a slap on his knees, he pushed himself up, then held out his hands to help her stand. She wasn't interested in seeing how her body would react if he touched her hand, so she waved him off. But the minute she got up, her feet forgot how to stand on the narrow blades. Her ankle rolled, and she began to tumble.

Until he scooped her up.

If her foot had betrayed her before with its tinglings, her arms were worse. How his hands under her elbows could shoot fireworks straight to her chest, she'd never know. But they filled her lungs with smoke, making it hard to breathe. Or maybe that was the wall of his chest in front of her face.

He was too broad for his own good, and all she could see was the navy-blue knit of his sweatshirt. All she could smell was the subtle fragrance of . . . *him*. Soap and the ice and something spicy that he must have put on after he shaved.

Eli towered over her, even with her skates on. But he leaned down, nearly pressing his lips to her ear. His breath stirred her hair, his words like honey and only for her. "Steady there." He squeezed her elbows, and she thought she might take another tumble. Only because she'd turned to jelly inside.

What ridiculousness.

Although, maybe for the first time, she had a bit of compassion for the girls hanging on his arm in the tabloids. Yeah, she could understand how all of this—all two meters of Eli Ross—could make a girl lose her mind.

But not Violet Donaghy.

She jerked back, stepping away in clunky, uneven strides. "I'm fine. I'm good."

Laughter filled his eyes.

Yes, she could definitely understand those girls.

Ellen from church—one of the team boosters—huffed and puffed around the outside of the rink. Her breathing reached them before the woman herself, her purse hooked at her bent elbow.

Ellen waved her free arm wildly, as though Violet and Eli hadn't noticed her approach. "Eli. Coach. Could I have a word with you about your strategy for the game next week?" Her words were innocuous enough, but her gaze left Violet with little doubt that she would be at the center of Ellen's questions.

Eli looked to her as though she might save him. Not likely.

"I'm going to go find a pair of gloves." Violet waved at them, giving a genuine smile in exchange for Ellen's fake one.

Ellen didn't even wait for her to clomp out of earshot before she asked, "Are you sure she's a good influence? What do you really know about her? What does anyone?"

Violet could feel Eli's gaze land on her, but trying to walk faster in skates only made her move more awkwardly. She forced herself to take even strides, even if it meant hearing his response.

"Well, I know she doesn't talk about people behind their backs. She's a class act."

She wasn't sure if he'd said that to put Ellen in her place or because it was true. As she turned down the hall toward the locker rooms, she hoped it was both.

She clomped into the supply room, looking for some gear. "Carson!"

He looked up from the boxes he was stacking, a bright smile on his face.

"Eli has roped me into skating today, and I don't have my gloves or hat with me. Do you have anything I can borrow?"

Carson's grin grew even wider.

Ten minutes later, Violet was dressed in a sweater, a toque to keep her ears from getting cold, and gloves that were just a little too floppy. But at least she was warm.

Eli was still stuck in conversation with Ellen.

A small crowd of locals had gathered—mostly kids and their parents—to enjoy an afternoon of fun. When the Zamboni puttered off the ice, Carson turned on music that filled the arena, and then he swung open the entrance. Little hockey players zipped away, their skates almost a blur, arms pumping back and forth.

Suddenly the Stars surrounded her. "Come on, Miss Donaghy."

"Just Violet. Please."

They didn't stop to listen, propelling her onto the ice and almost immediately leaving her in their wake. That was probably better. Let her get her feet under her. Or, rather, figure out how to keep her feet from flying out from under her.

She remembered her dad's instructions. Bend your knees. Lean forward just a little bit. Point your hips where you want to go. The muscle memory was there, but it was thin like a veil. Clearly Eli and the girls knew how to deal with the ice, but she'd managed to forget how terribly strange it was to lose all traction, to feel in her very core every bump and ripple of the frozen surface. And to know that each one had the power to send her crashing to the ground.

She glanced over one shoulder, then the other. No sign of Eli.

Good. She wasn't going to let him see her unsteady on her feet.

Push, push, glide. Push, push, glide.

Okay, she could do this.

She passed two kids hugging the wall. At least she wasn't *that* out of practice.

Madison and Chloe flew past her, brushing against the sleeve of her sweater and threatening to send her down. They spun and skated backward, waving and laughing and dancing to the music.

For a split second, Violet stood all the way up, locking her knees and straightening her back. Suddenly her arms flailed, her feet backpedaled, and she knew she was going to fall.

But she didn't.

Before she even looked up, she knew that Eli had rescued

her again, his hand on her back putting her to rights, keeping her steady. Huffing a strand of hair out of her eyes, she waited for his snide comment. It didn't come.

His smile was warm enough that she could almost take off her sweater. "You were right. You're not a bender. You have good form."

She wanted to ask just exactly what form he was looking at, because she felt like Gumby on stilts at the moment. But she bit back the question and said only, "Thanks . . . I guess."

"You want to skate together?" He reached out his hand to take hers, turning to face her as he skated backward.

The simple, quiet question almost knocked her flat on her backside. But this was not a made-for-TV movie, and they were not on a date. "You go ahead. I'm fine."

He gave her one more look, apparently deciding whether he believed her or not. Then he was off. His feet moved with such assurance, so much grace. Back and forth, crossing over and then back. He moved side to side, catching up with his team and then passing them. The girls chased after him, but they were no match for his speed and skill.

A whole lap later, Violet realized she wasn't the only one watching the team playing around. Moms and grandmas stood on the other side of the glass, hands clasped and hearts in their eyes.

The sudden clipped scrape of skates against the ice right behind her made her back stiffen. Then two hands grabbed onto her rear end.

Violet nearly jumped out of her skin, her blade catching the ice as she scrambled to regain her balance and her wits. She spun, a glare for Eli already in place. If he thought this was funny, he was wrong. And everyone in the rink was about to know it.

But he wasn't there. Or at least, not right behind her.

A boy of about six or seven, arms flapping like a heron in a hurricane, stumbled toward her. His feet slid back and forth, legs bending like putty as he reached for anything solid, anything to save a splat against the ice. His long hair hung in front of his wild eyes, and Violet could see the strain in the line of his lips as he struggled for control.

Apparently her bum had been the closest option.

A dark shadow silently slid behind the kid, strong hands slipping beneath his arms and lifting him off his feet. "Okay there, little man?"

The kid looked up into the face of his rescuer, the fear in his eyes immediately turning to wonder. "Eli Ross." His words came out in breathy awe.

Eli set the kid gently back on his skates, waiting while they skimmed over the surface until he regained his balance. "Be careful out there."

The kid nodded as he found his footing and sailed toward his friends, their excited chatter already overwhelming the audio system playing the latest from Taylor Swift. No apology or even acknowledgment that he'd copped a feel on a woman four times his age.

Ungrateful kid.

Eli's gaze stayed on the boy for a little while before he turned it on her. He met her stare for a quick second before looking pointedly at her hips. His grin barely contained the laughter sparkling in those too-blue-for-his-own-good eyes, the corners of his mouth fighting to release his humor. "Friend of yours?"

She fought the chuckle bubbling in her chest and spun again. She pushed off in the flow of traffic, refusing to give him the privilege of a shared laugh.

As far as escapes went, it wasn't her smartest. Within a second, he was by her side. His skates ate up the ice, his blades hugging the scarred surface.

He stayed right at her shoulder, just visible out of the corner of her eye, his own shoulders trembling beneath his sweater. "You get that a lot?"

The last time she'd skated, the kids had bounced right into her legs and tumbled off her and onto their own backsides. They'd also popped back up like balloons. This was the first time she'd been properly goosed by a flailing skater.

Not that she was going to say that to Eli. So she had no idea what compelled her to respond to his question with one of her own. "Why do you think I agreed to skate today?"

His blades cut the ice, shaving it as he came to a quick stop. His laughter echoed, bouncing off the glass and into the metal rafters and floating over them all. And finally Violet let herself laugh too.

ten

It's going to be how much?" Violet swayed, the number of zeros on the estimate from the electrician making her eyes blurry. It had to be a misprint, a typo of some sort. Maybe she was just missing a decimal point.

But the grimace on the grizzled electrician's face didn't give her much hope. "I'm sorry. I know it's a lot. But the whole building needs to be rewired to get it up to code." Glenn tilted his head toward the kiln. "Especially if you want to run one of those without starting another fire."

She put her hands on her hips and glared at the scorched wall around the socket, then at the useless kiln. Then back at the paper ticket in her hand.

The insurance adjuster had called Mama Potts just the day before. The payout, which was still weeks away, wouldn't even cover half of the rewiring, let alone the new kiln and their destroyed work. The payment was to cover the fire repairs, not bring an old building into a new century.

Glenn's pale green eyes looked up into exposed rafters, then down the walls, taking in the open room. "You probably don't have enough equity in here to get a loan."

Okay, that hurt. Even if it was true.

He twisted the corner of his graying mustache. "We can set up a payment plan if that'll help."

"How soon can you get started?"

Violet spun around at the sound of Eli's voice. She'd almost forgotten he was there, carrying now-empty shelves outside and breaking down the ones that couldn't be salvaged.

"Would you excuse us for a minute?" she said to Glenn, grabbing Eli's forearm and tugging him into the sunlight. "What do you think you're doing?" she said under her breath. "I don't have that kind of money."

"You also don't have another option."

Squinting at him, she crossed her arms. "What did I tell you about making valid points?"

His smile was sad. In his eyes, she could see he wanted to laugh but he didn't find any humor in this situation.

"This whole thing stinks," he said. "I know it and you know it. But you have a building that you can't use and a business with almost nothing to sell."

"Thanks for the reminder."

He reached for her with arms outstretched, almost like he was going to wrap her in a bear hug and make all of her worries vanish. She froze at the mere thought of being in his arms, every nerve in her body on high alert.

It was not where she belonged. Definitely not where she wanted to be.

Probably.

She let out a quick sigh when he dropped his arms and gave a quick shrug instead.

"It just seems like the only way forward is . . . well . . .

forward. Either you're going to let it all crumble around you or you're going to fight for it."

More with the valid points. Because not making a decision was still making a decision.

There wasn't a question in her mind or a doubt in her heart. The decision had been made from the first moment that Mama Potts invited a skinny, clumsy sixteen-year-old into her studio and showed her how to form something beautiful from a hunk of clay.

Violet told Glenn she'd figure out a way to make payments, signed his quote, and agreed on a start date a week out. As soon as he left, she marched through the studio door into the shop.

Eli chased after her. "Where are you going?"

She scanned a shelf of mugs, looking for her favorite before holding it up for his survey. "What do you think?"

"It's green."

"Very observant." She was already halfway out the front door, the bell above the frame jingling.

"Hey." When Eli caught up with her, he seemed almost out of breath. "What's going on? Aren't we going to finish cleaning out the studio today?"

"We will. I'll be back soon." She turned to go, but his hand at her elbow stopped her. His grip was gentle, but even the slightest pressure told her what it might feel like to be wrapped up in those arms, his touch like flames licking up a wall. Disaster.

"Violet?"

"I figured you'd be two steps ahead of me, since it was your idea."

"To see Jenny and Dylan." A smile stretched his lips, showing off his straight white teeth. "To ask them to carry your pottery."

She nodded, already heading up the road, but stopped as she realized he was right by her side.

"What?" He shrugged. "Like you said, it was my idea. Why should I get left out of this adventure?"

Adventure was much too strong a word for a brisk walk two hundred meters down the road, her face lifted to the sun.

As Violet reached the paved parking lot, each of its six spots empty, she paused. The doors of the three businesses were open, and the sweet smell of chocolate drifted from the farthest. But there was no one else around. No locals. No tourists. No customers.

Perhaps this wasn't such a great idea.

Eli was looking around and must have thought the same thing. "There'll be customers in a few weeks, right?"

"Of course." She spoke with more confidence than she actually felt. The Red Clay Shoppe had survived on tourist seasons for the last four years—tourism was the heart of the island. By the time Victoria Day weekend rolled around at the end of May, the roads were fuller, the storefronts buzzing with activity.

But remembering that in the face of empty parking spots and the electrician's quote stuffed in her pocket wasn't easy.

Forcing a smile onto her face, Violet marched through the center door and into a haven of wildflowers and spearmint. The smells immediately relaxed her shoulders, and she had a genuine grin for Jenny, who sat on a high stool on the other side of the wooden counter, her nose deeply embedded between the pages of a paperback. Jenny was probably in her forties, but her face was a testimony to her cleansers and lotions. She looked a few years shy of thirty, not a wrinkle on her face or a gray hair in her sleek black ponytail. Her head remained bent over the story unfolding in her hands, so Violet gently cleared her throat.

Jenny jumped, the legs of her stool clattering against the floor as she rocked back and forth. "Violet!" She hopped up and raced around the end of the counter, pulling Violet into a hug that pinned her arms down at her sides. "Oh, honey. I heard about the fire and Mama Potts's arm. How are you?"

Aside from being wholly immobilized by the woman's embrace, she was fine. Physically, anyway. She wasn't eager to analyze her mental or spiritual situation. Violet simply nodded in answer to the question.

Jenny stepped back, holding her shoulders at arm's length, her gaze unrelentingly inquisitive. "Seriously. Are you all right?"

Before Violet could respond, Jenny's gaze shot toward the doorway, and her eyebrows rose until they disappeared beneath her bangs. Dropping her hold on Violet, Jenny stepped around her and practically floated toward Eli. "You're . . . You're . . ."

"Eli Ross." He reached out to shake her hand. "Very nice to meet you."

Jenny fully ignored the handshake, instead using the opening to slip her arms around his waist and hug him just as tightly as she'd hugged Violet.

Eli froze, his arms at his sides, his eyes huge and filled with silent laughter. Violet slammed her hand over her nose and mouth to stifle the snort that threatened. *I'm sorry.* She mouthed the words before she realized he couldn't see them.

"I'm such a big fan. I mean, my boys and I, we watched all of your games. We were so sad when you retired."

Eli patted Jenny's shoulder with an awkward motion. Violet could see him working through the word Jenny had used. *Retired.* He hadn't retired. The rest of the world seemed to know it, but maybe his fans didn't care.

"I can't believe you're really here. In my store. Can we—will you take a picture with me?"

"I'm not really . . ." Eli motioned toward his threadbare T-shirt, which looked like it belonged to Levi, the leanest of the Ross brothers. It hugged every bit of Eli's torso, shoulders, and arms.

Not that Violet had noticed.

Okay, so maybe she'd noticed a little bit. It was hard not to when the guy wore a shirt like that.

Or any shirt.

No, that wasn't true. She hadn't given him a second look until today. And probably just because she wanted to know if the heather-gray T-shirt was as soft as it looked.

Now she looked a little closer because of the laughter in his eyes and the comical shock on his face as he stood there and let Jenny hug him.

Jenny pressed her ear to his chest and smiled up at him, a dream clearly fulfilled. Finally she pulled back but didn't let go. "Are you back in town? For good?"

"For better or worse."

As much as Violet didn't want to admit it, it might be the former instead of the latter.

"Is it true that you're coaching? I heard a rumor, but I couldn't believe it."

"Well, I won't be able to make practice this afternoon if you don't let go." His voice was flush with humor.

Jenny's laugh was as high and light as a hummingbird. She released her hold and stepped back, bumping into Violet. "I'm sorry. I'm just . . . I can't believe that you're really here. My husband, Dylan, took us to see you play against the Leafs a few years ago. You even signed a puck for my boys. Maybe you could sign one for me too."

The humor left his eyes, snuffed out in an instant.

Violet had a ridiculous urge to save him, to stand up for him as he'd done for her with Ellen. "Actually, he has to get to practice soon. But first, I came to ask if you'd carry some of our pottery in your store?" Holding up the teal-green mug with an outline of the island in red clay, Violet tried for an easy smile.

"Sell it here?" Jenny waved her hand toward the tables stacked with pyramids of body scrub tins and shelves covered in blocks of pink and blue soaps. "But it's not really what . . ."

Violet's stomach twisted painfully, and it must have shown on her face.

Jenny started over. "Won't it compete with your sales? We send visitors your way all the time."

"I know, and we really appreciate it." Violet sighed. "It's just that we can't reopen the store."

"You're closing the Red Clay Shoppe?" Jenny's voice ran up an octave. "You can't do that!"

Violet gave a violent shake of her head. "No. It's just until the whole building is rewired. But it'll take several weeks, and we need some sales to pay the electrician."

"Oh." Jenny didn't blink as she looked between them, then at the proffered mug, and finally around the open room—still without a customer. "I don't know how much help we can be. The truth is that Mama Potts has been her own draw to this area. The visitors we get are either coming to the theater or because someone in Charlottetown told them about your shop."

"Of course." Victoria was a little artistic haven, but Mama Potts's reputation around the island drew more visitors to the area than Jenny and Dylan ever could. Violet pressed her fingers to her forehead, smoothing out the wrinkle between her eyebrows.

"But we'll do whatever we can," Jenny rushed to add. She ran toward the mahogany bookshelf near the front door and immediately began clearing the tins of lavender face cream there. "You can have all these shelves. And we'll . . ." Her eyes darted toward Eli. "We won't charge you any commission. You set the sale price, and I'll give you everything you make."

Violet hadn't even dared to hope Jenny would be so generous. Sure, it probably had more to do with impressing Eli than it did with Jenny wanting to be neighborly. Violet would take it anyway.

"Thank you." She reached out to shake Jenny's hand. "I'll bring by some stock tomorrow."

"You both? You'll both be here?" Jenny had eyes only for Eli, who bestowed her with a rich chuckle.

"Yes. I'll be here too."

"You've got this, 11." Eli slid a puck to the shortest Star, who snagged it with the toe of her stick, zipped between the line of orange pylons, and finally shot it at the net. It clanged against the left post, flew toward the glass, and bounced back to the ice.

She dropped her stick and covered her face with her gloves. "I'm sorry, Coach."

"Don't be sorry. Make the shot."

"I can't!" she wailed, a sound that had always accompanied crying in his experience.

He froze, the puck he was ready to send to Madison stuck at his side. He shot a look at Violet sitting on the bench, hovering over her phone and swiping at the screen. This was supposed to be her area of expertise, but she was on the hunt for a new kiln, and he had a feeling all of her attention was focused there.

11 just kept shaking her head, holding up the line, until Madison put one gloved hand on her hip and pulled off her helmet with the other. "Get over it, Sophie," she said. "You can too make the shot. I've seen you do it. Now get back in line and get your head on straight."

Sophie looked straight at Madison, attitude all over her. "Just because hockey is all you think about doesn't mean it's easy for the rest of us."

"Well, maybe if you thought about it a little more, it wouldn't be quite so hard."

64 shoved Madison from behind, making her drop her helmet, which skittered across the ice. Throwing down her gloves, Madison rammed into 64, who toppled into the girls behind her.

"You think you run this team just because you were Coach Butler's favorite and he made you captain," 64 said. "News flash—he left, and you're not special."

Violet had been right. These girls didn't mess around. His teams had had their share of fights, but they were fists only. When the whistle blew, they were over. These girls fought with their mouths, every sneering word meant to knock another down.

He glanced toward Violet still engrossed in her online search. Then he looked at the moms in the stands, their heads all turned in his direction. He was supposed to do something before this turned into a yard sale, all the girls' gear strewn across the ice for anyone to pick up.

"Blue line!" His whistle pierced the air in a single sharp note, and each girl froze. Even Violet looked up.

He'd have made a few of his coaches proud with that one.

"Now!" he yelled. The girls scrambled to scoop up their sticks and buckets and shoved their gloves under their arms. When all of the girls were on the line, he dropped his voice so they had to lean in toward him. "Blue line to blue line and back. Until I tell you to stop."

The girls groaned, and he smiled, skating to the boards in front of the bench and leaning against them. He blew the whistle again, and the girls took off, the swish of their pants nearly drowning out the scrape of their blades.

"You look pretty smug there, Coach." The low words in his ear caused goose bumps that had nothing to do with the cold to race down his arms.

"Maybe if they're too tired to argue, they won't devour me—or each other."

Violet chuckled. "Nice strategy."

He smiled, his eyes scanning the far bleachers where Mable Jean and her posse had settled back into their own discussion. As his gaze flicked back to Violet, he caught a shadow beneath the bleachers. Just a silhouette, but it made his hackles stand on end. Maybe it was Carson.

But he knew it wasn't. The frame was too big. Too familiar.

There and gone. A ghost of his past. A reminder that he had to make something happen. Fast.

He clenched his fist beneath his brace. He missed the sharp pain that had greeted that motion for weeks. It was barely a dull ache now. A reminder of the passing days—a certainty that if he didn't act soon, he'd wind up with more than a broken wrist. Tony expected to be paid. Eli expected his first paycheck after the game next week. The problem was that the latter wasn't enough to cover the former.

Maybe the need to stretch his dollars was why his dad had tried to win a few wagers, bet on sure things. Only there weren't any sure things in gambling unless you had someone on the inside.

His stomach clenched, and his vision went blurry.

Placing a bet to try to increase his paycheck was a guarantee of one thing and one thing only. That he was as stupid as his old man. He had to find some other income. And he knew exactly one guy who might be able to help.

"You can't just run them ragged forever though."

"Huh?" Eli jerked himself out of New York and the memories there.

"The team." Violet crossed her arms. "They have their first game with you in a few days. What are you going to do if they start fighting each other then?"

In the middle of the ice, his two goalies lagged behind even the slower skaters, Madison clearly the strongest, fastest. Her arms swung side to side in perfect form, the strokes eating up the space between the blue lines. Her turns were practiced, sharp.

Right then, he knew her like he knew himself, just a generation removed—the same passion for the game enveloping everything she did.

Some of the other girls were good. Madison had greatness somewhere deep inside. Maybe he could help her set it free.

Eli blew the whistle again. "Good practice. Go home and get some rest."

The girls slumped off toward the locker room, their groans echoing all the way to the rafters.

He followed behind them, calling out to Madison before she could reach the yellow door. "17, hold up."

She turned around, her face red and sweat making the hairs at her temple curl. "Coach?"

"A word?" He nodded toward the side, and she stepped out of line, letting every other player file past her.

She didn't speak, her eyebrows raised, and he waited until there was no one else within earshot. Violet stood back near the entrance to the rink, her half smile hopeful. He wasn't sure what he wanted to say. What did he wish his coaches had told him when he was in a bantam league? What would he have actually listened to?

"Coach Butler was right to make you the captain. You're a strong player, and I can see how much you love the game."

Madison glowed. "Thanks, Coach."

"But from someone else who's used to being the best player on the squad, take it easy on your teammates."

Her smile faltered. "What do you mean? Sophie wasn't even trying out there. She should have made that shot. You know it."

"Maybe she should have—but just because you *can* make every shot doesn't mean you *do*."

"I know, but she barely puts any effort into it. She's letting me and the other girls carry her—mostly me." She thumped the numbers on her sweater.

Or maybe Madison was playing selfish hockey, refusing to pass the puck, looking to add to her own highlight reel.

He wanted to say it. He also knew it wouldn't be helpful. He took a deep breath and sent up a silent prayer for words to convince her. "You know what your job is as the captain?"

She patted the C over her heart but shook her head.

"It's not to score the most goals or make the most headlines. It's not to get the loudest cheers or the most recruitment letters. The captain's job is to help every other player on the team have their best game."

Madison's shoulders drooped. "But, Coach . . ."

He shook his head.

"But she doesn't try."

"Maybe she needs someone to believe in her."

Madison frowned. "That's what her family is for."

Eli had to bite back a smile as he leaned over her. "That's what her captain is for too."

"You want this C back?"

"Nope. I want you to show the whole team you deserve it."

She looked at her skates, digging the tip of her blade into the floor. "What about you?"

"I already know you deserve it."

Pursing her lips to the side, she wiped her forearm across her eyes. "All right."

"I'll see you at practice tomorrow." He dismissed her with a nod toward the peeling paint of the locker room door, and she quickly disappeared behind it.

"When did you get so wise?" Violet asked, suddenly at his elbow.

"You think all those valid points I've been making are a fluke?"

She shoved his shoulder. "I think these girls may be lucky to have you after all."

eleven

"I heard you got yourself a job. Figured I better come check up on you."

Eli felt the words slide down the back of his neck, greasier than the product in Tony Moynahan's hair. He cringed and turned toward the oversized luxury SUV in the rink's parking lot. Tony—wearing his signature leather jacket—lifted his chin from where he leaned against the grille. Through the open passenger window, Bobby waved a friendlier greeting.

With a glance over his shoulder to make sure that the girls and their parents were long gone, Eli ambled toward the brothers. "What are you doing here?"

"Checking on my investment. Making sure you weren't thinking you might take after your old man."

"I'm here. I'm getting my first paycheck next week. I'll get you your money."

Tony looked unimpressed. "You makin' fifty g's your first check?"

"No, but—"

Tony held up one finger, waving it side to side. "What I hear is you're making ten on this job."

Eli swallowed the retort that sat on the tip of his tongue and settled for a stiff nod. "I'll hand it all over to you as soon as I have it."

"But is that what we agreed on?"

Stabbing his fingers through his hair, Eli mumbled under his breath.

"What was that?" Tony asked, cupping his hand around his ear.

"No. It's not what we agreed on." But he didn't have it. He couldn't make money grow on a tree. Tony and Bobby could make blood come from him though. "Listen, I'm sorry. I'm working on some stuff, but I might need a little—"

Tony's laugh was ripe with derision. "Hey, Bobby. You hear that? Eli Ross wants more time."

Bobby's high-pitched chuckle floated out from the SUV. "Good one, Ross."

It wasn't a good one. It wasn't a joke. This was his life. Biting his lips closed, he forced himself to stay silent in the face of two men who had never learned the definition of grace.

Tony's false humor vanished, and he stepped forward, right into Eli's face. He was more than a few inches shorter, but he had all the bravado of a man who'd had to make up for his size his whole life. "Listen very carefully, Eli." He grabbed the front of his sweatshirt. "I want my money. I want it on time. And I want it in full. You got it?"

Eli ripped himself away, and the other man dropped his arm. "I got it," he said between clenched teeth.

"Because if you don't get me my money in four weeks,

I'm going to have to find it elsewhere." Something dark and sinister flashed in his eyes, turning them almost black. "And I'd hate for your mom and that pretty brunette who was with you inside to wind up in the middle of that mess."

Eli squeezed his fists so tight that his fingernails dug into his palms as he let out a slow breath. "You leave them out of this. They've got nothing to do with it."

"If you don't make your payment in four weeks, I'm going to choose who has something to do with it. And it'd be a shame to see that cute little shop have another fire."

Eli had no response as Tony marched to the driver's side of the SUV and climbed behind the wheel. Bobby waved and called out a friendly goodbye, almost like he didn't remember their encounter in a New York alley a month before.

But Eli did. He knew Tony meant business. And there was no way he was going to let Violet and Mama Potts wind up the victims. He'd find that money.

"Could I at least come by your store and show you our work? Everyone loves Mama Potts's pottery." Violet forced a smile, hoping it carried through her voice over the phone. "And we have lots of variety. Not just mugs. Platters and vases and spoon rests too."

"I'm sure it's great. But we already have an exclusive distribution agreement with a studio out of Summerside. Good luck."

She ended the call and pressed her head against her arm on Mama Potts's kitchen table. Fifteen shops across the south shore. Fifteen excuses not to even meet with her. They didn't carry pottery. They didn't have the space. They already had a distributor. From Summerside to Point Prim, no one was interested in carrying their pieces.

It seemed the only shop that wanted to carry their work was the one she'd nearly burned to the ground. Well, and Jenny's store, but that had more to do with Eli than the pottery.

"That sounds like it's going well."

She almost threw her phone in Eli's direction as he walked into the kitchen. "Yep. It's going great." She sat up and looked down at the list of local shops she'd scribbled onto a notepad, all but three of them crossed out.

"Maybe you need a new schtick." His head and shoulders disappeared into the fridge. He emerged with a pitcher of tea a second later and poured himself a glass. "Or maybe you're just giving them a reason to say no."

"I'm not. I've told them all about Mama Potts and why this is such a great opportunity."

"Uh-huh. But you're calling them."

"Right. It's rude to just show up."

He fell into the chair beside her, taking a sip of his drink. "But it's easier to turn someone down when you don't have to look them in the eye."

"How would you know that? Did you become a salesman since leaving the league?"

"I've sold watches and skates and even modeled for high-end gloves. They're called endorsements."

She snorted. "I'm sure you're a great hand model."

"Who's a hand model?" Oliver strolled into the kitchen from outside.

"Your brother. Turns out he's been holding out on us with his special skills."

Oliver raised an eyebrow. "Maybe you should take some pictures of him drinking out of one of Mama Potts's mugs. We could plaster that all over a billboard."

"Very funny."

"No, seriously. I've got it." He leaned back, stretching his hands across a make-believe marquee. "'Have a drink with Victoria's best hand model.'"

Eli scowled. Violet hooted.

Oliver nudged his brother's shoulder, an unexpected mea culpa.

Even stranger, Eli seemed to accept it with grace, his smile returning, his posture relaxing.

A slammed door drew every eye in the room, and Levi stopped short as he entered the kitchen, a few papers in his hands.

"Whatcha got there?" Oliver asked, reaching for what Levi held.

In a rookie mistake, Levi jerked them away, holding them out of Oliver's reach and basically handing them straight to Eli. Then again, he hadn't had to watch out for his oldest brother in years.

Eli jumped up and jogged away, his eyes scanning the pages. "Preapproval for a loan?"

Levi sighed, silently holding out his hand.

Eli kept reading. "It's all filled out. With your name." He whistled low. "That's a lot of money."

Oliver's eyebrows pinched together, and he sucked on his front tooth. "What's that all about?"

Violet couldn't help but roll her eyes at the hooligans. "Are you all blind? Levi's going to buy his own place."

Eli turned back to his little brother, his mouth open. "Really?"

Levi said volumes with a shrug and a low grunt.

Oliver slapped him on the back. "Well, all right. You have a place already picked out?"

Even if he hadn't nodded, the sheer joy in Levi's smile would have revealed the truth.

"But you never said anything," Oliver said. Eli snorted, and Levi shook his head at his brothers' jokes.

Violet shoved back her chair, trotted across the room, and caught the youngest Ross brother in a tight hug. "Ignore them. This is big. I'm so excited for you."

"Thanks. Me too." His whisper in her ear was soft, his voice always deeper than she remembered.

The clatter of a cane and uneven footsteps announced another arrival. Mama Potts couldn't sneak up on any of them—not that she needed to. Several seconds behind her ruckus, she appeared at the bottom of the stairs, hobbling into the kitchen. "What are you kids up to?"

"Learning that our little brother is about to be the first homeowner of this generation," Oliver said.

Mama Potts looped her good arm through Levi's and leaned in to kiss his cheek. "I know. Pretty exciting. Wait until you see it. It's the perfect bachelor pad—plenty of room for puppies and grandkids someday."

Levi jerked away, leapt to retrieve his papers from Eli, and bounded up the stairs. Apparently that was all the people time he could handle.

The rest of them chuckled as Violet found her seat again, and Eli touched the back of the chair in front of him. "Here, Mom." He squeezed her shoulder, and Mama Potts sat and patted his hand before he slid an extra chair in front of her and propped up her ankle.

There was so much tenderness between them now. But there had been many years of silent strain—so much loss and heartbreak. How could it all be gone now?

No, not quite gone. It was still there, just forgiven.

But it couldn't be that simple. Not after how Eli had left, how his silence had broken Mama Potts's heart. And Violet was certain that Mama Potts herself had been broken. After so many years, she was a vase that had been shattered and glued back together. Still useful, still beautiful, but unquestionably disfigured. Yet her affection for Eli hadn't diminished. She still held an overflow of love for her son.

Maybe a mother's love didn't end with heartbreak.

Violet couldn't help but hope that was true. Not just for Eli's sake. For her own.

"How's it going?" Mama Potts's words pulled Violet from her thoughts, but she couldn't quite make sense of the question.

"What?"

"You're calling stores, aren't you?"

Violet blinked down at the notepad before her, then back up at Mama Potts, all the *nos* echoing in her mind. "No one's interested. Most of them already have exclusive distribution agreements."

Mama Potts drummed her fingers against the table, pulling at her chin with her other hand.

"I think she needs to meet with them face-to-face," Eli said.

Violet sighed. "I'd be happy to go in person. I just don't think it's going to change the answers."

Mama Potts's fingers stilled, and she looked up, a half grin tilting her mouth. "Maybe a new tactic is exactly what you need. An edge." Her eyes darted to Eli.

He raised his hands in surrender. "What'd I do?"

Violet didn't know where this was going, but she already hated it. "Maybe I'm just asking the wrong questions. Store owners tend to know other store owners. Maybe they could point me in the right direction."

"Or maybe you should start with someone who's already a fan."

"I've been using your name all over, and several have recognized it. It just hasn't been enough."

Mama Potts shook her head and pointed to her eldest child. "I meant a fan of his."

Violet's stomach sank. She was supposed to be able to make a few calls, sell some pots, buy a kiln, fix the electricity, save the store. That was the plan. She didn't need Eli to accomplish it.

"I have a friend in Montague. We grew up together and had babies around the same time. She always loved little Eli, said she followed his career from the start. She owns a souvenir shop now." Mama Potts tapped her chin, slowly nodding. "I think a visit from him might be just the thing."

Violet could go. She could take care of it. She just couldn't be Eli. She crossed her arms and slumped back into her seat.

"You want me to go to Montague and talk about pottery?" Eli sounded about as confident as a first-time skater.

"No. I want you to take Violet to Montague so *she* can talk about pottery."

"Whoa." Violet shoved her chair back, balancing on the back legs for a split second before saving it from toppling over, the front legs clapping against the floor. "I don't think that's a—"

"It's perfect. Eli can drive you. Use my car."

Violet shook her head. "I'll take the bus. It'll be fine."

Oliver, who had remained blessedly silent for so much of the conversation, apparently decided it was time to chime in. "You're going to take all of your inventory on the bus? Yeah, that's going to work out well."

Violet rewarded him with an exaggerated roll of her eyes. "I'll figure it out."

"But that's still you without Eli. You have to go together."

She knew Mama Potts's words weren't meant to be a slap in the face. But somehow they were—a reminder that she wasn't enough.

Eli's gaze fell heavy on her, his scrutiny intense. She couldn't help but wonder if he, too, saw her missing pieces, saw what she lacked, saw what had made her parents so desperate for another child—her mom willing to try for and suffer the loss of six more.

His eyes were warm, filled with something akin to compassion.

He couldn't possibly know the whole truth. No one—not even Mama Potts—knew that. Still, he seemed to know her. And what she needed to hear.

"I'm willing to go if you are. I can't do it without you."

Squeezing her eyes closed, she let out a small sigh. She wasn't getting anywhere on her own. If Eli could help, it would be worth it. For the sake of the shop. "All right."

Eli stared at the phone in his hand. He pushed himself up from the steps beside the garage and paced the length of the lawn. Then back. And one more time for good measure.

The sun warmed everything in its path, making even the fresh-cut grass smell like perfume. He slowed his breathing to match the clapping of the waves at the shore, just beyond his mom's home and down a small bluff. He couldn't see them from where he stood, but he knew their rhythm. It was in his blood. No matter how far he'd traveled and how long he'd been gone, this was home.

The problem was he didn't deserve to call it home anymore.

Once upon a time he'd wanted to come back. He'd wanted to show his mom and brothers that he'd been a success. That he'd been right to leave. And that they should welcome him back.

But now all he had to show was a debt that he'd taken on, labeling him the fool that he was. He was almost out from under it, yet still so far from freedom.

Fifty grand from it, to be exact.

He sure wasn't going to ask his mom or brothers to help him. Mama Potts had enough financial troubles to think about with the studio, and while he now owned a lobster fishing license, Oliver was saving for his future with Meg.

There was no way he'd lend that kind of money to a brother who'd walked out on them. And Levi was about to take on a mortgage.

Eli was going to have to call in some favors. If he had any left.

Falling back onto the steps, he pressed the button to place the call.

He'd met Jett Haggerty at a party thrown by one of his teammates. The guy could get his hands on anything. Fast cars. Tickets to the latest Hollywood premier. An introduction to a former member of the Beatles playing the Garden.

The first favor was free. The next came at a price.

Eli hadn't minded. Not when he had money to spend and nothing to lose. When Haggerty started showing up at the same clubs and partying with the same people, Eli liked him. He was loud and rich, and the fun always seemed to follow him. Unlike everyone else in Eli's life, Haggerty never asked for anything except what they'd agreed on.

Eli had thought he couldn't get any lower after the commissioner kicked him out of the league. But realizing he had absolutely no one to turn to with that pain had been even worse.

Haggerty wasn't a friend. He was a businessman, and he'd never pretended to be otherwise. But he was still the most connected man Eli knew.

The other end of the line connected. "Haggerty. Who this?"

Eli swallowed the lump in his throat and put on every scrap of frivolity he'd once worn. "Haggs! It's Ross."

The silence was deafening.

"Eli Ross."

"Yeah, I know. Just didn't think you'd have the nerve to call me after that last game. And then you just disappeared." Haggerty swore under his breath, and Eli cringed. "Where'd you take off to, anyway?"

"Listen, I know. That game didn't go our way."

Haggerty smacked his lips, and Eli could hear him cracking his knuckles all the way from Jersey. "Maybe it went just how someone wanted it to."

Eli dropped his elbow to his knee and rested his forehead against his hand. "I know it's been a little while, but I need to make some money."

"How much?"

"Forty."

Haggerty whistled low and long. "Why not the old-fashioned way? I got a hunch you know someone who would place a bet."

"I'm not going to gamble for it. I can't afford to lose what I've got."

"Sounds like you're in a jam. Wish I could—"

"Wait." Eli scrubbed his hand down his face. "I'll pay you three percent of whatever I can make on the job."

"Your agent made five."

"Fine. All right. But I need money—fast."

Haggerty smacked his lips again. "What kind of work you looking for?"

Honestly, he'd dig ditches if it would get Tony off his back. "Whatever you've got. Anything in the game. Anything legal."

A footfall at the top of the stairs made Eli spin around. Oliver squinted at him, crossing his arms over his chest, and Eli quickly ended his conversation. "Call me when you have something."

Oliver's feet thumped with each step, his gaze never wavering. When he reached the ground, he stood toe to toe, eye to eye with Eli. "What are you into?"

"Nothing you need to worry about." Eli tried to dismiss his concern as easily as he slid his phone into the back pocket of his jeans.

"I am worried. I told you when you got here not to hurt Mama Potts or Violet."

"And I haven't, have I?"

"Not yet."

Eli stared him down, hating that Oliver's concerns were valid. Hating even more that his own stupidity might rain down shame or worse on his family.

Oliver brushed a long strand of black hair out of his eyes and tucked it behind his ears, which had always stuck out a little too far. "I don't get you, man. One minute you're joking and teasing with us like you've always been here, always been a part of this family. Then you're keeping secrets and making me question if I should trust you with Violet."

"I'm pretty sure Violet can take care of herself."

Oliver looked ready to spit. "Of course she can. But the two of you together all the way to Montague and back . . . I don't like it."

"What's wrong with you, man? We're just trying to save the studio."

"But you're clearly not telling us everything." Oliver waved toward the phone in Eli's pocket. "Why do you feel like you need to keep secrets? What's so awful that you have to keep it hidden?"

You have no idea.

Oh, how Eli wanted to tell his brother the truth. To tell him how their dad had showed back up in his life a little over a year before. To tell him what a stupid, trusting fool he'd been.

To admit that his heart had been broken all over again by the same man.

Oliver had known the truth about their dad before. He didn't say much after their old man took off. He didn't say anything, really. But Eli thought then—and still did—that Oliver blamed himself for the night their dad left. Whatever had made their dad leave, Oliver wasn't surprised by it.

He also sported a pretty nasty shiner for the following week.

Eli was afraid to ask if their dad had given it to him. Mostly because he already knew the answer. And he knew he should have been the one with the black eye.

He should have been there. He should have protected them all. It was his job as the oldest, the biggest, the strongest.

He should have been home. He should have saved Oliver from whatever it was that had caused everything to change that fateful night. Instead, he'd been at practice.

Taking a deep breath, Eli tried to let go of those regrets and just be in this moment—where Oliver looked ready to throttle him.

"I'm worried about Violet, all right." Oliver's fists clenched at his sides, wrinkling the brown fabric of his cargo pants. "What if your secrets aren't as contained as you think they are? What if she ends up hurt?"

"I won't let that happen. Besides, she's got plenty of secrets of her own."

Oliver lifted one fist, his arm cocked like he was ready for a real fight. "What's that supposed to mean?"

Eli clapped a hand to the back of his neck, ready to bite off his own tongue. He needed to shut up and go to bed and not get up until he had to be at practice the next day.

"I'm serious. What do you know?"

"Only what I don't know. I mean, how much has she told you about herself?"

"Enough."

"Fine." Eli held up his hands, taking a small step back, still in reach if Oliver decided he was crossing a line. "Maybe that's true. I know she's been part of this family almost as long as I've been away from it. But where is she from? Where's her family? I hear rumors—but they're just that. She won't confirm or deny any of them. Is she the daughter of a real estate tycoon from Charlottetown? An orphan? A runaway? Is she hiding from the law in the States? Too many parking tickets, so she won't drive? What?"

Loosening his fingers, Oliver dropped his arm and let out a dry chuckle. "She's not from the States. I heard her speaking French in her sleep one time when she took a nap on the couch."

"She speaks French? Maybe she's from Quebec." Eli raised his eyebrows. "That's the point. We don't know her story."

"I'm sure Mama Potts does."

"And if she doesn't?"

"I don't care. None of us care. She's been here every single day for the last ten years." Oliver swung his arm toward the house and its long shadow across the lawn, the setting sun painting the sky with spectacular pink and orange strokes.

"She helped us move in here. She found us cheap dishes and used furniture so we'd have someplace to sit. She made Mama Potts smile again. I don't care if she doesn't want to tell us her story."

Because being there—showing up even during the hard times—was what family did. The truth echoed unspoken between them.

Violet was family. Eli wasn't.

He looked away, listening to the waves slap against the sand when they reached the shore. "So I can blame that godforsaken couch on her?"

Oliver snorted. "Hardly. Mama Potts picked that one out on purpose. I think she didn't want her boys falling asleep on it."

Eli could still feel the couch's armrest digging into his calves, robbing him of a restful night. "She picked well."

"Eli, you know when you're ready to talk about your secrets, there are people who care about you. People who will listen."

"Sure. I mean, Levi hasn't said more than a word to me since I got back. I bet I could talk to him all day." There he went, cracking jokes when Oliver was being real.

Oliver poked his tongue at the corner of his mouth, a battle for the right words evident across his features. "I'm just saying that people care about you. And about Violet. So just be careful, okay?"

"I swear, I'll watch out for her."

A throat cleared behind him, and Eli nearly swallowed his tongue.

"I don't believe I need either of you keeping an eye on me."

twelve

"Wait!" Eli chased Violet down the locker room hall.

They'd hardly spoken in a day. Not since she'd stalked off after overhearing a conversation never meant for her ears. He knew she'd been working at the studio, had seen evidence of her presence. But she was never there when he arrived. To her credit, she'd shown up to practice, decidedly cool where he was concerned. But he didn't think the girls noticed.

Violet turned toward him, hands on her hips and shoulders rising and falling in dramatic fashion beneath her prim button-up sweater. "What is it, Eli? I've got to go check the mail. We're waiting on the insurance check. I thought practice was over."

"It is, but I just realized that . . ."

Her gaze jumped around, landing on anything but his face. Over his shoulder. At his feet. Even on the industrial ducts overhead.

"Violet, why are you so angry with me? I'm sorry if I crossed a line, or if Oliver . . . He's just worried about you."

"Yeah, well, he doesn't need to be. Neither of you do."

He nodded, but her words didn't fully make sense to him. He and Oliver hadn't said or done anything that would have evoked such a strong response. "But isn't that what family does? They worry about each other."

She stuck a finger into the middle of his chest, and he stumbled backward against the cement block wall. Not from the force of her touch but from the surprise of it. "You and I are not family. We're . . . we're . . ."

He searched for the word to fill it in for her, but he didn't have it either. They weren't family. But she was as much Mama Potts's daughter as he was her son. And maybe he had started out wanting to get close to Violet to repair his relationship with his family, but the truth was, he genuinely liked her. He liked spending time with her.

Still, *friends* was a little much for someone he knew so little about. Then again, she didn't know all that much about him beyond what anyone could have read in the papers. Or what Mama Potts had shared about his childhood. It wasn't like he was eager to fill in the gaps of her knowledge either.

"Teammates?" he supplied. They *were* working toward a common goal—a couple of them, actually.

She frowned, her eyebrows pinching together as she seemed to try out the word. Wrinkling her button of a nose, she sighed. "You have to trust your teammates, and I don't think either of us are there."

She was right. And when trust was lost, it was the hardest thing to rebuild. But in that moment, he wanted to be worthy of her trust. He wanted to do every bit of the hard work of proving to her that he wasn't the same kid who had walked out on his family. He wasn't the man who had broken his teammates' hearts. He wasn't the same fool who had blindly trusted his old man.

"How do we change that?" he asked.

Her eyes flashed. "You want to change that?"

"Sure. I mean, we have to work together. We have to road-trip together in a couple days." Taking a deep breath, he dropped his smile and reached for her arm. "I want you to know that you can trust me when I say that I'll protect Mama Potts's shop—your shop. When I say that I won't let these girls down. You can trust me."

Her gaze devoured his face, sweeping over every line and curve. If he'd nicked himself shaving that morning, he was certain she'd find the mark. "All right. Then leave it alone—my past, I mean."

"Okay. I won't push anymore. I'm sorry." If he was ever to learn her history, he was going to have to open up about his own. And that wasn't going to happen. They'd have to figure out how to build trust another way.

She tilted her head down, looking up through her thick black lashes. "Stop asking Oliver. And don't bother pestering Levi."

He laughed. "All right."

He meant it. He just had to remember as much. Because promising not to push was the surest way to pique his curiosity.

"I'll see you tomorrow." She turned to walk away.

"Wait." He reached for her arm, but his fingers found hers

instead. Long, slender fingers. Soft as a flower petal but agile and strong. She didn't pull away immediately, and he couldn't tear his gaze from where their hands met, his skin tan and rough, hers pale and porcelain.

Oh, man. She felt good.

He dropped her hand immediately. That was dangerous territory.

"The girls. The game. They have to dress for it." He pointed over his shoulder toward the yellow door, but it didn't help to clarify his stuttered words.

"Yes," she said, giving him an exaggerated nod. "They have uniforms for the game."

He rolled his eyes at himself. "No, I mean, before and after the game. When I played, we wore a shirt and tie and dress pants. I don't know if their last coach expected it, but I do. It's part of representing the team well, even at—maybe especially at—home games. Half the town is going to show up, if Mable Jean is right, and I want the girls to hold their heads high."

"All right." But she clearly didn't understand his dilemma.

"But girls don't wear what I did. What do I . . . how do I tell them . . . ?"

She laughed when it clicked into place. "Sunday best. Tell them to wear their Sunday best. No jeans."

He squeezed his empty hand, half wishing it wasn't empty. "Thank you."

"I'll see you tomorrow," she whispered.

He didn't want to admit to himself that he was already looking forward to it.

Violet needed her hand to stop tingling and her whole body to stop shaking.

The two things were completely unrelated, but they were interconnected. Her hand hadn't felt normal since Eli had decided it might be a nice time to hold it.

For the record, it was not. It would never be a good time for him to hold her hand.

So what if it was gentle yet strong, rough but tender? And so what if he'd backed off as soon as she'd asked him to?

Still, he'd looked into her eyes with his wild blue ones like he cared. Like he wanted to know about her past, not for his sake but for hers. Like he wanted to be able to make right what had been wronged.

Well, that was never going to happen. It couldn't.

Besides, why should he care? He barely knew her. He was probably just curious about the girl without a past. Oh, she knew the rumors, had heard them a hundred times. Sometimes they hurt, but mostly they just reminded her of what she'd rather forget.

But there was no forgetting the envelope in her hand—the cause of the trembling throughout the rest of her body. She couldn't hold it still, and she could barely read the return address. Not that she needed to. She'd recognize the vellum stationery and fine printed letters of the handwriting anywhere. And the return address hadn't changed since she'd lived there more than a decade before.

It was addressed to her, care of the Red Clay Shoppe. Just as every other letter had been for years. Before that, they'd been sent in care of Aunt Tracy. Two a year, every year, without fail.

All hidden away with her secrets in a buried box.

Violet glanced down the empty lane, then up toward Jenny and Dylan's stores. The lid to the black mailbox beside the Red Clay Shoppe's white front door creaked in the breeze, the only sound in any direction save the chirping birds and rustling leaves in the big spring trees.

Taking a deep breath, she slid her finger beneath the glued flap and pried it open. Then she pulled out the single sheet covered in perfect penmanship.

My dearest Violet,

I can hardly believe that another winter has come and gone without seeing you. I confess that with each letter, I pray that you'll come back to us. It's harder and harder every year to honor your wishes. Maybe it should be easier. They say that time heals wounds. I think it just makes me miss you more.

Sometimes I imagine what you must be like now, no longer the young woman you were when I last saw you. I was married and expecting you by the time I was the age you are now. Perhaps you're married too. Do I have grandchildren I don't even know about? Oh, I wish you'd tell us. Please, tell us you're all right. Tell us you're taken care of. Tell us you're happy.

I think many parents wish just for their children's happiness. And I do wish for you to be happy. But more than that, I wish that you'll find a peace that passes all understanding. A peace that you and I can't explain. It took me a long time to discover it, and many months of prayer. I begged God to understand why all this happened to us.

He didn't tell me why, but he filled me with his peace. That's the better answer, the one I needed.

Have you found peace, my dear daughter? I pray you will.

My letters never come back, so I have to hope you receive them. I hope you know that I've always loved you. Even through the grief and the pain, you were my girl. You still are.

As always, when you're ready, we're here. You can always come home.

Love,
Mom

The tears came then. They always did, arriving unbidden and unwelcome. How could her mom write such things? As though she'd forgotten that terrible day.

No. She hadn't forgotten. None of them ever would.

Sometimes at night, she thought she could hear her mother wailing like she had that morning, kneeling on the driveway, rocking back and forth. The sound had been enough to tear a body in two. And it had. It had ripped Violet's heart out. It had made her leave. Made her tell her mom and dad not to follow her.

How could she ever look her mother in the eye again?

That was what Eli wanted to know. Those were the secrets he wanted brought to light. Those were the memories he wanted her to relive.

He had no idea what he was asking. It was too much.

"Miss Donaghy?"

She swiped a hand across her eyes, praying they weren't red and her face wasn't splotchy, as she turned toward the voice. "Sophie?" She blinked the blurriness away. "What are you doing here?"

The girl stood with arms twisted before her, hands clasped, gaze fixed on the first step up to the porch. Her pixie cut was messy and still damp. Probably from a shower after practice.

"Are you all right?"

The girl nodded quickly, but her pointy shoulders twitched beneath a gray sweatshirt at least two sizes too big for her. It sported a CCM badge across the chest, just like most of the bags the girls carried their gear in.

"Did something happen?"

She shook her head quickly.

Violet looked toward the closed door, just about ready to invite the girl in. Except the only thing she had to offer was the lingering smell of smoke and partially empty shelves, having delivered several boxes of inventory to Jenny.

Instead, she pointed to the top step. "Do you want to sit with me for a bit?"

Sophie nodded, and they settled side by side on the cement. Violet lifted her face to the afternoon sun, letting it soak through her. The Prince Edward Island shore couldn't wipe away the past, but somehow its light had always eased the tender spots. The golden warmth made it possible to breathe again.

Maybe Sophie felt the same as she let out a big sigh. She kept her legs hugged to her chest, resting her chin on the torn knees of her jeans and watching the road in silence. A single car zipped by. Then all was silent for a long moment.

"Coach said we could . . . he said we should talk with you about . . ."

Violet nodded slowly. "Sure. What's on your mind?"

"It's not really about hockey, so I can't ask Coach. And I can't ask my dad. He doesn't have a clue. And the other girls . . ."

When Sophie fell silent, Violet slipped her arm around the girl's shoulders and gave her a quick squeeze. "Is this about Madison?" She'd seen the two go after each other at practice, but she hoped Eli's talk with Madison about leadership might have helped.

Sophie's eyes went big, and she curled her lip like that was a stupid question. "No. Madison can be a real pain, but she's a good player."

So this wasn't about Madison, and it was something she couldn't talk about with the other girls. "You have friends on the team, right?"

"Sure. Not like a best friend. Ian's my best friend—from school."

"All right, but you can't talk with him? Or with one of the other girls?"

Sophie pushed the toe of her sneaker against the cement step. "They've all got moms."

Violet's stomach knotted with a sudden memory. Sophie's mom had passed away a while ago, a few years after Violet moved to town. She'd gone fast. Maybe an aneurysm or something like that. Violet couldn't remember for sure. But Sophie had been small, had just started skating. She'd probably been five or six, about the same age as Garrett. Violet remembered seeing her at church and around town. She'd been raised by her dad and her four older brothers.

"Coach said we should wear our best church clothes to the game."

"Yes."

"He said no jeans."

Violet motioned for her to continue.

"But that's all I've got."

An image of Sophie's family in their pew flashed through Violet's mind. Stair-step boys who looked just like their farmer dad. Hair combed and gelled until even the orneriest cowlick couldn't retaliate. Clean plaid shirts. Jeans without a stain or frayed hem. Even their Sunday boots shone.

Then there was Sophie. Not as broad, not as tall, and a whole lot prettier. But she was dressed just like them, because five farmers didn't have a clue what to do with a thirteen-year-old girl.

"You need some clothes," Violet said, forcing the chuckle out of her voice.

Sophie lifted one shoulder up to her ear. "I guess. But I don't like dresses. I don't have to wear a dress, do I?"

Violet did laugh at that. "Only if you find one you like." She stood and held out her hand to help Sophie up.

"Don't worry. I won't."

Violet leaned over the boards and smacked her palms against the side of the rink, cheering a jumble of words that didn't make much sense as they came out. Next to her, Eli yelled, "Change it up." Half the bench scrambled over the side, changing places with the line on the ice.

Sophie yanked off her helmet and squirted water all over

her face. She'd shown up for the game in a sleek pair of burgundy pencil pants, a floral top, and black ballet flats—all of which Violet had helped her pick out at the thrift store in Summerside.

Madison fell to the bench beside her teammate. "Nice block out there, 11."

Sophie nearly glowed under the praise, her already red face turning a more pronounced shade of maroon. "You set it up for me."

"I'll set you up for a goal on the next line change. Be ready for it."

Violet caught Eli's eye and the twitch at the corner of his mouth as he tried to keep his surly, coach-appropriate expression in place. Giving him a dip of her chin, she winked her congratulations. Whether the score showed it or not, this was a win.

They were tied with four minutes left in the final period. Eli called for another line change, and Madison and Sophie hurdled the half wall, taking off on the ice. Just as she'd promised, Madison snagged the puck, passed it to Sophie, and took out a defender in three seconds flat.

If Sophie was surprised that Madison had come through, she didn't show it. Instead, she faked out her opponent—deked, as Eli called it—swung to the far side of the goalie, and took her shot.

Violet held her breath, a silent prayer on her lips. *Please. Please. Please.* She squeezed every muscle in her body tight as she waited for the clang of the puck against the goalpost. Instead the buzzer blew up, the flashing red light spinning across the ice. More than half the capacity crowd jumped to their feet, roaring until there was nothing but their thunder. Nothing but their elation.

She glanced at Eli to find that the firm line of his scowl had been replaced by a wide grin. Despite the suit he'd worn to match his players, he looked boyish in his joy. All the pain that had added lines to his face had vanished in the split second it took for Sophie and Madison to work together to score.

Suddenly he spun her, his strong arm around her back pulling her against a brick wall. No, not quite a brick wall, but a wall nonetheless. There was absolutely no give beneath the soft cotton of his white dress shirt.

Eli's shoulders shook. She couldn't hear his laughter, but she could feel it coursing through him and straight to the center of her chest. Her smile felt like it might crack her face, but it refused to be dimmed.

Whether her stomach dropped or his arms tightened first, Violet could never say for sure. But suddenly everything inside her was on fire, aware that the man holding her wasn't just any man. She wasn't used to anyone holding her. And certainly never like *this*. With this . . . awareness.

She felt like a rookie. A brand-new piece of clay. But the swarming in her midsection wasn't altogether unpleasant. She wasn't a large woman, and surrounded by the tree trunk that was Eli Ross, she felt safe. Protected.

Violet pressed a flat hand against his chest, forcing her gaze up to the point where his open collar met the tan column of his neck. His Adam's apple bobbed.

In the midst of the still roaring crowd, he didn't release her. And she didn't push him away.

She probably should have, especially in front of the team and the stands filled with Victoria's finest. She just couldn't put any effort into such a terrible idea.

Which was even worse. She didn't even *like* Eli Ross.

Except she kind of did. It would have been a lot easier to go on disliking him if he was the jerk she'd thought he was. If he ignored his mom. If he treated the girls on his team with less respect. If he didn't insist on being legitimately helpful and making valid arguments.

And if he looked incredible in a suit—even a borrowed one—well, she was just going to thank God that he and Oliver were pretty much the same size. The cut of that navy-blue suit over his shoulders made her wish *she* hadn't missed out on eleven years with him.

Thank goodness for the clatter of sticks and skates as the line returned to the bench, finally breaking whatever spell Eli had cast over her. Violet pulled away from what she hoped everyone else had seen as a celebratory embrace. When she caught his eye, his smile was gone, replaced with a hard line. His eyes flashed, but they were bright. Alive.

He'd missed this.

No matter what he said about being a player instead of a coach, he'd missed being part of a team. And he had something to offer these girls. Something that he might not even know he had.

"How'd I do, Coach?" Sophie danced from blade to blade, her stick thudding against the floor in front of the bench.

He gave her a solid fist to the top of her shoulder pad. "Not bad at all, 11. I knew you could make that shot. Way to put us up."

She glowed under the praise, her cheeks turning even redder.

Eli turned to Madison, who was hunched over on the bench, her face guard shoved up. "17, you okay?"

She nodded. "Wind. Knocked. Out." Gulping between each word, she tried to sit up but crumpled forward.

Eli called over his shoulder, "Audrey, get out there for the face-off."

The girl did as she was told, and the game resumed with just seconds left on the clock.

Eli slipped to Madison's side, Violet on her other. Their fingers bumped as they both patted the girl's back.

Violet pulled back as Eli found her gaze. She could feel his stare like she could feel his touch.

After a long second, he looked away. "It's going to be okay," Eli said to Madison, his voice soft. "It happens all the time. You make a hard hit and it just knocks the wind out of you. But that was a clean hit. You did a good thing out there."

Madison managed a smile but had no words.

The final buzzer sounded, and the fans jumped to their feet. The girls who had been on the bench swarmed the ice, Stars everywhere. The excitement was so loud Violet couldn't even hear herself think.

Then again, she wasn't sure she wanted to hear what was on her own mind. Not when she had to spend tomorrow afternoon with Eli.

thirteen

Eli drummed his thumbs against the top of the steering wheel for the fourth time in ten minutes. Those minutes had never felt so long. Not even when his team was one goal ahead with ten minutes left in the game. The handful of times that had happened, even those seconds had ticked by faster than they did now with him sitting beside a very silent, very awkward Violet Donaghy.

They were ten minutes outside of Victoria with more than an hour left in their trip to Montague, and she'd said exactly nothing except when she'd handed him a few boxes of inventory to put in the back of Mama Potts's small SUV. "They're fragile."

He'd said he would be careful and asked her how she was doing.

"Fine." She'd said the same thing when he sat beside her in the church pew that morning. She had opened her mouth—presumably to ask him a question—then closed it.

He searched for another question for her. The problem was that every question he thought of led right down the road he'd promised not to pursue. Everything he wanted to know about her had an awful lot to do with her past. So he kept his mouth shut. Clearly this was how it was going to be.

He didn't think she was angry. She was just silent. And fidgety. And apparently fascinated by the rolling green fields and round hay bales that lined the highway.

He cleared his throat. She didn't even glance in his direction. He was tempted to stomp on the brakes to get her attention, but that would only manage to extend this silent torture.

After another ten minutes, he'd had enough. "Did I do something to offend you?"

She looked at him, her eyebrows dipping and meeting in the middle. "No. Why would you think that?"

"Well, you've been not looking at me like I have a giant zit growing out of my forehead."

She blinked, and he missed the color of her eyes when they vanished for even a moment. But then her gaze settled on him in all of its vibrant glory, and he had to force himself to watch the road or else he'd put them right into the ditch.

She remained silent for several more seconds. Finally she volunteered four little words. "I was just thinking." Her voice was raspy, shredded. Like any good fan's after a big game.

He could work with this. "About what?"

"Things you probably don't care about."

Okay, he could not work with that. If he let her shut down, they would go back into silence, and he'd rather listen to nails on a chalkboard than silence for an hour. Because if there was nothing to listen to for an hour, then he was left to think on the things he'd so much rather forget.

"You might be surprised. Try me."

She crossed and uncrossed her arms, then gave a firm nod. "All right. I was thinking about the game yesterday."

"Was that your first hockey game?"

Her face twitched like he'd crossed a line into the verboten territory, but before he could backpedal, she said, "No. I used to go to games a lot. When I was a kid." Suddenly a smile split her frown, eliminating any shadow in the car. "But this was the first time I've ever been on a bench. Is it always so . . . so . . ."

He laughed. "Yes."

"Right? You know what I mean?"

He nodded. "It's electrifying. The energy is contagious."

"I mean, how else do you explain me pounding on the boards and screaming until I was almost hoarse?"

"It seemed like that might be new to you."

"Definitely." She glanced back out the window, and he hoped he hadn't lost her. Before he could figure how to keep her talking, she continued. "Was it always like that for you? Is that why you love the game? I've never seen you like that before. It was like you *belonged* there."

He sucked on his front tooth for a long moment, wishing he could ignore the question. But maybe if he opened up a bit about his own past, she'd return the favor.

"I always felt like I belonged out there on the ice. It's maybe the only place I did fit."

"Not with your family?"

He chuckled. "Mama Potts is artsy and creative. Always has been. But she didn't pass any of those genes on to me. Levi is the bookish one—always with his nose in a book and so shy I don't think we've ever had a full conversation."

"What about Oliver? Weren't you close?"

Eli gripped the wheel until his wrist burned deep inside. Then he flexed his hand, grateful for the freedom he'd gained by leaving his brace behind. "We were *brothers*. Not friends."

"What do you mean?"

"You must be an only child."

Her jaw clenched, her gaze dropping to her hands folded in her lap. But she didn't confirm or deny.

"We were so close in age, it felt like we were always competing. For my mom's attention, my dad's approval. If one of us liked a girl, the other was bound to go after her."

"I wonder who came out ahead."

He wanted to be smug about it, to say that he'd had no problem putting Oliver and his ears to shame. He was the star—first in town, then on the island, then in the whole NHL. Everyone knew his name. And some girls wanted to be with a guy like that.

Except it was all empty. None of it had filled him with anything but shame. And the shame was a whole lot worse than the fun had ever been pleasurable. A Sunday school teacher had once told him that sin may feel good for a little while, but it's never without consequences. When he thought about how many hearts he'd broken, how many women he'd hurt, he knew what his teacher was talking about. The pursuit of fun and feeling good had made him into a man he didn't recognize. One he hated. One who had been so focused on himself that he'd hurt every single person he cared about.

He cleared his throat. "Well, Oliver's clearly winning now. Meg is something else."

"Don't you wish you'd been close? Or could be now?"

Maybe this was why Violet didn't want to talk about her past. Drumming it up didn't solve anything. It just served to pick at old scabs.

He sighed. "It's too late for us."

It had been the moment he'd told Oliver he was leaving. The moment Oliver had told him they didn't need him. They hadn't. It had taken Eli all of twenty-four hours after his return to recognize that. The family had done just fine without him. Probably better than they would have with him.

"I don't think that's true."

He glanced at Violet out of the corner of his eye. "You don't know?"

Her mouth dropped open, and she slowly formed her question. "About what?"

"What happened when I left."

Violet turned in her seat, tucking her left leg beneath her so she could fully face him. "What do you mean?"

"I thought Oliver is like a brother to you."

"He is. But he's blood-related to you and you haven't talked to him in years, so I don't think we should go comparing conversations here."

He shrugged. "Fair point."

"But no, he's never told me about that. What happened? I assumed you just left."

Eli bit his lips closed. He should have done that twenty minutes ago. Right about now he could go for some silence. But he'd invited these questions, whether he wanted to answer them or not.

"My dad had left a couple weeks before."

"And no one has seen or heard from him since." She filled

in the rest as if it was the honest truth and didn't hit him like an illegal check to the glass. She thought it was true. They all thought it was true.

Only Eli knew what a snake his old man really was. And only Eli had been stupid enough to think his dad had actually changed.

He forced himself to hold still, praying that the look on his face didn't make Violet question her belief. Taking a deep breath through his nose, he squared his shoulders. "There was a scout from New York. He kept calling me, asking me to come to a tryout. He said he thought there was a place on the team for me. He said he thought I could be somebody."

She leaned forward, her tongue darting out between her lips. "And you wanted to be somebody, didn't you?"

"Doesn't everybody?"

She slumped back at that.

"Isn't that why you carve your name in the bottom of every mug you make, every plate you shape? So that someone will know you?"

"I don't think I ever thought about it."

He bit back another question that would dig deeper into her past and returned to his own. "I did want to be somebody. I wanted to be known. To be recognized. To put my family's name on the map. But mostly I wanted to play hockey. I loved the game, and I would have given—I did give—everything to keep playing."

"I see that with the girls—how much you love the game. How much you want them to love it too."

Something warm blossomed in his chest, flowing in every direction until it reached the tips of his fingers and toes. It swirled inside him, a single truth on repeat. Maybe this was what it felt like to be known. It wasn't a thousand strangers chanting his name or reporters telling what they knew of his story. Being known was about the small things, small moments. It was seeing the truth before he'd even put a name on it.

How could someone he barely knew see him so well?

"So what happened between you and Oliver?" Violet asked.

"He asked me to stay. He told me they needed me."

"And you left."

This time her assertion was true.

"I thought he was so selfish to ask me to stay. I thought he didn't care about my dreams or what I wanted." Turning off the highway toward Montague and its streams and rivers reaching out toward the bay, he shook his head and tried to release the whole terrible memory. "I didn't even consider how much they needed me. Or how much I nee—needed them." His voice cracked like a middle schooler, something clogging his throat.

For the first time since he'd hugged her at the game, she touched his arm. This wasn't about celebrating, but there were no fewer emotions, no less electricity coursing between them. Her fingers branded his arm, but he wanted to beg her to leave them there anyway. As long as she was touching him, he knew he was still alive. As long as she was there, he was more than his worst mistakes.

"When I told Oliver I was going anyway, he told me to go and not to come back. They didn't need me." He pulled off the road, following the GPS into the parking lot of a big yellow barn. He put the car in park and rested his forearms on the wheel, just staring through the windshield, afraid to meet her gaze. "I was so stupid that I believed him. When I turned my back on them, I turned my back on everything I'd been taught, everything I believed."

"So what changed? What made you come back?"

"My dad showed up."

Violet could manage only a squeak of a response. There weren't words. No one had seen or heard from Jason Ross since he'd taken off with Mr. Druthers's truck and gear and walked out on his family.

He'd vanished. Period. End of story.

Maybe she hadn't heard Eli right. "You mean . . . um . . . What do you mean? Not your *dad*, dad."

He poked his tongue against the corner of his mouth, a muscle in his jaw jumping. But he just shook his head, his lips closed tight. She was prepared to wait him out. Or rather, to push him until he started spilling answers.

"Eli Ross, did you see your dad?"

He chuckled then, low and free of humor. "You sound just like Mama Potts when I was a kid. Except it was 'Elijah Aaron Ross, what have you done now?'"

Only then did she realize her hand was still on his arm, and she squeezed it enough to get his attention. "I'm serious. That's big. That's *huge*. Have you told your mom?"

He finally looked in her direction for a split second, but it was long enough for her to see something in his eyes. Something that amounted to a whole lot of regret. It stole her breath.

A quick rap on Eli's window made them both jump, and

they looked outside to see a round, middle-aged woman wearing a smile even brighter than her neon-pink shirt. “Eli? Eli Ross? Is that you?” Her voice was muted through the closed window, but she had no problem making herself heard. “Your mama said you were coming, but I didn’t believe her. You’re all grown up, but I’d recognize those dimples anywhere.” She kept going, not bothering to take a breath.

Violet couldn’t follow what she said past the comment about his dimples. Because Eli wasn’t smiling. In fact, she’d never seen him look more miserable in the three and a half weeks she’d known him. Not even when he discovered he’d agreed to coach a hockey team of teenage girls.

She wanted to know why. What had his dad done that was worse than turning his back on his family, stealing from his boss, and leaving them all to deal with the rumors, whispers, and repercussions?

This wasn’t the time to ask. Not with an audience and work to be done. They had more than an hour on the road back to Victoria for her to push for more information. He couldn’t run then.

Violet opened her car door, stepped out, and waved at the woman still plastered to Eli’s window. “Hi. Mrs. Sanders?”

She looked up, her eyebrows disappearing behind her pale bangs as though she hadn’t even realized there was someone else in the car. But her mouth kept flapping. “Marty. Call me Marty. Everyone does. Even my husband. My name is really Francis, but my maiden name was Martindale, and all the kids . . .”

Violet nodded and smiled and tried to insert herself into the conversation, but the opportunities were minimal.

"You must be Violet. Mama Potts told me about you, but she didn't tell me that you were coming here with Eli. Oh, I can hardly believe he's here. He's really here. He was such a cute kid, and I watched all his games from his first to his last in the NHL. We were just so sad when he stopped playing. I wonder why he left. I mean, the sports reporters all had their theories, but you know, he never said."

Violet nodded. She did know that. And now she was wondering what his old man had done. She was pretty sure Eli's leaving the NHL had something to do with him.

For a moment she worried that Marty would ask Eli the questions he wasn't eager to answer. Then a slow smile fell into place. Marty could ask all the questions she wanted. She never stopped talking long enough for anyone to answer.

At this rate, Eli was going to be trapped in the car if Marty didn't leave his side. Violet walked around the car and put a hand on Marty's back, gently guiding her toward the trunk of the SUV.

Marty's only indication of surprise was the tiniest pause before she continued chattering.

Violet looked back just in time to see Eli escape his prison and send her a comically exaggerated sigh of freedom. She smiled, glad the pain she'd last seen in his eyes was gone, at least for the moment. But she wasn't going to forget it.

Eli stretched, lifting his hands high in the air until his heather-blue T-shirt lifted above the waistband of his olive-green cargo shorts, revealing a thin line of skin she had no business looking at. She had even less business wondering if it was made of the same granite as his chest.

Ridiculous. She was being absolutely ridiculous.

So what if he was handsome and fit and made her wish they'd met under very different circumstances? He was also hiding secrets that could hurt the people she loved. He'd already proven he could do it once.

Except when he'd shared today about how he'd hurt them, she'd seen how the regret still stung. He knew what he'd done, and he didn't like himself very much for it. Because of that, she couldn't hate him too. Besides, she had secrets of her own. And when he told her about his regrets, it made her wonder if maybe he was a safe place to share hers.

"Oh, you *are* Eli." Marty threw her arms around his waist, holding on for dear life. "You were just such a small thing the last time I hugged you. But look at you. You're even bigger than you look on TV. Or maybe you've put on a few kilos since you left the NHL?" Marty patted his belly like he was a pregnant woman, and Eli looked over her head, biting back laughter that made his shoulders quiver.

If Eli had gained any weight since leaving the game, Violet hadn't found it. Not that she'd been looking.

If they were going to have any chance of getting back on the road and home before nightfall, she had to make a move. Opening the gate of the trunk, she cut Marty off. "We brought you some samples. And if you find something you like, we have some inventory to get you started."

Marty blinked and released Eli, apparently only then remembering that he hadn't just come for a visit. "Oh—oh yes. Debi did say that you'd bring some samples. But, oh my. We don't have room for all of that inventory. I did tell her we only have a small space. Bring the samples and come inside."

Marty hooked her arm through Eli's, propelling him toward

the converted barn, its yellow exterior as bright as the woman who owned it. He looked back, an apologetic smile on his face. Violet waved him off. She hoisted the sample box, closed the trunk, and followed behind. Her feet thumped against the wooden boardwalk that led to the front door, and when they made it inside, she knew that Marty's definition of "a small space" and her own were vastly different.

The vaulted ceiling seemed to reach all the way into the heavens, and Violet's studio could have fit inside the room two or three times over. The barn could have held every citizen of Victoria by the Sea with room to spare. It housed at least one of every single trinket, gadget, and *Anne of Green Gables* doll available on the island. This was a tourist haven, and Violet couldn't keep from turning in a slow circle, taking in the spinner of island-shaped magnets and the table of kitchen doodads featuring lobster-claw oven mitts and potato-shaped potato peelers.

She didn't even hear Marty's chatter, able only to take in the room around them. Table after table. Rack after rack.

And it smelled like heaven. Sugary sweet. The case of fudge near the register made her mouth water.

When she made one more turn, she spotted a corner shelf packed with PEI coffee mugs. Her stomach hit the floor.

"Do you already have a distribution deal with an island artist?"

fourteen

Marty sputtered to a stop, and suddenly the room was silent save for the wind chimes hanging at the back door. The silence dragged on for ages, and Violet hugged her box of samples against her stomach, each second twisting her insides tighter.

What a waste. Mama Potts had sent them on a wild-goose chase when Marty already had a ceramics artist. Violet could have spent the time searching out other opportunities.

Steeling herself against the defeat, she said, "Okay, we won't waste your time."

When she caught Eli's eye, he shrugged. The simple motion seemed to scream that they should still ask. It wasn't time to give up just yet.

Marty, clearly afraid of losing Eli so quickly, revved up again. "But only for coffee mugs. I can still carry your plates and your vases."

"Spoon rests?" Eli asked.

"Oh yes! A customer just asked about one last week. And I

didn't have what they were looking for. Maybe you do. Please." She tapped the wooden counter next to the fudge case. "Let's have a look. Debi told me about the fire and your situation. I want to help."

Violet could only muster a tired smile as she slid the box onto the counter and unwrapped each piece.

Marty's oohs and aahs echoed through the store. She picked up a blue glazed serving platter, her fingers circling the smooth edge with an affectionate touch. "This is gorgeous." She traced the island's outline in the middle of the plate. "I had one like this—not nearly as pretty—but my son broke it. I'll take it."

"For the store?"

"No, for my kitchen." Marty chuckled before waving toward the bowls and vases. "But I'll take all of these for the store. Do you have more?" For once, she stopped and waited for the answer, chin jiggling with excitement.

Violet didn't know whether to be overjoyed or terrified. "No, but I can make more."

"Good. Get to work."

"Only . . ." Violet stopped, and Eli finished her thought.

"We're without a kiln at the moment. Do you know anyone who might have one?"

Marty plucked at the loose skin at her neck, her gaze rising to the bare boards of the ceiling. "Let's see. Well, there are several studios up north and a few in Charlottetown, though I doubt they'd be able to share their kilns. But there was someone selling one . . . Now I can't remember who." She pulled harder at her skin, stretching it out. It didn't seem to help her memory. "It was . . . it was . . . Oh, I can't remember, but do you know who would know?"

Violet and Eli shook their heads.

"Aretha Franklin!"

Violet thought she remembered that the famous musician had passed away a few years before. And besides, what would a world-famous singer know about the arts scene on PEI?

"The singer?" Eli asked.

Marty giggled and pushed at his arm, suddenly a smitten teenager. "Of course not. Aretha—well, it's Sloane now—she owns an antique store up near Rustico, and she plumb knows everyone on the island. Oh. Oh!" Marty's giggle was gone, her eyes wild. "Maybe she knows someone in Rustico who would sell your stuff too. You should go see her. Go see her now." She hurried around the edge of the counter, digging through some paper and receipts on a shelf under her register.

She came up waving a business card. "This is her store. Aretha's Antiques. It's right there on the main road. You can't miss it. There's not much else in the area, except they have an inn now. Have you been up there? To the Red Door? It's just beautiful. Hank took me for our anniversary. Best breakfast I've ever had. And we took one of their cooking classes. And—oh! Aretha is related to the inn's owners. I can't remember—it's her son or nephew, or Jack's? Oh, I can't remember. Just go see her. Tell her I sent you."

Marty wasn't appeased until both Violet and Eli assured her that they'd do so. It took another hour for them to make the arrangements for Marty to carry the Red Clay Shoppe's pieces in her store, and even longer to finally make their escape. But not without a few hugs. Well, one for Violet and too many to count for Eli. He took them with grace, promising he'd make the trip when it was time to drop off more inventory.

Before they left, Marty tucked a wad of colorful twenties into Violet's hand. "An advance on these. They're going to sell in a flash."

When they were finally seated in Mama Potts's car, Violet covered her face with her hands and broke down laughing. It wasn't because the encounter had been particularly funny—although she'd rather enjoyed watching Eli squirm a little bit under such attention. She just needed a release of the emotions that had been building for hours.

Eli joined her, his chuckle bellowing through the car. "What just happened?"

"I have no idea." She dropped her hands and twisted to get a good look at him. His hands were on the wheel, but he hadn't even turned the car on yet. "If she can afford to keep that kind of inventory for her shop as a whole, she must be getting good traffic. I've got to start replacing the inventory that was ruined."

"Maybe Mama Potts can help?"

"I think she'd try if I asked her, but she needs to let her hand heal."

He nodded thoughtfully. "Maybe I can help?" She raised her eyebrows, and he shrugged. "You could teach me."

Her laughter sounded like the wind chimes in Marty's store. "I appreciate the offer. But first we have to find out about that kiln. Maybe Oliver can take me—"

"I'm suddenly not good enough to be your chauffer?"

"No." She rolled her eyes. "I didn't say that. I was just . . . I didn't want to impose. Besides, don't you have practice?"

He grinned. "I gave the girls a day off this week because of their win."

"Trying to earn some brownie points with the team, eh?"

"Nope. They already love me."

"They think you scowl too much."

He shrugged. "I do. But they won their first game with me. They'll always love me for that."

Oh, to have the confidence of an NHL star—to be certain of love, at least where the Stars were concerned. He didn't have to put on a facade and pretend to be someone worthy of their love.

For a single moment, she wished she was half as worthy.

"So, what's it going to be?" Eli asked.

"What do you mean? It's the middle of the afternoon. If we leave now, we'll make it back to Victoria before dinner."

"Or . . . we could go to North Rustico. We could find this Aretha Franklin and find you a new kiln."

"Are you serious? Right now?"

"Why not? We'll be back home tonight. And we don't have practice tomorrow."

Why not? Why not? She scrubbed her brain for any valid reason.

Why was she looking for a reason not to? This was her chance to get him to open up. To get him to tell her what had really happened with his dad.

"All right. Let's do it!"

Eli had forgotten how beautiful the island was, how green and lush and utterly peaceful. Some in New York tried to claim that Central Park was enough green for the whole city. It wasn't. And it was missing all the other rich colors. The brilliant yellow of the canola fields. The untarnished blue of the sky, completely indifferent to the occasional cloud. The similar but different blue of the lakes and rivers that reached in from the sea. And of course, the rich red soil.

It was a rainbow of color. A feast for not only the eyes but also the spirit. He had a hard time watching the road as they wound their way to Charlottetown, then north.

He wasn't quite as eager to talk now, not after he'd divulged too much to Violet on their earlier ride, so he kept his gaze outside the car, soaking in the golden sun, letting it warm his skin through the window.

Violet sat silently too—but watching. Gone were her fidgeting fingers rolling into the hem of her shirt. Gone was the uncertainty between them. She had him in her sights like a fisherman reeling in a tuna. And if he didn't strike first, she was going to.

"Well, that was something else back there at Marty's."

"You certainly have a fan."

"Only one?" He meant it as a joke, but deep inside he felt the loss of the cheering fans, the longing to be admired. To be loved. And he was afraid that he'd laid the truth out bare.

"Mama Potts loves you too, you know."

Well, this had gotten a lot more serious than he was hoping for. He scrambled to find something to distract her. "You said earlier that you used to go to hockey games when you were a kid. What was that like?"

"So is this what we're going to do? You're just going to avoid talking about the bomb you dropped earlier?"

He tried for a nonchalant look that said he had no idea what she was talking about. Her scowl assured him that he'd failed. "You're sure one to be pushing," he said, "especially when you told me not to."

"But this affects your whole family. My history is only about me. You have to tell Mama Potts."

"No. I don't." He twisted his hands against the wheel, his face so tight he could almost feel it cramping. "He's never coming back. And trust me, no one wants him to." His words at the end came out as more of a growl than he'd expected them to.

She huffed, turning back to square herself in her seat, staring straight through the windshield. "Fine. You want to know about the hockey games we went to? My dad played."

"What?" His arm jerked in surprise, nearly taking them across the center line of the otherwise empty road.

"Not like that. Not at your level or anything. But he was always in a local league of some sort—probably still is—and my mom and I would go see him."

Eli couldn't make sense of all the information she threw at him in one seemingly innocuous sentence. There was so much to unpack, so many contradictions to the rumors that swirled about her history. Most of all, her parents were still alive—or at least her dad was. She wasn't an orphan. She hadn't been one when she'd shown up in Victoria as a sixteen-year-old kid.

After a short pause, she said, "Okay. Back to you."

"Whoa. That's not on the same level as my miscreant father making a reappearance."

"And who made you the commissioner?"

He shot her a side-eye. "I'm the one who knows what happened. So I think *I* get to decide what will make me spill more."

"Well, I don't think that's fair at all. You could just say that nothing I shared is equivalent to your story. And before you know it, I'll have told you everything and you'll have told me nothing."

"All right. How about this: One question at a time. Back and forth. When one of us decides not to answer, we stop. No pressuring. No complaints."

The tip of her nose wrinkled, her lips moving back and forth. She crossed and uncrossed her arms around her slender middle before finally giving a single decisive nod. "Agreed."

"My game. I go first. So, your parents aren't dead real estate moguls from Charlottetown?"

Violet waved a finger at him. "That's like four questions all rolled up into one. That's not fair."

She had a point. "Um . . . what do your parents do?"

"My dad is a CFO and my mom volunteers."

He opened his mouth to ask for more clarity, but she cut him off.

"My turn. Where did you last see your dad?"

"New York."

"Huh-uh. I need more detail than that. New York State is bigger than all of PEI. And the city probably has more people than Canada."

He shook his head. "You asked. I answered. Now it's my turn." He tapped his chin, searching for the right way to phrase the question. "Have you seen your parents since you moved to Victoria?"

"No." Her voice was really quiet, thready, and he wished he'd come up with another way to get her to open up to him. Holding his own secrets as ransom wasn't going to make her trust him. And it sure wasn't going to make her want to share.

He had a bad feeling that she'd end up hating him for getting her to reveal something.

"You know what? This is stupid. My dad found me when I was living in New York—still with my team. And he . . ." Eli licked his lips before biting into the bottom one until he could taste blood.

It was always so much harder to admit his failings than it was to celebrate his successes. Maybe he didn't have to tell her everything. Maybe he didn't have to go into exactly what he'd done. He could tell her what his dad had been up to—and still spare himself the memories that haunted him.

"He was in bad shape."

Violet's face twitched, and he could see her fighting back the questions that pressed.

"He owed some bad guys a lot of money."

"Gambling?"

Ah, so she'd heard the whispers of his transgressions too. They had just started to come to light when he left.

"The last thing I heard about him before I left the island was a rumor that he had a gambling problem. But I didn't know how bad it was until I saw him in New York."

"How'd he find you? I mean, was he in touch?" She leaned forward, pulling her knee clear to her chin and wrapping both arms around it, almost like she needed something to hold on to.

Eli shot her a look that he hoped told her he'd answer all of her questions in due time, and she quickly apologized.

"I hadn't heard from him since he left. But a little over a year ago, he showed up at this gym I sometimes went to during the off-season. One of the trainers there was a former teammate who helped me stay in shape. It wasn't hard to track me down, probably. What with a million paparazzi lingering outside the gym." He gave a rueful smile. "Not for me. A lot of actors and socialites went there. The paps liked to get pictures of them without their hair and makeup done. But truthfully, I probably looked better after a training session than I did in the middle of a game. Someone somewhere probably tossed a few bucks at a photographer for a pic of me walking out of the gym. And then one day I stepped outside after a hard session, and there he was."

Eli didn't need to close his eyes to see that moment again. To see his dad standing before him in a skeevy gray suit.

"It was like I couldn't place him. I knew I was supposed to know him. I just couldn't figure out how this ghost from my past could be right there in the middle of my actual life. It looked like he was trying to appear that he had his life together. He was wearing a suit, and his shoes were polished. But his whiskers were uneven, and his hair was unruly and unwashed. I just kept staring at him, thinking he had to be a figment of my imagination. And then he spoke."

Violet let out a little gasp. "What did he say?"

Eli did his best impression of the grizzled voice. "'Hey, Son. Remember me?'" Even now it made his skin crawl. Because he had remembered him. "I wanted to walk right by him. Or tell him off. Or pretend he didn't mean anything to me. But, man . . . he was the first family I'd seen in a decade."

"What did you do?" Violet's voice had turned husky, and he checked on her to make sure she was all right. He wasn't sure what he'd expected, but it wasn't to see her fists pressed against her mouth, her eyes bigger than the platter Marty had purchased.

"The worst thing I could have done. I asked him what he wanted."

"And?" She scooted toward him, leaning over the center console until he could smell the soap on her skin. She was like Jenny's soap store personified, and he leaned into the clean scent for a long moment, letting it wash away the stench of old memories.

"They all wanted something. No one ever came to me for nothing. The guys wanted tickets to a game. The girls wanted to be seen with a professional athlete. The reporters wanted the scoop on this drama or that player. No one ever just wanted me for me. So for a minute, I let myself believe my dad was there just for me. That he'd missed me. That he'd missed being part of our family." Eli couldn't help the scoff that followed. "I was so stupid."

He jumped when her hands snaked around his arm, her forehead pressing to his shoulder. The weight was new, strange. It was different from the other weight he carried. It replaced the old with something new, a pressure that sat on his heart but didn't hinder his breathing. It was heavy but not unpleasant.

This was just Violet being Violet. And suddenly he knew exactly how she'd stepped into his family's life. She hadn't filled a hole. She'd just begun to carry the weight of their burdens. To let them set it down, even for a minute.

Eli leaned over until his ear rested on her head. If he listened hard enough, maybe he could hear her thoughts. Maybe he could hear her picking up what he'd been carrying around.

Instead he heard her quiet whisper. "He left again, didn't he?"

"He always does."

fifteen

They arrived in Rustico in silence. Violet hadn't asked any more questions of Eli. How could she, when she'd begged him to bare his soul and then refused to open up in return? So they'd sat in silence for the last fifteen minutes. It wasn't awkward or strained as it had been earlier that afternoon. But it was heavy. It was real. It was raw.

She had eventually let go of his arm and sat back in her own seat. Her palm still tingled where she'd held on to him.

She'd wished she could promise him that his dad would never disappoint or leave him again. But those were promises she couldn't make, and she had no other words to offer. So she bit the tip of her tongue as he steered them down the main road.

Marty had been right. There wasn't much to North Rustico. A bank and a Lion's Club on one side of the road. A bakery up ahead—she could already smell the cookies and sweets. And off to her right a simple white building with a gray roof. Beside the front door, a red painted banner said ANTIQUES.

"I guess that's it," she said. Eli was already turning into the parking lot, just one of its three spots open.

When they got out, Violet stretched, bending and twisting to loosen her back. Only then did she realize she'd smelled merely a hint of the bakery from inside the car. Out here it smelled of cinnamon and sugar, nutmeg and ginger. She could nearly taste them in the back of her throat.

"Can we stop by that bakery before we leave?" Eli asked.

Violet laughed. "I was thinking the same thing."

Eli said something about great minds before giving her a little bow and a wave to indicate she should lead the way. She had expected it to feel dark inside, out of the sun, which spread its warmth as it arced across the sky. But the walls were bright white and cheery. And despite a maze of furniture covered in every historic knickknack ever found on the island, the single room felt spacious.

The bell over the door had just finished jingling when a grandfatherly voice called from an unseen corner, "Welcome. Come on in. I'll be right with you."

They followed the maze, winding through a series of bookshelves covered with clothbound editions of L. M. Montgomery's famous tales. An old typewriter sat in the middle of a cherrywood desk, and Eli pressed his finger to one of the perfectly rounded keys. The letter flew up to meet the white paper in the scroll, its solid clack still familiar a century after it had been made.

"That's amazing," Eli whispered. "Can you believe this thing still works? Such craftsmanship."

Violet had always loved art, even before Mama Potts taught her how to throw a pot. This store was lush with it. Whoever had accumulated these items had an eye for beauty and grace. From the old sea lanterns to art deco lamps, something caught her eye with every turn.

"Do you think Aretha Franklin picked all these pieces?" she said to Eli.

"Sometimes she lets me have a say."

Violet and Eli both jolted, spinning toward an old man whose face was more lined than a map, his shock of white hair standing up in the back.

"Jack Sloane." He shook hands with her and then Eli.

"Sloane?" Hadn't Marty said that was Aretha's new name?

"Just so. How do you know Aretha?"

Violet pressed a hand to her chest and shook her head. "Oh, we don't. We just met a friend of hers in Montague—Marty. Sanders."

"Oh, for sure. We know Marty."

"And are you . . . how do you know Aretha?"

Jack laughed. "Well, on the good days, she still claims me. We've been married five years now."

Violet didn't know why that surprised her, except that it seemed like someone his age should have been celebrating forty or fifty years of marriage. But there was no mistaking the joy in his eyes at the mention of his years with Aretha.

"Is she around?"

His face fell just a bit. "I'm sorry. Not today. She's at an auction over in Summerside, and she's staying the night. But she should be back tomorrow."

"I don't suppose *you* know anything about an artist selling a kiln."

The crevices around Jack's mouth deepened. "I'm sorry. I

don't. But if you come back in the morning, Aretha will be here."

Violet looked at Eli. She couldn't ask him to drive her back to Victoria and then to Rustico again tomorrow. The trips weren't long, but he'd already gone out of his way.

"We're from Victoria by the Sea, on the south shore."

"Over by the bridge. Of course. I've been through there. Lovely community. Beautiful little theater."

Violet bloomed under the praise of her adopted home. "Yes, it is."

Then Jack seemed to understand the problem. "You're not staying in the area, are you?"

She and Eli shook their heads.

"Well, could you? I mean, my nephew and his wife, they run Rose's Red Door Inn just a half a mile down the road. I'm sure they have empty rooms. They could put you up for the night."

The line of Eli's jaw turned sharper, more pronounced, and she knew that he felt the same fear she did. Neither of them had two loonies to rub together. And she couldn't possibly spend the first payment from Marty on an unnecessary room at the inn, no matter how lovely it might be.

"Um, thank you, but—"

"Nonsense. It'll be our treat to host you. They always have empty rooms this time of year, and Caden is just back from Toronto, so you know the kitchen will be cookin' up some real treats."

Violet knew no such thing. She only knew that there was no way a stranger could be this giving. Most families she knew weren't this generous with each other.

"Come on," Jack said.

Before she knew it, he had ushered them out the door, flipped the CLOSED sign, and bustled them toward the boardwalk. It curved around a pretty bay, mussel boats weaving between their markers in the center. It was picture perfect, the sun beginning its descent and glistening across the rippling waves. They passed a white gazebo and wrought-iron streetlights. It was like they had stepped back in time.

A shiver raced down Violet's spine as the wind swept in over the water, and she huddled deeper into her sweater, wishing she'd brought a jacket. The island was always finicky in May, unable to decide whether it wanted to embrace the warmth of spring.

She tucked her hands into her sleeves. Whether Eli noticed, she couldn't know, but he stepped closer to her, his body a natural heater in the evening hours.

"This way." Jack pointed toward a set of wooden steps that cut a path up the grassy bluff to the street above.

Violet had made it halfway up before she was struck immobile by the big blue house on the hill. It wasn't that it was so much larger than its neighbors or that the white trim glowed any brighter. It wasn't the early spring flowers blooming in boxes beneath the windows or even the brilliant red door tucked into the wide front porch. It was none of those things individually but all of them collectively that stole her breath.

It was like an entrance into a storybook. One that the island had been keeping secret from her until right that moment.

Suddenly the red door burst open, and a little boy with dark brown curls ran onto the porch. "Papa Jack! Papa Jack!"

Her eyes burned, and she frantically wiped at them, expecting to find mascara trails on her fingers. But her eyes remained dry. She blinked hard against the tears, praying they would hold off until she had a private moment.

The boy looked just like Garrett. The same unruly hair and lively eyes. The same button nose and bow lips. She was transported back to Montreal. Back to her family. Back to that day.

But no one else knew. No one else felt that jarring thud that terrible day. She was all alone in her memories and all alone in the present.

Jack raced across the street, picked the boy up, and swung him around. "Little Jack!"

A smaller version of the boy—this one a girl—toddled out behind him. Her eyes were wide, her smile mischievous. She latched on to big Jack's leg. He brushed her hair out of her eyes and smiled down with such love. Family. This was what it was supposed to look like.

And the family just kept growing, as a pretty woman with a round middle waddled after her kids. She kissed Jack's cheek and picked up the little girl, a miniature version of herself.

"I brought some friends," Jack said. "They came to see Aretha, but she's not back yet. Do you have a room for them?"

Jack waved them over, but Violet couldn't get her feet to move. She'd likely have been stuck there forever if Eli hadn't tucked his hand under her elbow and given her a gentle nudge.

"Do we need to go?" he whispered. "We don't have to stay."

She shook her head. She just needed a quiet place, an alone place, where the tears could come and the memories wouldn't scare anyone off.

When they reached the stairs in front of the porch, the woman smiled brightly. "I'm Marie Sloane. Welcome to the Red Door Inn."

Eli had never seen anything like it. He'd never been to this inn, yet he felt like he'd missed it for years. It was hot chocolate and summer nights and his blades on the ice all rolled into one. And the smile from Marie Sloane made him feel like a long-lost friend who'd finally found his way home.

He could sense in Violet the same hesitation he felt—the same longing for home. He knew why he didn't deserve it. But he couldn't figure out why Violet could ever feel unworthy of a family's love.

Marie waved them up to the porch. "Come on in. We weren't expecting any guests, but I'm sure we can find a bed or two for you."

"Two," Violet said rather quickly, and Eli had to hold back a snort.

Marie raised an eyebrow. "So you're . . ."

"Just friends," Eli said, surprised that it was true. After their conversation in the car, there could be no doubt. He would never have shared the truth with someone who wasn't safe. And he knew deep in his gut that Violet was safe.

"Oh, I've been there." Marie chuckled, leading the small parade into the air-conditioned foyer. "I'm sorry it's so cool inside, but I'm about ready to pop, and I can't work in anything less than igloo temps."

"Anything to keep my girl happy." A guy—clearly Marie's husband—walked in through a swinging white door from the back of the house and kissed his wife on the forehead. She leaned into him, lifting her glowing face to accept his offering. It was a strangely intimate moment to witness between virtual strangers. Even worse, it gave Eli a picture of what it would be like to kiss Violet just so.

Maybe he should have done that at the game when he'd simply hugged her. Although there his feelings hadn't felt very simple while she was in his arms. She had felt good and right and like she fit into all of his hollow places. For the first time in his life, he'd wanted to postpone turning back to a hockey game. He'd wanted to hold on to her forever.

But people left. They always did. There was no use getting his heart mixed up in something that was guaranteed to hurt. Not that he'd ever gotten his heart involved where a woman was concerned. But with Violet—well, it was the first time he'd been tempted.

"This is my husband, Seth." Marie patted the man's chest. "And of course, these are our kids. Little Jack and Julia May."

Eli introduced himself and Violet and shook the other man's hand. It was hard and callused, like he worked with his hands every day.

Turning back to her husband, Marie smiled. "Can we put them up for the night? We only have the Grissoms in the blue room."

Seth's smile turned apologetic. "I moved the furniture out of the three rooms in the back corner so I can run new pipes to all those bathrooms. I thought I had a few more weeks before we needed them."

Eli patted Violet's arm, and she tugged on his shirtsleeve. "We don't need to stay," he said. "We'll just—"

"Don't be ridiculous. We still have the Montgomery Room." Marie's eyes sparkled. "And we can roll Taco Bed into an empty room." She smiled apologetically. "For Eli."

"Taco Bed?" The name itself sounded delicious, but the way she said it, Eli thought he might end up being dinner.

"Taaaccccooooo Bed!" Little Jack singsonged the name.

"Come here, you little squirt." His dad scooped him up and tickled him until he screamed with joy. "I'm going to get dinner for these two." He ushered his kids toward the swinging white door but looked over his shoulder before he disappeared. "Just so you know, Taco Bed is guaranteed to make you feel like ground beef after just one night."

"Oh, you!" Marie swatted after him, his laugh lingering even after he'd disappeared. "It's not that bad." She cringed. "Okay, it's not great. But I'm afraid it's all I have."

"I don't mind the floor," Eli said.

Violet, who had been strangely silent, chose that moment to speak. "I can take the floor. It was my idea to come here."

"Ah, no. I'm pretty sure it was my idea," Eli said. "And what kind of gentleman would I be if I let you sleep on the floor?" With a conspicuous nudge of his elbow, he added, "You're going to make me look bad."

Violet chuckled. "All right. Fine."

"Wonderful. Make yourselves at home. Whatever you need, help yourselves to whatever you find." Marie clapped her hands like she was legitimately delighted. "Let's bring your stuff in."

Eli looked at Violet, then back at Marie and Jack. "We don't really have things. We weren't planning an overnight trip."

"Oh, that's all right. I probably have a pair of prepregnancy pajamas that will fit Violet." Marie's gaze turned to him, her sweeping survey turning her smile doubtful. "I don't even think my pregnancy pajamas will fit you."

Violet crawled into bed later that night wearing the borrowed pajamas, which were soft and cozy and fit just about perfectly. She pulled the quilt stitched with quotes from L. M. Montgomery to her chin and sank into the softness of the bed. When she closed her eyes, she saw Little Jack's smile, which was suddenly replaced by Garrett's and his laughter the last time she'd seen him. Alive.

Her eyes flew open, and she stared at the single patch of moonlight on the ceiling. Almost immediately the edges began to blur, and she pressed the heels of her hands to her eyes, praying the burning would stop.

It didn't. Blinking rapidly didn't help either. It only released rivers that flowed down each side of her face and pooled onto the pillow.

Flopping to her side, she tugged her knees to her chest and tried to take a few deep breaths.

Don't think about him.

But telling herself not to had never stopped her. In fact, her counselor had suggested setting aside time specifically to remember him, giving herself time to cry and grieve. And she had for years.

Seeing Marie and Seth and their sweet, joyful family was a perfect picture of what could have been. What she'd taken away.

She jumped from beneath the warmth of the quilt, slipped

her sweater over her head, and pulled on her socks. The cold of the wooden floorboards seeped into her toes as she shuffled from the window to the door and back, arms wrapped around her stomach. But there was nothing to warm the cold within.

Seconds turned to minutes to nearly an hour, and her mind only played on repeat the life that might have been.

Pressing her hands to her face, she let out a silent scream. This was why she kept melatonin on hand. She didn't have any tonight because she hadn't planned on spending the night. What a stupid idea.

But maybe Marie had some. Or at least some bedtime tea. And she had told them to make themselves at home.

Cracking open the door to her room, Violet poked her head into the hallway. The second story was nearly silent save for the intermittent snores coming from behind the door she assumed belonged to the Grissoms, though she hadn't seen the other guests. A window at the end of the hallway cast a pale beam halfway across the floor, but the other direction—the one that led to the back stairs—was pitch-black.

She tiptoed in that direction, her fingertips trailing along the faint texture of the wall until she reached the open doorframe. With light footfalls, she made her way down each step, and when the stairwell curved, a dim light at the foot beckoned her. She was nearly to the bottom when she stepped on a wooden floorboard that seemed intent on announcing her presence. Its creak echoed back up the stairs and all throughout the house, and Violet held her breath, praying everyone else would sleep through it.

After a long moment where only the sound of the wind off the shore whipping around the house greeted her, she scurried the last few steps into the kitchen. The light on the hood over the stove had been left on and cast the whole room in a soft yellow glow. White cabinets gleamed, and even whiter counters held every necessity.

Except a teakettle.

She made a slow circle beside the island, checking every corner and cranny of the counters. Nothing.

She glanced at the stairs, dreading a long night of lying in that bed, no matter how comfortable and cozy it was. As long as she was awake, she wouldn't be alone.

"Whatcha looking for?"

Violet jumped and spun toward the doorway between the kitchen and the dining room, where Eli filled the entrance, his shoulder still holding open the swinging door. He rubbed his eye with one hand and his lower back with the other. But it wasn't his semi-sleepy state that made laughter bubble out of her.

Eli stood in borrowed pajamas—a pair of gray sweats that would have been perfect in a flood and a white T-shirt that left absolutely nothing to the imagination. He looked like a kid forced to wear the clothes he'd outgrown.

"You look . . ." She tried to hide her relentless smile behind her hand.

"I look like I just got out of bed? Is that what you were going to say?"

"Um . . . sure. Something like that."

His chuckle was low and throaty as he slipped into the kitchen and leaned his hip against the nearest counter, looking perfectly at ease. Except . . . well, he'd told her enough that she knew he wasn't.

He crossed his arms over his chest, the T-shirt clearly about to give in under the stress of his flexed shoulders. A sudden thought popped out of her mouth. "You've been borrowing a lot of clothes lately."

"Yep."

"What happened to yours? Why didn't you bring them with you?"

"I sold them."

Her mouth opened, but no sound came out. He'd sold all of his clothes? Then the truth struck her, the pieces of his story beginning to come together. "When your dad came to see you, he owed people money, didn't he?"

"A lot of it."

She sighed, knowing that Eli couldn't have walked away without helping his dad. He'd turned his back on his family eleven years ago, but she was starting to suspect that he had carried the pain of that choice too. Maybe it had looked different from being evicted from his home and having to start over completely like Mama Potts, Oliver, and Levi had. But it had left him no less affected. And when he came face-to-face with his dad, he hadn't wanted to make that same mistake again.

"Your dad—did he have something to do with you getting kicked out of the NHL?"

"Everything."

There was so much pain, so much real in that single word. Violet had a strange urge to walk over to him and wrap him up in a hug, to tell him that his dad's actions didn't define him. But that was a terrible idea. "I was in the mood for some tea." She swept her arm around the room. "But no kettle."

Eli's eyebrows rose slowly.

"What? Marie said to make ourselves at home. And I'm not the only one wandering about the house in the middle of the night."

With a soft snort, he shook his head. "Yeah, but at least you weren't forced to sleep on Taco Bed—or *attempt* to sleep, anyway."

She cringed. "That bad? Do you want to trade? I'm not . . ." *Sleeping anyway.* She didn't want to confess the rest. If she did, he'd ask why. And then . . . she wasn't sure she had it in her to keep him from being the one person on the island who knew her story.

Eli took three quick steps toward her, his eyes darker than usual, focused on her. Violet scuttled back, bumping into the island and holding her breath for some reason she could not explain.

Maybe it was his breadth or his height. He seemed to surround her. But fear wasn't the reason her heart thudded heavy in her chest and echoed in the back of her throat. He wasn't scary. He was safe.

Maybe that was worth being afraid of.

Stretching his arm toward the ceiling, he kept his gaze on hers. It was tangible, sweeping over her from head to toe—a rush of warmth that completely disregarded the layers of fabric between them. It was heavier even than the unspoken words she so desperately wanted to share. Because in that moment, she knew they shared heartbreak. It wasn't identical, but it was enough.

Which meant she wasn't alone.

Her gaze followed his arm to the pots and pans hanging from the rack suspended from the ceiling. When he brought his hand down, he held a copper kettle. Grabbing it with both hands, she cradled it like she had the first vase she'd made on her own.

"Thank you." She turned to fill the kettle up with water. Now she just had to find some tea.

By the time she'd set it on the stove, Eli had already opened and closed upper cabinets, finding two mugs and a variety of tea boxes. "What kind do you want?"

"Chamomile or some bedtime variety."

He held up a box, and she glanced at it before giving a quick nod. She had the same kind in her apartment. With the simple white mugs on the counter, tea bags awaiting the boiling water, he hopped up onto the island counter, his long legs swinging, his face half in moonlight and half in shadow.

"So why are you having a hard time sleeping tonight?"

She fiddled with the knob, adjusting the stovetop burner. "No reason."

"Is this a regular thing for you?" His voice was low, so there was no fear of it carrying to other parts of the house. Yet there was a steel to it that compelled her to give him nothing less than the truth.

"Yes."

She waited by the stove, listening for the rolling boil that would come right before the whistle blew. Staring at Eli's reflection in the copper instead of at the man himself didn't save her from more of his questions.

"You want to talk about it?"

"No." Maybe. A little.

"Okay."

No. Not okay. The memories that kept her up most nights were always going to be there, always haunting her.

"It's just, sometimes . . . I don't know." He cleared his throat, but his words were still raspy. "When I told you about seeing my dad, it's like you were sharing that weight. I didn't mean to put it on you. I just wanted you to know that if you have something you want to share, I can carry part of it too." He made an odd little noise, and she could picture his smile. "I'm pretty strong."

The kettle began to rumble, and she snatched it off the burner before its whistle could wake the rest of the inn. Keeping her back to him, she poured water into each mug and set the kettle back on the stovetop. Eli must have chosen a mint tea, and she inhaled the soothing steam as she finally turned toward him, his mug in her outstretched hand.

"I was sixteen." She hadn't meant to say it, but as long as she could focus on the dip and swirl of her tea bag and not on him, the words seemed far too eager to spill out.

"Hmm?"

"I had just gotten my driver's license." She waited for him to crack a joke, but he didn't. He seemed to know that she couldn't get through this without his silence. "I was . . . I was going to the mall to meet some friends. I swear I was paying attention. I checked all my mirrors and all my blind spots. But all of a sudden— I didn't even get out of the driveway, and there was this thud. And I knew. I mean, I just knew that life as I knew it was over.

"My parents had tried for twelve years after they had me

to have another child. Garrett was their miracle." The tears came then. Rolling down her cheeks and splashing into her tea. Her throat was full, crackly, and she tried to clear it, tried to soothe it with the chamomile. But no more words would come out. They were stuck in the knot in her chest. The one that caught every other breath.

Refusing to look up from her tea, she felt more than saw him approach. His big arm reached around her, his mug clinking against the counter, and he relieved her of her own drink. Leaving her with only her hands to stare at. Then his joined hers, warm and strong, gentle and firm. Just that was a little like knowing she had a home.

It wasn't enough though. Leaning forward, she reached for him. And he was there. She hadn't doubted he would be.

Burying her face into his neck, she wrapped her arm around his shoulders and held on as her sobs grew louder and her eyes caught fire. "Garrett was play—playing on a scooter. He always stayed in the yard where my mom could watch him, and I didn't see him. Mom looked away for only a second. The police ruled it an accident. But how could I face my parents every single day when I'd taken the child they'd wanted so much?"

He was silent for a long time except for a few audible swallows. She could feel the muscles of his throat working against her temple. She wanted him to say something. Anything—except that it was all right.

It wasn't all right. It had never been all right. And it wasn't going to be again.

She'd seen the trauma therapist and talked until she was hoarse. She'd cried on Aunt Tracy's lap until she was nothing more than jerking shoulders and silent sobs. She'd sat in that pew every Sunday and begged for forgiveness.

None of it had changed what had happened. Nothing could.

Time had worn down the sharp edges like glass in the sea. The broken pieces were smoother now. No less broken, but not as painful.

Mama Potts had played a big part in that, giving Violet something to focus on, teaching her how to find joy again. But she couldn't pretend that everything was fine. That she hadn't severed the lifeline between her and her family. That she didn't regret the little life lost every day. That she didn't open that box of Garrett's pictures and watch them absorb her tears.

Slowly, almost thoughtfully, Eli's hands slipped around her waist, his arms protecting her from all the ugliness that the media and strangers had hurled at her. And somehow protecting her from the worse words she'd screamed at her own reflection.

Her breath caught on a half sob, and she pressed her face into the damp spot on his collar.

Eli didn't tell her it was all right. He didn't say anything at all. He just held her a little closer, pulled her a little tighter. Just enough to remind her she wasn't alone. Enough to invite her to keep going.

"My great-aunt Tracy lived on the island, not far from Victoria. She invited me to come stay with her, so I did. I couldn't bear the sadness in my mom's eyes every time she looked at me. She didn't see me. She didn't see her daughter. She saw the girl who had killed her son." Violet let out a trembling breath, sinking even deeper into him. "And after a little while, that was all I could see in myself anymore too."

"I'm so sorry."

She couldn't see his face from this angle, but he was so close she could feel his warmth and smell his toothpaste. He brushed her hair from her face, tucking it behind her ear and sliding his fingers down her neck. If he noticed the damp spots from her tears, he didn't say anything. He just kept running his fingers through her hair, cupping her cheek, soothing her stuttered breaths.

"I mean, how does someone forgive you for something like that? Is that even possible?" The words in her mom's letters flashed before her. They couldn't be true. "How could God forgive me for that?"

He rested his chin against the top of her head. "I ask myself that too. Could God ever forgive me for what I've done? But my choices were selfish and prideful. Yours was an accident."

"Leaving Montreal wasn't. Staying away wasn't. But I can't go back. I can't risk seeing that sorrow in my mom's eyes again."

He nodded. His thumb followed the line of her jaw to the middle of her chin, flames licking in its wake. He raised her chin and traced the bottom of her lower lip from corner to corner. It was sweeter than a kiss, comforting and thrilling all at once.

"We both have some shattered edges," he whispered. "But maybe God isn't afraid of our brokenness. I hope he's not, anyway."

sixteen

Eli didn't so much wake up the next morning. He just got up. He hadn't slept after Violet's revelation. He'd simply lain on the aptly described Taco Bed and stared at the dark ceiling. After more than an hour of just lying there, he did something he hadn't done in a very long time. He prayed for someone else.

He still believed God was present and was listening. He always had. For so many years, he'd been too focused on himself to care. But with the kind of pain Violet was carrying around, there didn't seem to be anywhere else to go. Nothing and no one else could ease that burden and give her the peace she wanted. And oh, how she longed for it. He could hear it in her voice. An absolution, a relief. She craved forgiveness.

He recognized that cry in his own heart, to be free of the weight of regret and shame. He knew he needed God's forgiveness. And he wanted to know that Mama Potts and Oliver and Levi could forgive him too. That they could love him in spite of his miserable choices. That he belonged to them no matter what.

But Violet needed something different. She needed to forgive herself. Maybe then she could be certain of God's forgiveness and discover if her parents could forgive her too.

He wanted to wrap his arms around her and hold her until all her pain eased. He longed to promise that the pain would heal. He couldn't heal it for her, but maybe he could help her find the thing that could.

She'd trusted him with her deepest pain, so maybe it wasn't too late to tell her the whole of his regrets. By this point she could probably put most of the pieces together. But if he told her the rest, she might look at him differently.

He met her in the hallway outside the dining room. She wore the same clothes as she had the day before, her long hair wet and darker than usual from a shower. She rubbed her eyes, which were free of makeup and rimmed in red.

She looked absolutely beautiful.

He had no business thinking things like that. And he'd keep telling himself that until those thoughts quit showing up.

Still, she was objectively pretty. Even through the redness, her eyes shone like freshly polished gemstones. Her features were almost regal, her hair always smooth and shiny. And those lips. Perfect pink lips. So what if he wanted to kiss them good morning? It was a nice thing to do.

She gazed up at him, her palms covering her cheeks. "I must look like a mess."

"Not even a little bit."

"You're a terrible liar."

"What? I'm being honest. You look . . . you look brave." He squinted at her, inspecting every one of her features. "It's not easy to face your past. Trust me. I know."

Violet waved away his words, but the pink creeping up her neck wasn't his imagination. "You don't have to . . ."

Whatever she was going to say was drowned out by the commotion of the dining room as the door flung open and Little Jack flew between them. Clattering plates, lively voices, and a Broadway musical soundtrack were underlying it all. *Les Mis*, if he wasn't mistaken.

"You must be Eli and Violet!" A short woman with white curls and a warm smile rushed forward to meet them. "Jack told me to head straight over here as soon as I got home. He wouldn't hear of me even opening the store until I'd talked with you."

Marie hurried to their sides. "Aretha, let them at least sit down and have some breakfast. You can chat with them while they have their blueberry pancakes."

"Oh, you've already been so kind," Violet said. "We couldn't—"

A voice from the kitchen cut her off. "I've already made your plates, so sit down. I'm not wasting this food."

Marie offered an apologetic smile and a hushed excuse. "That's Caden, our chef. She's wonderful, and a little bit pregnant with her first. You know, the hormones."

"A little bit pregnant, my *foot*!" A curvy woman appeared in the kitchen doorway, her blond hair swept up in the back, a floral apron tied above her slightly rounded belly. She carried a steaming plate in each hand. "If you can eat and keep it down, you eat. Okay?" There was no room for argument in her tone, and Eli liked her immediately.

Violet apparently did too, as she rushed to sit at the closest four-top. Eli joined her as Caden set plates before them.

Violet poured hot maple syrup over her pancakes and shoveled an enormous bite into her mouth. Suddenly her chewing stopped, her motions stilled, and she made the sweetest sound at the back of her throat.

Eli had the strangest urge to get her to make that sound again. Someday. Some way. Whatever it took, he'd make her hum that note of pure bliss.

Before he could dive any deeper into that thought, he took a bite of his own short stack, and he knew just what had caused her response. This was heaven on a plate. The blueberries ripe, the pancakes light and fluffy and filled with a flavor he'd never had. Nutmeg maybe, or pumpkin spice. He couldn't place it. He could only put more in his mouth. The rich and sticky syrup coated his tongue, tying it all together.

Eli was mopping up the last drop of syrup with his final bite of pancake when he looked up to see Aretha, Marie, Caden, and Violet all staring at him. "What?" he asked before shoveling in the last bite.

Violet chuckled. "That was quite the show."

Her plate still held half her pancakes, and he poked his fork in her direction. "You need some help with that?"

She deflected his attempt with her arm. "Nice try. You had your own."

"Do you want more?" Caden asked. "I have the batter. Adam hasn't come over yet, and the Grissoms already left for the day."

Oh, if Eli didn't already like Caden, he would have loved her right then and there. "I shouldn't—"

"Adam will never know," she said, turning back to the

kitchen and humming along to the drum-filled song coming from the speakers.

"I'll never know what?"

Eli turned to find a guy in a leather jacket, sunglasses hanging from the front of his T-shirt.

"Welcome home, sweetie," Aretha said, bestowing a kiss on his cheek. If she wasn't everyone's grandmother by birth, she'd apparently given herself the role and brooked no argument. Adam didn't seem to mind, wrapping an arm around her shoulders and squeezing her tight.

"I missed you. All of you." His gaze dropped to Eli and Violet at the table. "Except, I don't know you. But I think one of you is about to eat my pancakes."

Eli laughed and stood. "Guilty." He shook Adam's hand and saw his eyes flash with recognition.

"You're Eli Ross."

"Guilty of that too."

"What on earth are you doing in North Rustico?"

Eli motioned to Violet and then Aretha. "We're looking for a pottery kiln and heard Aretha might have a line on someone selling one. And if she maybe knows of any stores in the area that might be willing to carry some pieces from Mama Potts's Red Clay Shoppe."

"We had a fire," Violet said around another giant bite.

"Sorry to hear that," Adam said, but he still looked confused. "So you work at this red clay place?" he asked Eli.

"Mama Potts is my mom. I've been helping out since I got back to the island."

"I love her stuff!" Caden arrived with a fresh plate of pancakes and slid them into his spot. She ran back to the kitchen, one hand on her back and one holding her belly. When she reappeared, she had a stack of bowls in her hands. "I have matching coffee mugs and plates too."

Eli picked up one of the blue glazed pieces and looked at the bottom. Beside the Red Clay Shoppe stamp were two tiny letters. *VI*. "I believe Violet made these."

She looked up, appearing almost guilty, like she'd been caught about to lick her plate clean. Maybe she had been.

"You made these?" Caden asked. "They're amazing."

Violet looked down at her empty plate, a simple white dish. "But you made those. And I could eat them every single day."

Caden tittered with delight, sliding into the seat beside Violet. "I'm so sorry to hear about the fire at your store. Will you be able to reopen?"

"Not until we get the whole building rewired. Our electrician is supposed to start on it this week, but until then . . ." Violet shrugged, and every face in the room registered understanding.

"We've been there," Marie said. "Ours was a busted water pipe. But we know what it's like to wait and not know where the money is going to come from."

Suddenly Caden sat up a little straighter, her gaze bouncing back and forth between Marie and Violet. "We can help. We get hundreds of guests every summer, tourists who love to take home souvenirs. We don't have a store exactly, but what if we put some of your pieces on display here in the dining room? I bet we could sell them in a second. What do you think?"

It wasn't clear who she was asking, but Aretha clapped her hands. "Splendid idea."

Marie's smile was all agreement.

"You all work out the details," Aretha said. "I'll call around to see if anyone is selling a kiln. I might know of someone down near Summerside."

Violet couldn't understand how so many perfect things had come together while her soul still felt so freshly filleted. How could she be both jubilant and devastated in the same morning?

"I can't believe they took all the mugs we had left," she said to Eli as he pulled Mama Potts's car back onto the main road, heading south toward Victoria.

"I can. You and Mama Potts do great work. Plus a chef loves to be recognized for *her* great work. I don't think I've ever seen you so happy as you were with those pancakes."

"Excuse me. I'm not the one who ate two plates."

"Well, it would have been rude to turn down her offer."

"You ate her husband's breakfast."

"Yes, I did." Eli held up a finger. "But in all fairness, she was going to make him something else. Probably."

Violet giggled, the sunlight through the car window warming her skin and something new within making it easier to breathe. It was refreshing not being the only one to know her secret. But it was also a little terrifying.

"Listen, Eli. About last night."

He looked at her for a brief second before focusing back on the road. For just that moment, she could feel his thumb against her lip, his fingers on her skin. And she remembered the fire. It had been there when he'd hugged her at the game. Different. Joyful. But no less consuming.

There was something between them. She hadn't wanted to admit it before. She still wanted to deny it wholeheartedly. Except for that little bit of her spirit that wondered, that wanted to know if their kiss would burn as bright as his touch.

What a stupid thought. Of course it would. And it would burn out just as fast.

When he was done here, he'd walk away again. There was nothing keeping him. He could leave and still keep in touch with his mom and brothers. He could leave on good terms this time. But he would still leave.

Victoria was her home. It was just a safety net for him. He was there only as long as it took him to figure out where he was going next.

"Yeah?"

His low voice snapped her out of her thoughts, and she realized he'd been waiting for her to continue. "What I told you last night—about my brother and my parents—no one else knows."

"Not even Mama Potts?" His voice rose in disbelief.

"No one."

"All right."

"Can we keep it that way?"

He was silent for a long time, and she stared at his profile, memorizing the outline of his day-old beard. Deep inside she expected him to tell her he couldn't keep this secret. After all, he hadn't asked her to keep his. She just knew that she should.

Finally, he let out a long breath. "I won't tell anyone. But I think you should."

She hung her head and twisted the edge of her sweater

into a tight screw. "I don't think I can handle Mama Potts looking at me the way my mom did."

"Maybe it's not about Mama Potts. Maybe it's about you."

"Me?"

"It just seems like it's been eating you up inside for years. Maybe you should tell someone else. Maybe you should reach out to your parents. I mean, obviously you miss them. I missed Mama Potts when I was gone."

When she blinked, her mom's most recent letter flashed on the back of her eyelids. An invitation, a cry to restore their relationship. But it couldn't be true. It wasn't. Fists shaking against her knees, she managed a soft whisper. "They don't want anything to do with me."

"But it's been years. And they love you. They're your parents. Don't you even want to try?"

Oh, this man. How could he be so tender with her the night before and push so hard on old scars this morning? "Can you just leave it be?"

"You're right. I'm sorry. I didn't mean—"

"Besides, you have plenty of secrets about your dad, and you haven't even told his wife. You know, they're still married."

Eli blinked several times, his jaw dropping. Then, oh so quietly, he said, "I never thought about it."

"Your mom told me last year. He's never been pronounced legally dead, and she's never filed for nor received divorce papers. They're still married."

"Do you think she still loves him?"

"I think . . ." Violet watched the pine trees along the road fly by, searching for answers among them, but there were none. "I think love is hard. It's more commitment than butterflies.

He gave her you three boys, and she loves you. And as far as I know, your dad used to be a good man."

"Yeah, well, I can assure you, he's not now."

"Those men who were here—I mean, at the studio. The ones in the red sports car. Is that who your dad owes money to?"

"He doesn't owe them money anymore." There was a certainty mixed with grief and regret in his words, and a thought so terrible came to her mind that she needed him to contradict it on the spot. But she was afraid to ask for fear that he wouldn't.

"Eli?"

"Please don't ask." His voice was husky, ragged with honesty.

"Eli?"

Suddenly he whipped the SUV into a small turnout, a gravel parking spot big enough for four cars and a view of the river. It was perfect for tourist pictures. And for Eli to throw the car into park, get out, and pace the length of it. There was nothing around them except green fields. The road was empty in both directions as far as she could see.

But all she could really see was the line of Eli's mouth, the hardness on his face, the trembling of his fists. She was almost certain it wasn't the cool morning air making him shiver.

If he wanted her to be scared of him, she intended to disappoint him. Marching up to him, she stood in his path and faced him down. "What are you so afraid of me knowing?"

"I'm not afraid of *you* knowing anything." He stepped around her, his stride growing longer, eating up the ground beneath his feet.

She tossed up her hands and threw back her head. "Then what don't you want to tell me? What are you so afraid I'm going to ask that you don't want to answer?"

His back to her, hands on his hips, he stopped beside the car, hunched forward, and sighed. "You already know."

"It can't be. Really?"

"You sound so surprised. I thought your opinion of me was pretty low."

She stepped toward him, then back. It had been low. In the beginning. "I guess some things change."

"Ha." The noise barely qualified as a laugh. It was more like an involuntary breath.

"Tell me about it."

"Why?"

She did reach for him then, resting her hand on his shoulder, trying to soothe away the knotted muscle there. "Because sometimes it helps to speak the truth. Sometimes it feels better to just get it out."

"Do you feel better—after last night?" His words were hushed, sincere.

"Strangely, a little bit. I don't feel great, but I like being able to say Garrett's name without fear that you'll find out what happened."

He released a pent-up breath, his shoulders stooping even more. "When my dad found me, he was half a million dollars in debt. Gambling. He swore it was an addiction. He would get help. I'm not sure I believed him, but I had no doubt when he said his bookie was going to kill him if he didn't pay up."

His muscles tensed, and she could do nothing to ease his pain but slip her arms around his waist from behind. Resting her ear against his back, she heard his heart thudding hard in his chest and the catch in each breath. His sweatshirt was soft, warmth flowing from him.

"They were going to make an example of him. No one got away with not paying their debts. Especially to Tony Moynahan and the men he works for."

"The man in the red car."

He nodded.

When he didn't continue, she did it for him. "So you . . ."

"I should have told my dad it wasn't my problem. I should have gone to the cops. I should have done any number of things. I didn't."

seventeen

Violet couldn't believe Eli was telling her the truth about his dad. All she could do was hold on to him while it spilled out.

"He was family. The only family I'd seen in ten years. The Lord knows I wanted to believe that he was going to get help, that he'd had no control over his addiction."

Eli stepped to the side, dislodging her grip as he leaned against the car and pulled her to his side. He didn't seem to want to look at her, but neither did he let her go. So she wrapped him up in a hug and pressed herself into his shoulder.

He crossed his long legs at his ankles and leaned into her. "I guess I thought if I could make things right for him, I could make things right with the rest of my family. If I came home with Dad, maybe they'd forgive me. Maybe they'd welcome me back, and we could be a real family. All of us."

He worked his jaw side to side. "It was stupid. It was the most stupid thing I've ever done. I told him I'd meet Tony and we'd try to work something out. After all, I was living in a 1.5-million-dollar condo. I didn't have a penny in savings—because who needs savings when the contracts keep coming?" He shook his head. "I was not very smart."

Violet wiped some dust off his cheek, scratching his prickly beard, and wished she could remove his regret just as easily. Nothing about regret and shame was easy. The voices in her head kept repeating her sins even after more than ten years. She didn't have a brilliant word of wisdom or a tip for silencing those accusations. The only thing she could do was listen as he revealed the whole ugly truth.

"So whose idea was it for you to take on your dad's . . ."

"We met up at this seedy bar—me and my dad and Tony. It was all dim lights and shady deals. Tony was quick to suggest that I didn't have to pay off my dad's debt. He could make it all go away. He just needed five games. Five losses. Then we'd be square.

"I could see the hope in my dad's eyes. He was a man on death row looking for a pardon. I was the governor with the stamp. I felt so powerful. I just kept thinking about all the times my dad had let our family down and how I could change everything. My choice could change him for good. It was only five games, after all. It wasn't like we were going to the playoffs—not with our record that season. But as soon as I started trying to talk myself into it, I knew I was just digging a bigger pit."

Eli kicked at the dirt beneath his feet. "Still, I didn't see another way to help my dad. I knew it was wrong. I knew I was breaking every major rule of sports. You never fix a game. Everyone knows that. You don't lose on purpose. You work your tail off so you can hold your head high no matter what. And so you know you didn't let your teammates down."

"You meant to lose?"

"I agreed to Tony's terms. I would make sure we lost the next five games. The first two, we were going up against the toughest defenses in the league. It didn't take much to lose those. A few extra penalties, a couple of missed shots. And I just kept the spread wider than most of the bets."

"You could have been arrested for that."

"Like I said, I wasn't very smart. I wasn't thinking about anything but being a family again. And after I'd agreed, after I'd taken on my dad's debt, it was too late to change my mind."

With her ear against his chest, she could hear his heart rate pick up and the shallow catch of his breath.

"That first game, in the locker room. I couldn't look any of my teammates in the eye. I could barely breathe. I thought I was going to pass out. How could I have promised away their games? I wasn't just messing with my own career. I was risking theirs too. Except it was life or death—*my* life or death—at that point. I had to keep going. But I swore that it was the end. I was going to retire. I was going to quit the game. If I couldn't trust myself, how could I ask any of them to trust me either?"

"So, what happened at the third game?"

"There was no third game."

She leaned forward to look into his face. "But . . ."

"I wasn't as sly as I thought I was, or as good of an actor. Coach accused me of tampering with the games. He took it to the commissioner's office. They kept everything hush-hush, didn't want me to tarnish the organization's reputation.

I knew it was over. I was gone. I was never going to suit up again."

"But Tony . . ."

"Yeah, he still wanted his money, and according to him, I still owed three hundred grand."

"But shouldn't your dad have—"

Eli sighed, his voice going guttural. "He split. I haven't seen him since the bar that night when I agreed to take on his debt."

"That rat!" She threw her fists down to her sides and imagined how satisfying it would be to punch Jason Ross in the nose or kick him in the shins. Oh, he deserved it. He deserved so much worse than that too.

"So you sold everything you owned to try to get out from under it," she said.

He confirmed with a simple nod. "Turns out everything to my name wasn't enough. I sold my condo fully furnished. But I only had about two hundred grand in equity. Put all my electronics on the market. Took my suits to a consignment store. I even tried selling a few of my signed jerseys to collectible dealers. Not that anyone wanted them at that point. But no matter what I did, there just wasn't enough."

It was the catch in his voice that stopped her breathing. He ached in the deepest part of his soul, and she just wanted to fix it for him. She wanted to heal that wound, to make it possible for him to go back in time and make a different choice.

It was her turn to pace, and she marched the length of the car and then back to him. "It's not right. It's just not fair. Doesn't Tony get it? This is your dad's fault."

"It *was* my dad's fault." He hung his head, his hair blowing in the gentle breeze. Still leaning against the car, he rested his hands on his hips and lifted his shoulders nearly to his ears. "I made it my own."

"No. I refuse to accept that."

He smirked at her. "I hate to say it, but I don't think Tony much cares what you accept or not. He wants his fifty grand, and he's going to get it. One way or another."

"And he . . . he beat you up, didn't he? He's the reason you had a black eye, and he broke your wrist." She slammed her fist into her other palm, wishing she could show Tony just what she thought of thugs like him. She wasn't exactly one for violence—save the occasional entertaining fight during a hockey game. But this Tony character needed to know they weren't going to stand for this anymore.

Eli pushed himself forward, blocking her path, towering over her. He crossed his arms, and she could see how an opposing team might be intimidated. She was not.

"Eli, we have to do something."

"I am doing something. I'm earning back the money so I can get rid of Tony for good."

"But will he really stay gone?"

He scrubbed a hand down his face. "I don't have anything else that he wants."

"But you're never going to . . . you can't ever play in the NHL again. It's not fair."

He grabbed her arms. His hands were huge, nearly wrapping all the way around her biceps, but his grip was gentle. Firm yet soft. "Don't you get it? This is on me. This is my fault. I took on my dad's debt when I was too proud to ask for help. I should have told my coach or called the police or reached out to anyone. Instead, I thought I could fix it all on my own. There's only one reason I'm never going to play in the NHL again. And it's me."

She gripped his wrists, holding on to him so he had to look into her face. Unmoving, she stared him down. "Don't *you* get it? You don't have to be in this alone. You're not on your own anymore. Your mom and brothers . . . We'll help you."

"I'm not going to let anyone else get involved in my mess."

"It's too late. I'm already involved."

He took a step toward her, and she matched it going backward. Suddenly he was too close. Too big. Too much. He used up all the oxygen and left her head spinning and her knees weak. She stumbled back into the side of the car. She couldn't get any farther away, and he just kept coming for her, closing the space.

But she wasn't some weak-kneed ninny, so she pushed herself forward. Then there was nothing between them, not even a breath of air. She arched her head all the way back so she could see his face, but her gaze landed on his Adam's apple, which bobbed several times. His chest rose and fell, matching the rhythm of hers. Fast. Strained.

Finally her eyes met his. He consumed her, devouring each angle of her face, his breathing growing more and more erratic.

Maybe she should have been worried, but she wasn't. His fingers still held her with such restraint. And the longing in his eyes wasn't to be rid of her. It was for more of her. More of them.

That should have concerned her. But really, she just worried how much it didn't bother her. How the idea of the two of them made her heart sing.

When he spoke again, his voice sounded like it had been dragged over a gravel road. "Why do you want to be involved? You don't even like me."

She lifted one shoulder. "I like you enough."

His eyebrows rose, and that satisfied grin fell into place.

"You know, enough that I don't wish you any more bodily harm."

Suddenly he let go of her arms, one hand sliding to the small of her back. He gave her a quick squeeze, and her air vanished for as long as it took her to scream, "All right!"

He raised his eyebrows, a silent challenge.

No ninny behavior today. It was time to own up to whatever was happening between them. At least, what she hoped was between them.

"All right," she whispered. "I like you. Period. End of confession."

His nod seemed satisfied. His hands slid to either side of her waist, giving her a gentle push against the car. She squeaked when she bumped against it, her heart thudding in the back of her throat. It was so loud, he had to be able to hear it drowning out every chirping bird and passing car. There was only her pounding heart. And his. She could feel it beneath her palm, because at some point she'd put her hand on his chest. She glanced down at it and decided it was a perfectly fine resting spot.

When she looked back up, his eyes were fire.

It took her a long moment to realize that it wasn't his gaze that was blazing a trail across her cheek. His thumb was to blame for that. It stroked back and forth as he bit his bottom lip.

"I'm going to kiss you now."

Her stomach swooped. Of course he was going to kiss her. The sheer certainty of his statement made everything inside her tingle. She had to fight to keep her eyes open, because she just wanted to *feel* this moment. But she also didn't want to miss a second of his embrace.

Eli cleared his throat. "If you don't want me to, tell me right now."

Her eyes flew open, and she almost pushed him away for delaying the inevitable even one more second. Instead she grabbed the back of his head and pulled him right where she wanted him, pressing her lips squarely against his. They bumped against each other, bouncing like pinballs, seeking—and not quite finding—the right fit. She wiggled against his sharp angles and unforgiving chest, two pieces from very different puzzles.

He pulled back and chuckled.

Well, that could hurt a girl's feelings. It had been a while, but she couldn't have turned into a terrible kisser. Or maybe she had.

Before she could push him away for real, he cupped her cheeks, held her face still, and settled back in. His lips were firm and warm, and he knew exactly what he was doing. His touch was as gentle as goose down yet fiercely protective. Like a storm brewing over the bay and then rolling in to consume her.

With him, there was no room to consider the lies whispered in her ears or question the choices she'd made after her world had crumbled. There was only Eli Ross, his arms now around her and his heart in sync with hers.

She was stuck in the best possible way. Between him and the car. She ran her fingers through his thick hair, trying to get more of him. Trying to take his regret from him and replace it with joy.

And if she took her own enjoyment from this moment too? Well, that was part of being in his arms.

She was completely surrounded. Sheltered. Secure. She didn't doubt for a second that he would do whatever it took to keep her safe.

Hugging his waist, holding him just as tightly, she hoped he knew she would do no less.

~

Eli couldn't hold her any closer. But he kept trying.

This connection was unlike anything he'd ever experienced. He wasn't a facade or a figurehead. He wasn't a trophy to put on the shelf, a picture to show off to friends.

He was the very worst thing he'd done, and she still cared about him.

She tasted of maple syrup, only made sweeter by her own essence. She smelled of fresh air and clean skin and this scent that was wholly Violet. He had smelled it on her at the ice rink once or twice, and now when it filled him, it took him back there. To the place where he was most at home. Violet and the ice.

Sliding his hands up her back, he leaned in just a little bit more. She shimmied against him, and then she made that sweet sound. The one she'd made while eating Caden's pancakes.

But this time it was all because of him, all his doing.

His heart slammed against his rib cage, his eyes fluttering open and then closed. Longing to savor the moment but wanting to see her enjoy it too.

Her hands had found their way back to his chest, and he kept waiting for her to shove him away. Only she didn't. Her fists tugged at the fabric there, like she would refuse to let him go should he try to pull away.

As if he'd be that stupid.

Suddenly a car flew past, the driver laying on the horn.

He and Violet both jerked back. She was gasping for breath. To be fair, he was too. The distance between them was too great, so he pressed his forehead to hers, watching the quiver of her lower lip as she tried to regain some control. That lip was too tempting to be left alone, so he swept his forefinger across the bottom ridge, pressing ever so gently at the center. He missed its taste already.

That was ludicrous. He had no business thinking such things.

But he couldn't stop his thoughts. Not when he no longer had to wonder if the sizzle in their banter would translate to their kiss. What was between them was more than . . . well, it was just more.

"Eli?"

"Yeah?"

She nibbled on her bottom lip. "Maybe we should get back on the road."

"Probably." He didn't move.

Her laugh was as sweet as blueberries. "Eli." She pushed at his shoulder but didn't put any real effort into it.

One more. He just needed one more kiss.

When he pressed his lips to hers, she sighed into him.

It wasn't enough. And he had a terrible feeling deep in his gut that one more would never be enough. He would always want more. But he pulled away, opened the passenger door for her, and watched her slide in before closing it with a soft tick.

He took his time strolling around the back of the car, reining in every errant emotion and crazy desire. This was Violet, and he'd treat her with every ounce of respect that he'd failed to show to the girls who had come before. He couldn't wipe away his past, but he could choose to start over now.

And he would. He wouldn't have any regrets with Violet. Even after it ended.

And it had to end.

When he was back behind the wheel and on the road, Violet watched him closely. She seemed to catch every movement of his hand, every twitch of his chin.

"What's wrong?" he asked. "You afraid I'm going to go lightheaded and take us into the river?"

"Well, I mean, it was a pretty good kiss."

He tossed back his head and laughed right into the roof. "I thought it was a little better than 'pretty good.'"

She grinned. "Me too. But that's not what I'm afraid of."

His eyebrows pinched together, and he could feel the wrinkles in his forehead. "What is it? What are you afraid of? Us?"

"No—wait, is there an us?"

He choked on a breath, hacking until he was pretty sure at least one of his lungs had come loose. He was not prepared to define their relationship, which he hadn't allowed himself to give more than a passing thought about until right that moment.

"Never mind," she said. "Let's table that discussion. I'm worried about you. I'm worried about Tony. I'm worried about why you won't let us—your family—help you come up with that money."

He could offer only a shrug in response.

"And I'm worried that the police are going to come asking questions about those games. I'm worried that something is going to drag you away and break Mama Potts's heart all over again. I'm worried that—"

Eli pressed his hand to her knee, adding some pressure and, he prayed, passing her some peace.

When she stopped, she just stared at him in the silence.

Finally, he offered her the only thing he could. "It'll all be all right."

"But it's not all right. None of it."

"Maybe not yet, but it will be."

She shook her head, clearly unable to believe him. "You have to tell your mom."

Oh, no. They were right back where they had started, and his decision about that hadn't changed. "I can't let her worry about me the way that you do. I can't add that pressure to her life."

"But what if you can't make the money and Tony comes after you? Or—or us? Or the Red Clay Shoppe?"

"I won't let him."

"But it's not your decision. I mean, it's not like you let him break your arm, did you?"

Her words packed a wallop, the truth like a wrecking ball.

Maybe his very presence put Mama Potts and Violet and his brothers in danger. Maybe it would be better if he left, at least until he could finish paying off the debt.

He refused to ask if Violet thought he should go.

"I think if anyone can help—if anyone knows what it's like to be saddled with your dad's debts—it's your mom."

Perhaps she was right. But telling Mama Potts the whole sordid story would guarantee at least one thing—losing whatever respect he'd regained.

"If I don't tell her, are you going to?" he asked.

Violet shook his hand off her knee, curling in on herself. "Please don't ask me to make that decision."

eighteen

After sharing so much, stuck in such close quarters for two days, silence was a strange visitor. An unwelcome one.

Eli had hoped to see Violet at practice. She wasn't there. He'd expected her to come around the house. She didn't show up there. So he'd gone to the studio. She wasn't there either. She hadn't even shown up to see the girls win their game the day before.

He didn't know where else she could be hiding. He only knew she was hiding. There was no way she could stay gone in a town this size for days without trying. So he sat in Mama Potts's kitchen, sulking like a little boy who'd lost his best friend. Maybe his only friend.

Mama Potts started down the stairs, a box in her good hand, her limp a little less pronounced. Her appearance jerked him from his memories of that car ride back from North Rustico, from that stop on the side of the road. And yeah, that kiss. Every perfect moment of it. While he wanted a second one of those—and a third and a fourth—he needed to find Violet first. Preferably without alerting his mom and his brothers to the fact that he'd lost her.

"Hey, let me help you with that." He hopped up and was halfway up the stairs before his mom assured him she was fine.

"Sit back down. I can do this myself."

"But I'm already here." He reached for the box, but she swiveled it away from his grasp.

"You and your brothers. Always trying to take care of me. It'd be sweet if it wasn't so annoying."

He snorted, then pictured Levi verbally offering his help and laughed harder. "I'm sorry?"

"I've been an invalid for a month now, and I'm tired of it. So don't treat me like I'm useless. Just be normal."

He considered scooping her up and carrying her—box and all—to the kitchen. But one look in her eyes and he decided that wasn't worth it. Instead he slowly backed down the stairs, his hand on the railing, ready to catch the box should it begin to teeter.

It didn't. Mama Potts was a strong woman. She was used to taking care of herself. Something he would have known if he'd been around for the last eleven years or looked up from his stick for the eleven years before that.

She set the box on the table, and he snuck a peek inside. Whatever he'd been expecting, it wasn't the clutter of broken pottery pieces that filled the bottom. All different shapes and sizes and colors. The remnants of the studio that he and Violet had collected.

"You want me to toss this?" he asked.

Mama Potts looked downright offended. "I most certainly do not. That's my project."

"Which is . . ."

"Which I'm still figuring out. But just because I haven't figured out how I'm going to use these doesn't mean they aren't beautiful. I just need to play with them some more." She plopped down into a chair. "Now, would you please get me a pillow off the sofa so I can put my foot up?"

Balancing a heavy box down the stairs she could handle, but a pillow required help? He chuckled but did as she asked, propping it on an empty chair and helping her rest her foot on top.

When she was settled in, she began pulling ceramic shards from the box. Green and purple and blue and yellow, all with red centers made from PEI's clay. She was so busy rearranging them on the tabletop that he assumed she'd forgotten he was even there.

"So what's going on with you?" she asked. "You've been pouting like a first grader ever since you got back from your trip."

"Nothing." His voice was an octave too high, and he cleared his throat so he no longer sounded like a first grader. "And no I haven't."

She shot him a sharp look, a familiar one. He was surprised how much he'd missed it.

"I've been busy."

"With?"

"Practice and getting ready for the tournament and . . ." And looking for Violet when he should have been looking for more work, another job. Not mooning over the girl. Not wondering if he'd made the worst mistake of his life.

He'd put all of his ammunition in Violet's hands. Now he was just praying she wouldn't shoot him in the back.

"Did something happen on that trip? I mean, aside from Marty sending over the money and your connections in North Rustico."

"No. Why? Did Violet say something? Have you seen her lately?"

He would not have done well in police interrogation.

Mama Potts slowly lifted her eyebrows and stared down the tip of her nose at him. "Start talking, young man."

"There's nothing to tell. We had a little adventure. We met some interesting people. And we're waiting for a call about—"

As if on cue, his phone rang with an unknown number. He jumped up and darted for the door. "I've got to take this."

He stepped outside into the brisk evening air as he pressed the phone to his ear. "Hello?"

"That's the best greeting you've got for an old friend doing you a favor?"

His stomach sank. He'd been waiting for Jett's call but hoping for one from Aretha. Still, he put on his best show. "Hey, man. How's it going?"

"Better." Jett left it to be determined whether his response was an answer to Eli's question or an assessment of his greeting. Eli decided he didn't really care.

"You found something for me?"

"You, sir, owe me one—or maybe three."

His gut clenched. "That wasn't our agreement."

"Well, you can't get something for nothing. That's not how the world works, man. You know that." Jett sounded like a teacher talking to a preschooler.

"We agreed to five percent of whatever I make. That's what I owe you."

"Oh, you're cute. Mistaken, but cute."

Eli pounded his fist silently against the wall of the cottage, pressing his forehead next to it. His breath came out in quick pants. "What is it you want, Jett?" Even as he asked the question, he was transported back to that dark room, the back corner of the seedy bar where he had asked Tony the same thing.

"Only what I'm owed," Tony had said.

Eli had a hunch that Jett was thinking exactly the same thing. Everyone thought they were owed something. No one ever gave something for free.

Except for Aretha and Jack and Marie and Caden. They'd asked for absolutely nothing in return for a night in their inn and the best breakfast he'd ever eaten—not that he'd ever confess that to Mama Potts. So maybe there were a few truly kind people in the world. But they weren't the people he could ask for favors. And favors weren't supposed to come with strings attached.

"Aren't you even going to ask me what I found for you?"

Eli took a steadying breath. "All right. What is it?"

"A team that's looking for a center."

His stomach clenched, hope flickering and then doused in a moment. "I can't play in the league anymore."

"What kind of fool do you take me to be?" Jett swore loudly, and the bawdy laughter behind him reminded Eli of the life he'd once lived. The one he'd left everything for. He was never going back.

"Then what kind of team is it?"

"Latvia."

"I'm sorry, what does that mean?" Eli couldn't make sense

of the word. Though of course he'd heard of the country, he couldn't pinpoint it on a map.

"There's a team in Latvia in need of a center. They're not picky. They don't mind a player with a little history—especially one of your caliber."

He should be overjoyed. This was a chance to be back on the ice. Not as a coach but as a player, to use his skills and take care of the debt he owed. This was his shot. Instead bile rose in the back of his throat. He spat on the ground, but it wasn't enough to rid his mouth of the bitter taste.

"They're willing to offer you a signing bonus. Seventy-five grand. It's basically your whole salary for your first season, but they'll pay it up front. You can get out from under Tony's thumb and be done with the whole thing. Besides, I hear Latvia is beautiful."

"No, you don't."

Jett cackled. "You're right. I've never heard a thing about Latvia. It's probably cold and barren and miserable. But it's that or the business end of Bobby Moynahan's fists. So it's your decision."

"When do they want me?"

"Their season starts in three weeks."

"You're kidding me. I can't be there in three weeks." The calendar in the locker room at the rink flashed before his eyes. His girls had two more games and a tournament in three weeks to wrap up their season. He couldn't just walk away from them before that.

Jett scoffed. "You got a better offer?"

"Well, no. But . . . I have commitments. I have some things I have to wrap up here."

"Those things gonna pay you seventy-five grand?"

"No." Eli stabbed his fingers through his hair and turned around to lean against the wall. He slid down it until he sat on the ground.

"Hey, man, you called me. I found you what you're looking for, now you're not sure?"

"Can I let you know?"

"They won't hold it for you." Jett sighed. "But it's not like they have a lot of guys signing up for a spot on the Latvian home team."

"And just what favor would I owe you?"

"We'll figure that out later."

Eli hung up but held on to his phone, his arms resting on his knees. The sun had nearly set, and the shadows stretched across the lawn toward the garage, leaving him in the dark. Just where he always seemed to end up.

Well, this was a fine mess. He had an offer that would cover just what he needed. It would also require him to do the thing he'd sworn he wouldn't again. He'd have to leave. Then what?

A truck rumbled down the driveway, and he squinted into the headlights that stopped near the garage. The engine stilled, and the lights flicked off. The door opened and then slammed shut, heavy footfalls landing on the gravel.

For a second, Eli hoped his brother hadn't seen him. But Oliver walked right in his direction.

Oliver towered above him, and before Eli could offer an invitation, he dropped to the ground and leaned back against the house too. "Hiding from Mama Potts?"

Eli shook his head. "No, I was just taking a phone call."

"Doesn't sound like good news."

"Actually, it kind of is."

Oliver lifted one knee and rested his arm on it. "How's that?"

"I got an offer to play again."

"NHL?" Even in the fading light, he could see Oliver's raised eyebrows.

"I'm afraid that ship has sailed. This is for a different kind of team, but it's a good offer."

Oliver clapped him on the back. "Well, that's exciting."

The question he didn't ask hung between them, and Eli wanted to swear that he wouldn't leave again, that he was going to stay put. That he wouldn't hurt Mama Potts or Violet. Like he'd promised.

Except he didn't have that choice.

And a little bit of him longed to be back on a team, to prove that he was more than the betrayal of his last sweater and all that it stood for.

"I didn't expect you to be here again."

Violet looked up from the page in her book. The one she'd read five or six times. She still didn't have a clue what it said. Sticking her finger between the pages to hold her place, she tried for a natural smile. "I'm sorry. I know I've been here a lot lately. I can go if . . ."

Meg tossed her school bag into the corner of the quaint living room and flopped onto the other end of the sofa. "I don't mind that you're here. I *like* having you around. It's just . . ." She tapped one finger to her lips. "Well, ever since you got back from your road trip, you've barely left."

"That's not true."

Meg gave her an authentic teacher stare, right down the ridge of her nose.

"All right. I haven't felt much like going out. It's just that I got into a little bit of a . . . of a thing with Eli."

Meg jumped up, crossed her long legs underneath her, and clapped her hands. "Tell me everything. Did you guys make out? He's been eyeing you since he got here. I knew it was only a matter of time."

"It wasn't like that." But her neck flamed, and pressing a hand to cover it only made Meg's eyes shine brighter. "Okay, but you can't tell a soul—not even Oliver."

Meg chewed on the corner of her lip. "But if Oliver finds out from someone else—say, his older brother—we can talk about it?"

Violet shook her head and laughed. "It's really not a big deal. We just kissed a little bit." Except it felt like a big deal. Not because of the kiss—which still made her feel a little light-headed—but because before that, she'd told him her worst secret. And he hadn't run screaming or called her every name she'd called herself since she was sixteen. Instead, he'd told her his deepest secret.

And she'd threatened to reveal it.

Oh, she was some piece of work.

Meg bounced in her seat. "And then what happened?"

"And then we got into a fight."

Meg's joy seemed to leak out of her, slowly at first and then all at once, leaving her slumped against the seat. "So you've been hiding out here, avoiding him."

Violet nodded.

"So, no more kissing?"

"No." Not yet anyway. But she certainly wasn't opposed to it.

All right, that was not entirely true. She was downright *interested* in revisiting that specific activity.

Meg reached out and patted her knee. "What did you fight about?"

Violet shook her head. She couldn't tell Meg. She wouldn't tell anyone. His secrets weren't hers to share.

"All right. I won't press." Meg looked down at her hands folded in her lap. "But can I just say that you can't hide forever. I mean, you're welcome here as long as you like. But eventually you're going to have to face Eli, and the longer you wait, the harder you're making it on yourself." The corner of her mouth quirked. "Besides, making up can be a lot of fun too."

Violet couldn't contain her snort of laughter. "Meg Whitaker, do you have anything else on your mind?"

"Well, if you were going to marry one of the Ross brothers in one month and nineteen days, then you might understand."

They dissolved into giggles, schoolgirls again.

But Violet was certain of one thing. She was not going to marry any of the Ross brothers—especially not the prodigal son. Even if she did owe him an apology.

When Eli's phone rang during practice the next day, he scooped it up, hoping to see Violet's name there. It wasn't. It was a number he didn't recognize.

His stomach clenched, a name flashing before his eyes. Tony.

But it was an island number, and he doubted that Tony had given up his New York area code. So he called to the girls to keep slapping pucks at the net as he skated to the bench. With a modicum of privacy—the eyes of every mom in the stands on his back notwithstanding—he pressed the phone to his ear. "Hello?"

"Eli Ross?" The voice on the other end was so sweet it practically chirped. It was also vaguely familiar.

"Yes."

"It's Aretha, dear. How are you?"

"Aretha!" Joy nearly strangled him. "I wasn't exp— I was hoping you'd call."

"Of course I called. And with good news!"

His low laugh echoed off the bench, and he glanced over his shoulder. A few players had given up on the drill to stare at him. He jerked his head toward the net, and some of them took the hint. But for a moment he couldn't care that the others didn't. "What kind of good news? Do you have—did you find a kiln for us?"

"I sure did." Aretha kept going with details about her friend in Summerside who was retiring and willing to sell them her kiln at a screaming deal.

Eli only caught about every third word as he whipped around, looking left then right. He wanted to pull Violet in for a hug, to tell her the good news, to celebrate a win. But she wasn't there.

His gut hurt again.

After promising to call Aretha's friend and arrange to pick up the kiln, he hung up. But he couldn't focus on the team or the drills or preparing for the upcoming game. Everything inside him buzzed to tell Violet the good news, to track her down and fully celebrate with her.

And if he kissed her again . . . well, that would be just fine with him.

nineteen

Violet pumped her foot against the pedal of her wheel, letting the table pick up speed. Her lump of clay was still that—a lump. But she scooped some water over it, pressing her thumbs into the center as she cupped her fingers around the edges. Slowly the clay began to take shape as it spun around and around, smooth and cool in her grasp.

There was something hypnotic in watching the clay begin to resemble a coffee mug, to watch something beautiful come from nothing. After she'd taken Violet under her wing, Mama Potts had often spoken of the beauty in making something brand-new.

But what of the already broken?

Violet loved the way she could mold the clay into whatever she wanted it to be. The spiritual illustration wasn't lost on her. Pastor Dell had preached on Jesus being the potter and believers the clay. He molded each heart into the shape he wanted.

But what happened after the clay was fired? Violet had seen enough shattered pieces of pottery to know that they didn't come back together. Even if the pieces fit, there were always cracks, evidence of the brokenness.

Like suggesting that she'd tell Eli's mom the truth if he didn't.

She wanted to smack her forehead against her wheel. She had no business threatening to do that. So what if she saw so many of her own regrets mirrored in him? So what if she wanted to save him and Mama Potts from more heartache?

Like the heartbreak she'd left behind in Montreal.

Pot, meet kettle.

She couldn't try to fix his family just because she'd irreparably broken her own. There would be no reshaping, remolding. No matter how many letters her mom wrote. No matter how much she wanted to believe the words were true. She'd left behind only shattered pieces. What had been couldn't be salvaged without the scars to show it.

"Thinking about something important?"

Violet jumped, sticking a finger through the wall of her clay. She looked up to see Eli leaning against the open doorframe. "What makes you think that?"

He pointed to his eyebrows, scrunching them together.

With conscious effort, she relaxed the muscles of her face and ignored the hole she'd just punched in her mug. "Hi."

"Hey." He didn't move from his post, outlined by the evening sky, the orange and gold of the setting sun above his left shoulder casting a halo over his black hair. "You're here late."

She waved toward the wall where the electrician had cut out large strips of drywall. "I can't really work when he's here during the day. It's too dusty."

He nodded slowly. "You're not easy to find. You been avoiding me?"

Looking back at her mug, she worked the clay to fix her mistake. "A little bit."

His snort of surprise made her heart thump a little harder, but she refused to look at him again.

"Any particular reason?"

She nodded, but no words followed.

He seemed content to wait, and she could sense his gaze heavy on her. Her knee bounced under his surveillance, breaking the rhythm of the pedal and the spinning of the wheel. Then her fingers began to tremble, caving in the lip of the mug.

Well, this wasn't going to work.

Toppling her piece, she formed it into a ball before getting up to put it into storage.

Still his eyes followed her. She could feel them roaming across her shoulders and down her arms, analyzing her every movement. Suddenly she couldn't keep from twisting her hands together, working the red clay deeper under her nails and into her skin.

She marched toward the sink at the back of the room. Shadowed by the steps that led to her apartment above, she thought she might have a moment free of his scrutiny. But his steps followed hers across the cement floor. Her stomach twisted and her throat closed. She tried to gasp a breath, but it wasn't there.

All she could take in was a faint scent of *him*. Through the sharp smell of the glazes and the lingering scent of smoke, she knew him. He smelled of that borrowed aftershave and soap. He smelled of skates and sweaters and the ice.

He was so close that she could feel his presence, shivers racing down her spine. Whether they were trying to get her closer to him or away from him, she didn't know. But they meant he was near, close enough to stir her hair with his breath.

"Did I do something, Vi?" His voice was soft and throaty, coming from somewhere deep in his chest. Somewhere near his heart.

He'd never called her that before, and it was sweeter than maple syrup. He thought he'd offended her when it was so obviously the other way around.

Turning slowly, she kept her head bowed over her hands still covered in red. With a tiny shake of her head, she whispered, "I'm so sorry. I should never have tried to force your hand with your mom. Of course I won't tell her about your dad. I mean, I still think you should tell her. I think she might be able to help you deal with Tony and all of your dad's debts and everything, but I never should have threatened to tell her. It's not my place, and I won't say anything, and . . . and I'm just really embarrassed. You listened to all my secrets—and never judged me." Her throat began to seize up, but she pushed through on a wheeze. "You deserve the same."

After her verbal flood, she expected him to say something. Anything. But he let the silence linger, only the dripping faucet behind her and the chirping crickets outside filling the quiet moment.

Slowly—so slowly—he brushed the tips of his fingers through the strands of hair that had escaped from her ponytail. Tucking them back, he dragged his thumb around the rim of her ear. Her neck burned, all her skin aflame, and if she looked at him, she knew with complete certainty that she'd lose whatever footing she had. So she kept her eyes glued to the red spots that had fallen on the tops of her once-white trainers.

"Aren't you going to say something?" she whispered, barely able to hear her own words over the rush of blood in her ears.

"Anything in particular you want me to say?" His voice bordered on a growl—not angry or wild, just deep and slow. She could feel his words all the way to the core of her chest, inviting the unruly rhythm of her heart to return to the familiar.

She needed to regain some control over her body, which insisted on reacting to his mere presence. He'd barely touched the edge of her ear, and she was basically a puddle.

In her defense, his voice did things to her insides that she could not be blamed for. She could listen to him read the dictionary and she'd like it.

Still, the man had hardly strung two sentences together tonight. So what was her excuse?

"Vi?"

She nodded to let him know she'd heard him, but she still couldn't meet his gaze.

"Hey." He caught her chin with a crooked finger, tilting her head up until he could look into her eyes. "I was never worried that you were going to tell Mama Potts about all of that."

"You weren't?" She hated how surprised she sounded.

"You—more than anyone else I've ever known—know why people carry secrets. You'd never be careless with one. Not even mine."

No one had ever said anything so sweet to her. She didn't deserve his kindness, but neither would she waste it. Grabbing him by the front of his shirt, she launched herself up, her lips crashing into his. He didn't hesitate for even a moment. He wrapped his arms around her until she couldn't move. She didn't want to anyway.

She could barely breathe, but she didn't care much about that either at the moment. She just wanted to be close to him, to be near to someone who knew the truth and liked her anyway.

And he definitely liked her. The gentle pressure on her back and the low hum in the back of his throat didn't lie.

Even if she didn't want to admit it, she liked him too. She'd been so afraid that he would hurt her family—tear apart the ones who had put her back together piece by piece. But he wasn't that man anymore.

If she was completely honest with herself, Eli had found some broken pieces she'd long forgotten. He'd started putting them back into place, fitting them into the holes. His return felt like a promise that nothing was too far gone. If Mama Potts could welcome him back with open arms, maybe her own mom really could welcome her home too.

Maybe if Violet could restore her relationship with her parents, there was hope for a future family of her own.

She gasped, pulling back from their kiss. She should not be thinking about the future and family and whatnot—not while Eli had his lips pressed to hers.

She was still in his embrace, her hands on his chest as it rose and fell in quick succession. She couldn't blame him. Her breathing wasn't any less erratic, and it caught in her throat.

A low-watt grin tugged at the corner of his mouth as his

eyes flashed a deeper shade of blue. He didn't look smug, just satisfied. "I've been wanting to do that since the first time."

She giggled and pushed against him, but he didn't budge. If anything, his arms held her a little bit tighter.

"I'm serious. I've never met anyone like you."

Laughing him off, she gave him a playful swat. "I bet you say that to all the girls."

His grin faded, and his dimples went into hiding. But his gaze never wavered, and she was locked under its weight. "I've done a lot of stupid things in my life—I mean, you know a lot of it. But one of the things I most regret about my life before was the way I treated women. I thought we were having fun—I guess it felt fun at the time. But now I know what kind of scars it left on me, and I can't imagine how many women I hurt along the way."

He swallowed thickly, and she leaned in just enough to encourage him to go on.

"When I hit my lowest point, I remembered all those Bible verses Mama Potts had prayed over me. I remembered all those Sunday school songs about how much God loves me. I thought I didn't deserve any of it. I didn't—I still don't. I still have so many jagged edges. But one thing I know for sure, I won't hurt you like I hurt those other women. I won't be cavalier or casual about your feelings. I'm going to protect you."

She didn't know what to say, which was probably best since she couldn't say anything anyway. Her throat felt like she'd swallowed cotton.

The sincerity in his eyes made her own burn, and she

pressed her face into his neck. Talk about undeserving. She hadn't earned any of this—especially this man who cradled her heart so well.

He held her close, resting his cheek on the top of her head. The cracks and the scars were still there, but he made her feel a little more whole.

After a long silence, she stepped back, and he dropped his arms. Only then did she realize he was covered in the remnants of red clay. Lifting stained hands with a shrug, she said, "I'm sorry about your shirt."

"It's Oliver's anyway."

The next few days were filled with practices. Eli spent hours with the Stars, running drills, scrimmaging, preparing for the next game. They consumed his days. Strategy. Plays. Game film.

Sure, they were thirteen- and fourteen-year-old girls, but for most of them, bantam-level play would decide whether they'd continue the sport. The outcome of this season could be what kept them lacing up their skates or made them turn in their blades.

Eli did not want to be the reason they gave up.

After each practice, there was one person he couldn't wait to see. One person he wanted to tell everything to. But he had to wait until after practice to track her down at the studio, where the new-to-them kiln had been installed.

Violet had spent her days hounding the electrician to finish. All of her nights had been at the wheel, spinning beauty out of nothing.

His presence was probably more distracting than helpful, and he didn't want to disrupt her work. Just not enough to stop showing up when he knew she'd be there. Not enough to stop watching her work her magic. Definitely not enough to stop listening to her tell her stories.

Once she'd laid bare the very worst, the most painful, she was like a fountain that couldn't be turned off. There were childhood tales of her dad's hockey games, going to the zoo, falling asleep as her mother read *The Secret Garden* aloud. There were stories of Aunt Tracy, who had welcomed her into her PEI home and given her a haven to grieve. And there were stories of Oliver and Levi—stories he should have been there for himself. Adventures he'd missed out on. The one about Oliver trying to save a fox that had made a home under his stairs, only to get bitten, made Eli laugh.

Violet had a way of rounding out all of the jagged parts in his heart. All the regrets, all the pain he'd caused—none of it felt quite so sharp when she was nearby.

At practice one afternoon, he couldn't wait another minute to see her. Blowing on his whistle, he dismissed the girls. "That's enough for today."

"But we still have fifteen minutes left," Madison said.

Sophie tossed a puck at her teammate, giving her a hard glare. "Be quiet, Madison."

"Consider this a pregame gift. Get some rest before tomorrow. Go to bed early. Iron your clothes so you look less like a bunch of hooligans."

Madison and Audrey beamed under the moniker, and he waved them toward the locker room.

"Nobody irons anything anymore," Chloe mumbled.

"Fine." He laughed, feeling twice his thirty years. "Do whatever it is you do to get ready for a game."

The girls started toward the exit and the locker room beyond, but Sophie stopped sharp, ice spraying from beneath her blades. Some of the others nearly tumbled into her, but she just stepped out of the way as she pulled her helmet off. "Why?"

Eli had skated toward the wall behind the net to scoop up some of the wayward pucks, but he spun at her question. "Why what?"

"Why are you sending us home? Do you have somewhere to be? Somewhere you'd rather be?"

Yes, as a matter of fact, he did. But it was none of their business. He squinted at Sophie, but she didn't back down. She didn't even back away when Chloe jabbed her in the side with her elbow. Chloe whispered something and jerked her head toward the locker room.

"No, I want to know," Sophie said to the rest of the team. "Don't you?"

Abandoning the pucks, Eli skated in their direction. "Know what?"

The closer he got, the less steel there was in Sophie's backbone. Some of the girls put their heads together, their words flowing together in a hushed hiss. No one could look at his face.

He licked his front teeth, leaned on his stick, and tried to ignore the growing knot in his stomach. "17, what's going on here?"

Not even Madison could look him in the eye. "It's nothing, Coach."

"This is more than nothing."

Audrey stared toward the ceiling. "It's not strictly hockey related."

"All right. Well, there's obviously something bothering you, and since Miss Donaghy isn't here, I'll have to do. Spill the beans?"

From the back, Layla said, "You mean the tea?"

Was he a hundred years old? "The beans. The tea. The cookies. I don't care. Someone just tell me what's going on."

Every gaze remained on the floor or the ceiling.

"As far as I'm concerned, this is about hockey." His tone surprised even him. It was all coach—a conglomerate of every coach he'd ever had. "If it's bothering the whole team, it's going to affect your game, so let's get it out in the open."

Madison sighed and rolled her eyes. He wasn't surprised she was the one motivated by the game. "So, Sophie overheard—"

"Madison," Sophie hissed.

"Well, you did," Madison replied before turning back to him. "*Someone* heard that they're looking for a new coach for us next year."

Whatever he'd expected to come out of her mouth, that wasn't it. Eli couldn't get a response past the lump in his throat. He couldn't even get air past it. He tried to formulate a response, but he felt like he'd been hammered into the boards, his head bouncing against the ice without his bucket.

Jett.

Eli ground his molars.

Jett had to have told someone, who told someone, who knew someone on the island. No one else knew about the offer from Latvia. No one except Oliver, who wouldn't tell anyone. Eli hadn't told Mable Jean and her boosters. He hadn't even told Violet yet. He kept telling himself it was because he hadn't made a decision. But with each passing day, he knew what he needed to do. There were no other options, no other way to pay off Tony and keep Mama Potts and everyone else—especially Violet—from being hurt.

Sure, maybe leaving might hurt. Him more than them, probably.

But as he looked into the wide eyes of every girl on the team, his stomach sank—leaving that knot behind. These girls counted on him. He'd promised that he'd show up, that he'd be there for them.

He just didn't have another option. And he was afraid it was written all over his face.

Maybe they didn't know why he might not be there the next year, but the whys didn't matter much at that age. What mattered was showing up.

Madison's eyebrows veered down. "Some of the parents said you weren't going to be here next year, but that's a lie, right? Tell them it's just a stupid rumor. You said we had to show up to practice because you'd show up. You said you'd be here for us."

Technically he hadn't agreed to more than the rest of this season. But somewhere along the line, these girls had reminded him of what it felt like to be part of a team. He'd already let one team down, and he was going to have to do it again.

He forced a breath out between tight lips. "That's something you've got to know about hockey. There are always rumors. Always someone trying to throw you off your game. You can't let it ruffle you. Tomorrow you just have to go out there and play your best. Forget about everything you've heard, and play your game."

Looking at their wounded faces, he knew he'd never be able to take his own advice. How could he play in Latvia if all he could remember was breaking eighteen little hearts?

twenty

"This place looks almost good enough to reopen."

Violet didn't look up from where she set a stack of fired plates—fresh from the new-to-her and fully functioning kiln—on display in the shop. "You mean, the fact that the drywall guy patched and repainted all the holes improved the look of the place?"

She waited for Eli's chuckle. When it didn't come, she glanced over her shoulder to the door that led to the studio. Eli leaned against the frame, his hands shoved into the pockets of his jeans, his shoulders hunched under a weight that wasn't there the last time she saw him.

"I'm sorry I missed practice." She shuffled in his direction. "How was it?"

He looked up to meet her eyes, but there was a sadness deep inside, a tightness to his mouth.

"Eli?"

She reached for his hand, and he grabbed it like his ship was sinking and she was the only lifeboat. Her breath caught in the back of her throat, and she knew with utter certainty that she was not going to like what came out of his mouth.

"Eli?"

He nodded toward the studio. "Come sit with me for a minute?"

With a glance over her shoulder, she surveyed the empty shelves that needed to be stocked before the reopening. As if there was an actual choice to make. She followed quickly behind him and pulled out a stool at the closest wooden table.

The faint remnants of smoke still surprised her, but something else made her eyes sting. A quick swipe of her hand across them didn't do much to alleviate the pain, but she forced herself to meet his gaze.

"You excited about the reopening party?" he asked.

Not what she'd expected, but she nodded slowly. "I guess. Mama Potts just wouldn't let the idea go. Do you want to see the invitations?"

"Sure."

She ambled across the room, grabbed her purse, and returned to his side. When she tossed her bag down, it tipped over, envelopes and invitations spilling across the tabletop. She scrambled to collect them all, but Eli snatched the one that didn't belong with the recycled brown ones she would soon be mailing out. Of course he did.

He flipped over the cream vellum envelope, his eyes scooting across the address label. "What's this?"

"None of your business." She made a grab for it, but he raised it over his head, out of her reach. Scrambling for it, she nearly crawled up his side, yanking on his iron arm. "Eli. Come on. Give it back."

He laughed, his dimples on full display, his eyes sparkling brighter than diamonds. "Why don't you try a little harder?"

She laughed too as she realized her arms were looped around his shoulders, her face millimeters from his. She was wrapped around him, but he surrounded her, his presence holding her close. Even as he teased her, she knew she had nothing to fear.

He wanted her to try harder? She couldn't possibly best his physical strength, so she did the only thing she knew would throw him off balance.

She kissed him.

Eli froze for a second, then let out a quick laugh before dropping his arms and wrapping them around her back. He pulled her close, pinning her to him as he kissed her. Sweet and slow. His lips moved with a subtle assurance, making her pulse pound until she could hear every single beat in her ears.

He kissed her until she forgot why she'd even pressed her lips to his in the first place. Worse, she didn't even care that she couldn't remember.

All she could focus on was the feel of his gentle hand cupping her cheek and the way his thumb brushed beneath her eye. The tip bumped into her eyelashes, and he pulled away only long enough to press his lips to her closed eyelid.

She was a puddle, completely melted.

Sucking in a ragged breath, she pressed her face into the spot where his neck and shoulder met. Warm and strong. Safe.

"It's a letter from my mom," she blurted out.

Eli's chin jerked, bumping against her head and then pulling all the way back. "What?"

"It's from my mom."

Eli shoved the letter back into her hands. "I'm sorry. I didn't mean to play around with something like that."

She held the letter in both hands, staring down at her own name written in her mom's perfect script. "She misses me. And she wants to see me." She shoved it toward him.

Eli held up his hands in surrender, his face a comedy of confusion. "I can't read your letter."

"Why not? I want you to."

"But . . . isn't it personal?"

She lifted one shoulder to her ear. "There's nothing in there you don't already know."

His smile then was just for her. It wasn't flashy or overwrought. It was simple. Sweet. Knowing.

There was something incredible in being known. Something amazing in not having to hide the truth and being loved anyway. Not that Eli loved her. She didn't expect that. And she certainly didn't love him.

Except just a little bit. Because he knew her and he hadn't run. Because he'd let her know him too.

And because he had the power to break her heart.

She had a terrible feeling he was going to do just that. But maybe she could put it off a little longer.

She motioned to the letter, and Eli nodded, his thick fingers so out of place against the delicate stationery. He unfolded the single page, his eyes skimming the words she'd nearly memorized after so many readings.

The other letters had been read once and stored in her box. She'd dug up the box to add this letter to it, but when she'd started to bury it again, she couldn't. She didn't need to hide this—or any of her memories—anymore. She wasn't afraid they were going to come to light. They already had. She'd told the truth, and there was a freedom in that that she'd never known.

She had set the box on a shelf in her apartment and kept the most recent letter always at hand, desperate to believe it might be true yet certain that her mom couldn't have forgiven her. The top left corner of the page was bent where she'd plucked at it, the bottom crease beginning to tear at the edge of the paper.

"This isn't the first letter you've gotten from her." He looked up, then back down, his eyes shifting back and forth. "How many more?"

"Every six months since I left."

He dropped the letter, shaking his head, a dry laugh making it past his lips. "You've got twenty of these letters? Twenty times your mom reached out to you?"

"Sometimes my dad wrote too." She hated how small she sounded, but there was no pride in literally burying the letters.

"Violet, what are you thinking? Go. Call them."

"It's not that easy. And you of all people should understand that."

He huffed a sigh of disbelief, pushing himself up to tower over her. "Are you serious right now? Do you know what I would have done if Mama Potts or Oliver or Levi had ever written me *anything* like this? I mean, look what I did for my dad. The minute he showed up, I gave up everything for him." He stabbed his fingers through his hair. "No, not for him. For family. For a chance, at least."

His words stabbed at her heart, the knife twisting until she couldn't breathe. "You don't know . . . You weren't here to see how broken Mama Potts was. You don't know that look of pain when a parent loses their child. You never had to look your mom in the eye to see the pain you caused. I did. I saw what your leaving did to your mom. And I know what I took from mine."

Eli stomped two steps away. Then two steps back. Pressing his fingers to his temples, he released a long sigh. "You're right. It's not easy. I dreaded coming home, facing the people I had hurt. That first day—that first week—I was waiting for Oliver to turn around and tell me to stay gone. I was waiting for Levi to find his voice and lay into me." He flung his arm in the general direction of his family's home. "And every day I'm terrified that Mama Potts—that *you*—are going to realize that I don't have anything to offer, that I'm too far gone to be worthy of being part of this family."

Eli's eyes flashed. "I've been hiding my secrets because I knew if anyone discovered the truth, they'd never be able to forgive me. But that letter . . ." He jabbed his finger at the paper. "Your parents love you so much. You don't have to worry that they won't forgive you. They already have."

Lord, could it be true? She'd been so scared that she was too far gone to be forgiven, when the truth was that forgiveness had already been offered. She just hadn't accepted it.

Violet sat and slumped against the table, laying her head against her crossed arms. For ten years her parents had been reaching out. For ten years she'd doubted that they could actually mean it.

A stool scraped against the cement floor, and suddenly

Eli's arms wrapped around her. Brushing a few escaped hairs into her ponytail, he kissed the spot right behind her ear. A gentle warmth seeped through her, easing even the tightest knots in her neck.

"I think maybe forgiveness isn't sweet because it's earned." His voice rumbled so low that it vibrated in his chest. "Forgiveness is sweet because none of us deserve it."

She pulled away from him just far enough that she could look right into his eyes. "How can you say that and not see how much Mama Potts loves you? How your brothers would rather pay Tony out of their own pocket than risk losing you again? They didn't forgive you because of something you did but because they love you."

He didn't meet her gaze then. "I can't ask them for help. I can't put them in that situation."

"So, you think my mom loves me more than Mama Potts loves you?"

Eli's chuckle was sad. "I have no idea. I just know that your mom already knows all of your stuff."

"And your mom doesn't know most of yours—but she wants to. She just wants to know what's going on in your life. She wants to know you."

Narrowing his gaze at her, he slowly shook his head. "I thought I was the one who was supposed to make unwelcome—but valid—points."

She grinned, pressing her palm against the stubble of his cheek.

"I can't remember the last time I had a real friend," he whispered, a touch of awe in his voice. It made her insides tremble and her lip quiver.

"Is that what I am? Your friend?" Oh, how she wanted to know, and how she dreaded his answer. She wanted to be so much more than that.

Pursing his lips to the side, he seemed to fight a full smile. "Violet Donaghy, you're something else. You're smart and creative and so kind." Running his fingers across the hair above her ear, he bit his lip. "You're stunning, and sometimes it catches me off guard. Sometimes when I haven't seen you for a little while and you walk into a room, it's like I forget how to breathe."

She knew that feeling. Something as natural as inhaling and exhaling completely confounded her when he looked at her the way he did just then.

Something like pain flashed across his features, and he opened his mouth. Whatever he was going to say, she had an aching suspicion that it would cut her deeper than she could survive, so she pressed one finger against his lips, shaking her head furiously. "Don't. Please. I can't handle it. Just promise me—talk to your mom, tell your brothers."

He squeezed his eyes closed, leaving deep lines at the corners of them. "All right."

Violet tiptoed into Mama Potts's house two days later, closing the door silently behind her. Eyes closed and ears open, she waited to hear Eli's deep voice. It didn't come. She opened her eyes and crept another step, still listening.

"That you, Vi?"

Of course Mama Potts had heard her. Or maybe she was just so used to having Violet around that she could sense her presence. At this point it didn't really matter.

Hugging her notebook and the box of stationery to her chest, Violet stepped past the entry wall and into the kitchen. It was empty except for the smell of something rich and meaty coming from the oven and Mama Potts sitting at the table.

She shuffled to Mama Potts's side and pressed a kiss to her cheek before setting her stuff down. "All by yourself today?" She sounded a little too hopeful, even to her own ears. Mama Potts mumbled an agreement, and Violet let out a little sigh. It was just that every time she saw Eli, she ended up kissing him.

The kissing was good—seriously excellent—but it also muddled her thoughts and made her question everything she'd known to be true. And, oh, how she'd questioned, tossing and turning the entire night away. She was just thankful to be back in her own bed, in the privacy of her own apartment, so she didn't keep Meg awake too.

Eli had made it all sound so easy for her to call her mom and dad and invite herself back into their lives. But what if it didn't work? What if her mom didn't know what she was asking? What if her seeing Violet again just opened up all the old pain?

What if it ripped open her own wounds?

She just needed a little fresh air. She needed a bit of time to think about anything other than her mom and dad.

As if she could. But she could pretend at least.

Mama Potts's box of broken pieces occupied the chair at the head of the table, so Violet fell into the one across from her—the seat so often occupied by Levi. Flipping open her notebook to a blank page, she looked up. "I thought we could work on the guest list for the reopening. Meg printed out the invitations."

Mama Potts set down the bottle of glue in her hand and reached out for one of the invites. Her eyes grew wide as she gently patted the colorful vases printed on the corner of the card stock. "Lovely." She smiled and handed them back. "Who should we invite?"

"You start talking, and I'll write them down."

Mama Potts nodded, her fingers absently going back to the shattered pieces spread out before her. She'd already put half of a blue vase—its bottom and part of its neck—back together, but she'd set it aside. Now she pieced together the parts of something that had been green and something else purple.

Violet couldn't make out what the new thing was meant to be, but Mama Potts didn't suffer the same. She didn't even bother looking down as she flipped and turned the pieces to find their spot, like she already knew exactly where they fit.

"Well, I suppose the boys will come. But don't waste an invitation on any of them."

Violet chuckled.

"I'm sure Meg would like one, even if she's already seen them."

She nodded and jotted down the name.

"And Pastor and Mrs. Dell, Walt and Sandra Whitaker, and I suppose Mable Jean Huxley." Mama Potts ticked off the names of friends from church on her fingers.

Violet scribbled away, adding a few of her own names when Mama Potts paused. "I'd like to invite the girls on the team and their parents."

"Of course. And Jenny and Dylan."

Violet smiled as she added, "And our friends from the inn up in North Rustico."

They went back and forth, adding more and more names to the list until it was two full columns in her notebook. But when there was no more room on the page, two names still ran through her mind.

Saying them out loud felt somehow like a betrayal, as though Mama Potts hadn't been more than her surrogate mother for the last ten years. As though she hadn't been the one to bind up those gaping wounds in the early days. As though she hadn't loved Violet like her own flesh and blood.

"Would you mind if I invited my mom and dad?"

Mama Potts's hands stilled, and the easy rise and fall of her shoulders stopped. She pressed her lips together slowly, almost cautiously. Finally she whispered, "I've waited a long time for you to talk about them."

Violet nodded, her eyes suddenly burning and her tongue mute.

"I wasn't sure . . . Your aunt Tracy told me once that they were still alive. Up until then, well, I thought you were all alone."

"I know." Her swallow was so thick that she was sure Mama Potts heard it. "I just wasn't ready to talk about them."

"Do you want to tell me what happened?"

Her history flashed across her mind's eye. Her mom and dad. All those years of trying for a baby and only disappointment. Then Garrett's sweet, smiling face. His chubby cheeks and roly-poly thighs.

Then only darkness. Until Mama Potts came onto the

scene. There had been joy and laughter again. Little brothers and family dinners.

Then there was Eli, and his face, his presence, outshone everyone else. He made her less afraid to face all that had come before him. He made her want to have a future. Not one that buried the past but one that accepted it. Grieved it. Refused to let it define her.

All of a sudden, she was spilling everything, from the beginning all the way to Eli. All the way to his kiss and his sweet embrace.

Everything but his secrets. Those weren't hers to tell. But the rest of it belonged to her. The way he made her feel. The way he'd shown her that he could care, even when he knew—perhaps because he knew—her worst.

Maybe that's why she loved him. Because she saw her own brokenness reflected in him, and it didn't scare her anymore.

Mama Potts sat in silence, her hand finally creeping across the table, outstretched and open. Violet tucked her fingers into the older woman's grip and held on as the words kept spilling out. Some were like white-water rapids, others a gentle stream. Mama Potts waded through them all, only the pressure of her hand changing, infusing courage when it was needed most.

Finally, when there were no more words, Violet tried to pull her hand away, but Mama Potts didn't let go, her fingers strong enough to throw a thousand pots, strong enough to hang on.

"I'm so sorry for what you've been through. And I'm sorry I didn't know." Mama Potts smiled but let it quickly fall away. "No, it was probably better. If I'd known you weren't talking to your parents—who desperately want to see you—I'd have called them myself. I don't think I'd have been able not to."

A hiccupped sob escaped, and Violet clapped her free hand over her mouth.

"Honey, there's nothing you could do that would ever make me love you any less. You may not be my flesh and blood, but you're my daughter. How much more do your mom and dad love you?"

"But how? I just don't understand." She wanted to. She longed to. If only someone could spell it out, show her in exact terms how a parent could forgive so much. "How did you forgive Eli?"

Mama Potts let out a soft laugh, her eyes rolling toward the ceiling. "That boy. He does try me. I love him because he's mine. But I don't choose to forgive him because I love him or because he deserves it. I forgive him because I've been lost too. I've walked away too. I've been welcomed back too. None of us deserve to be forgiven. That's why it's called mercy."

Violet couldn't stem the flow of tears. They rushed down her cheeks, spilled onto her hands, and wrinkled the page of her notebook, blurring the names she'd written there. But she picked up her pen and added one more line to the bottom of the list, cramped in the margin.

Conor and Joanna Donaghy.

twenty-one

As they always did when there weren't enough of them, the days flew by. Violet scrambled to get the shop ready for the reopening, the Ross brothers chipping in as they were available. If only she could train them to make the shop's signature pieces. But Violet was alone in that since Mama Potts's wrist was still in a brace, her hand immobilized. At least she could sit in the studio and paint on the glaze after Violet's pieces dried enough for the next step. But that morning, when all of the pieces had been glazed, she excused herself, saying she had a project to work on and calling Levi for a ride home.

He arrived ruffled and wrinkled, with barely one eye open. But he'd silently helped his mom into the car with such tenderness.

The three Ross brothers were so different, but they had one thing in common beyond their dark hair and rich blue eyes. They loved their mom. All of them. In their own way.

Even Eli—maybe especially Eli.

Violet's paintbrush flicked a drop of glaze, just missing her apron and landing on the front of her T-shirt. It looked blue against the yellow shirt, but when the chemicals reacted in the firing process, it would dry into a rich orange, warmer than the island's morning sun.

She smoothed her brush along the rounded lip of the mug, filling in each groove, carefully going around the handle and every crevice. The longer she worked, the more glaze ended up on her front, adding to the splotches on her jeans. Her pants had become a canvas, rivaling the work of Jackson Pollock.

When the glazes were set, she loaded them into the kiln and turned it on. Usually they only fired the oven overnight, but she didn't have that luxury at the moment. Not when there were still empty shelves in the shop and Marie Sloane from the Red Door Inn had called about getting another box of inventory. They'd already sold most of the coffee mugs and several of the vases she and Eli had left behind.

The shop was reopening before the rush of the tourist season. There was more demand than ever for their product. Mama Potts was healing—albeit slower than she wished. All good things. So Violet couldn't explain the knot in her chest, the low-level fear that had been simmering since she'd dropped a handful of invitations in the mail.

Don't be obtuse.

She wasn't. She honestly didn't know where the anxiety came from.

Of course you do.

Okay, so she wasn't sure what she was going to do if her parents showed up to the party. Or worse, if they didn't. She hadn't exactly figured out what she was going to say to them. How did one begin to apologize for more than ten years of silence?

Note to self: ask Eli for tips.

Oh, he'd like that. He'd like thinking he could swoop in and rescue her. Not that she needed to be rescued, precisely. But if she was wholly honest with herself, she liked it when he swooped in. It wasn't like he thought she couldn't handle things on her own. He just seemed to like caring for her. And after so many years, it was kind of great to have someone special care for her.

That he did it with broad shoulders she could lean on and dimples that made her insides melt—well, that wasn't her fault. A girl couldn't be held responsible for finding him a little bit attractive.

More than a little, maybe.

Violet was so lost in her thoughts that she barely heard the gentle tapping coming from the shop's front door. It could have been going on for a second or a full minute. But it stopped just as she stood and set down her project.

It had to be a tourist. No one in Victoria would knock. They all knew to come around the back. If anyone was here when the shop was closed, they'd be in the studio.

She wiped her hands on a rag, leaving behind a blue streak before tossing it on the table. "I'm coming," she called. She hurried across the studio. Her hand was on the knob to the door into the shop when she heard a low voice from the direction of the back door.

"Excuse me. I'm looking for Violet Donaghy."

Everything inside her froze. That voice was part of so many

childhood memories. The voice in her ear as she learned to skate and the one practicing her French lessons with her. The one that had read her a book, then said her prayers with her before tucking her into bed.

She turned around slowly, afraid to see his face yet desperate for even a glimpse.

He stood beneath the open garage door, his hands in the pockets of his khaki pants. His dark hair was still thick and full but now with a touch of gray at the temples. If there were a few more laugh lines at the corners of his amber eyes, they only made him look more handsome. The rest of him hadn't changed, and she wanted to run to him, throw her arms around him, and beg him to forgive her. For all of it.

She knew the moment he recognized her, his blink of surprise and open mouth unusual for the perpetually collected CFO.

She wondered what she must look like to him. Her hand was already running over her ponytail when she realized she might have added a blue stripe to it. She was a mess. This wasn't how she'd wanted to see him after all these years, but she couldn't keep from running toward him.

"Dad." Her word came out on a sigh.

At the same moment, he yelled, "Joanna! Come here! She's here!"

Suddenly his arms were around her, and she was cradled against him, his chin resting on her head. "We're here. We're here." He'd said those words over her when she'd cried as a child, and it wasn't until she made that connection that she realized she was crying again, weeping into his shirt. Tears of regret and joy and an emotion too strong to name.

Another set of arms joined in their embrace, and Violet turned to her mom, holding her as they both shook with silent sobs, her dad surrounding them both. Her mom smelled sweet, like vanilla and cinnamon, a scent Violet had nearly forgotten until that moment.

She sank into them, holding on until her arms trembled. "I'm so sorry. I'm so, so sorry."

"Hush," her mom whispered. "We're here now."

That quiet assurance was everything she needed—to know that they weren't going anywhere.

They stood locked together for what felt like hours. The moment was gone all too soon when her mom pulled back, cupped her cheeks with both hands, and stared into her eyes. "You're all grown up now."

Violet giggled and dropped her gaze, but it immediately popped back up to take in her mom's features. Delicate and refined, her skin like porcelain. Her blond hair was cut in the same bob that just brushed her jawline, and she looked like she had the last time Violet saw her.

Except for one thing. The pain that had haunted her mom's eyes was gone, replaced by the peace she'd written about. The peace she'd prayed her daughter would find.

"I've missed you, Mom."

"You have no idea." Joanna sighed, pulling her back in, breathing deeply.

When the tears finally slowed, the sobs nothing more than ragged breaths, Violet pointed inside the studio. "This is where I work. Do you want me to show you around?"

Her parents hung on her every word as she gave them a quick tour of the space, pointing out her most recent pieces and even showing them her apartment. She told them about the fire and all that it had taken to get the studio functioning again. And about her family here on the island—how she'd become an honorary Ross.

"It was Eli, actually, who told me to write to you."

"Smart man," her dad said. "Will we get to meet him?"

"Is someone talking about me?" Eli swaggered into the room with all his usual confidence, but he staggered to a stop a few steps in. "Pardon me." He looked at her, his forehead wrinkled in a silent question.

Violet stepped forward, grabbed his hand, and tugged him to meet her parents. "Mom. Dad. This is Eli, my—" Oh dear. She didn't really know what to call him. "He's my best friend."

"Mr. and Mrs. Donaghy." Eli shook both of their hands, a warm smile in place.

"We're so happy to know Violet's"—her mom's gaze swung back to her, a knowing look in her eyes—"friends."

"I was hoping I'd get to meet you. You're early for the party."

"We got on a plane as soon as we got the invitation." Her mom squeezed her hand. "We wouldn't have missed it."

Violet couldn't stop the rush of heat up her neck, but she didn't care, because right in this room were the most important people in her life. And all those broken pieces inside her were starting to be made new.

The next day the Stars won their game, but Eli wouldn't have known it from the sideways stares coming from the boosters. There were enough stink eyes to clear the whole rink. Apparently the girls had told their parents that Eli wasn't going to be there for the next season.

Mable Jean scurried up to him after the game. "Mrs. Baker told me that you're not coming back next year. That must be a misunderstanding. The girls are doing so well. Of course you'll come back. Right?"

Eli tried for a smile, but he could only shake his head as Mable Jean's smile tumbled. He planned to call Jett that night.

But first, he'd made a promise to Violet.

He waved to the girls as they filed into the locker room. "Good game."

"See you at practice, Coach?"

The truth lodged somewhere between his head and his heart, and he couldn't get himself to be honest. He wouldn't see them again. He wouldn't get to finish the spring season with them. And he'd miss their last tournament.

He'd told them to show up because he would. And he was about to break that promise.

It made him feel seasick.

This wasn't running. It was different from last time. This was a necessary evil, a requirement for survival. He had to do this to protect Mama Potts. To keep his sins from hurting her or the shop. To keep his promise to Violet.

She was going to leave anyway. He'd seen the way she was with her parents—the light within that hadn't been there before. She'd go back with them. She'd rediscover her home in Montreal. She'd forget about whatever had been between them. Whatever he might have meant to her.

People left. It's what they did. His dad had proven that. Twice.

Then again, he'd proven it too. But he could do things differently. He didn't have to vanish, turn his back without a word of warning. He could explain the situation, help his family understand that this time he wasn't leaving because of his own selfishness.

The girls deserved the same.

That truth echoed deep in his spirit, and after he called Jett and told his brothers the truth, he was going to tell the girls. Even if it meant knocking on every single door, facing down every angry booster.

They didn't need the whole truth. But they deserved more than a vanishing act.

By the time Eli got home from the game, his stomach was in knots and his mind was spinning. He wanted to lie down on the sofa, bury his head under a pillow, and stay there forever.

It wasn't asking too much to be able to stay.

Except it was. He couldn't live with himself if he didn't get Tony out of their lives—forever. This was the only way.

When he walked into the kitchen, he fell into a chair across from Levi, who looked up from a book on interior design long enough to raise his eyebrows in a silent question.

Eli wanted to brush him off. But maybe Levi was the break he needed. Oliver would interrupt him. Mama Potts would cry. But Levi would silently listen to the whole story. Assuming he was more interested in that than making plans for his new home.

Eli cleared his throat and sat up a little bit straighter. "I saw Dad last year."

Something flashed across Levi's face. Pain mingled with regret. A familiar mixture Eli had seen in his own mirror.

"He came to see me in New York." Eli shook his head, crossing his arms on the table and hunching his shoulders. "No, that's not right. He didn't come to *see* me. He came to ask me for a favor."

Levi set his book to the side, closing it without even marking his place. He never looked away.

"Dad had gotten himself into some debt—gambling again. And he couldn't pay back the half a mil he owed."

Levi's low whistle broke the air.

Eli sighed. "Yeah. It was bad. So being the superb idiot that I am, I said I'd help him. I took on his debt."

"You have that kind of money?" The tenor of Levi's voice always surprised Eli. He used it so little that Eli expected more bullfrog than stage actor, but it was smooth and rich.

With a scoff and a shake of his head, Eli said, "No. But the bookie was happy to let me work it off, to let me make sure that my team didn't win a few games."

He knew the moment that his brother understood. Levi sported angry eyebrows and flaring nostrils. Eli just wasn't sure who or what they were directed at. Probably him.

"You could have gone to jail for that." There was a subtle question in Levi's statement.

"There wasn't much evidence. It wasn't a big conspiracy—just me making a fool of myself. And at the end of the day, the front office and the league just wanted to be done with it. To be done with me." Eli pushed himself up, suddenly unable to contain the energy coursing through him. He marched across the room and then back again, all the way imagining having this same conversation with Mama Potts and Oliver. Maybe he should have gotten them all together.

Or maybe he'd thought Levi would be the first to forgive him.

"That was a really stupid thing to do."

Eli jerked toward the voice coming from the entryway. He hadn't even heard the door open, but it was clear Oliver had heard enough.

Crossing his arms, Oliver stood like a sentry, like it was his job to protect this home and everyone inside it. "Do you still owe that bookie money? Is that why you took the coaching job?"

Eli shoved his hand through his hair, hung his head, and squeezed his eyes closed. "It's not enough. I still owe fifty grand, and . . ."

"Then you've decided to take the job you were offered," Oliver said.

Eli nodded. "I'm going to play in Latvia. They're giving me a signing bonus, and it'll cover what I owe. And then Tony won't be coming after—well, everyone I care about will be safe."

Levi grunted, his eyes narrowing, and Oliver's massive paw clenched into a fist. They could read between the lines. They knew everything he wasn't saying—that he'd invited danger into their lives, that his very presence was a threat to everything they and Mama Potts and Violet had worked so hard for.

He waited for those same hissed words that Oliver had said all those years ago. *"Go. We don't need you. But if you go, don't bother coming back."* He steeled himself against the crushing pain they would bring, the reminder that he didn't belong, that no matter how hard he tried, he didn't have a family anymore.

Oliver's giant hand clamped on his shoulder. "Why didn't you come back sooner? We could have helped. We still can."

The words felt like a punch to the kidneys, a cheap shot when his back was turned. They couldn't be true. Oliver couldn't possibly mean them. He didn't know what he was offering. And Eli didn't know how to respond in the face of that.

Apparently Oliver didn't need him to. "What I said, when you left—" His shoulders rose and fell as he took a deep breath.

Eli glanced at Levi, who didn't look away. Had Oliver told him about that final night? Did Levi know why Eli hadn't said goodbye?

Oliver didn't look at his younger brother, and Eli took the full brunt of his gaze.

"I was angry about Dad leaving, and I lashed out at a lot of people. Especially you." Oliver's jaw twitched. "I thought that I meant what I said. I thought we didn't need you, but I was wrong. And I'm sorry."

Eli had waited more than a decade for those words, but whatever he'd thought they'd feel like, he'd been wrong. Shortly after he'd left, he played the scene out in his mind, imagining his satisfaction with a solid "I told you so." Later—much later—he thought there was no way that Oliver could possibly offer an apology.

But the sincerity in Oliver's tone wasn't fake. He hadn't manufactured an apology on the spot, and the truth of that sank deep. Eli could feel it through his bones, and he only had one choice.

"I'm sorry I stayed away so long." His gaze flickered to Levi, half expecting his little brother to have picked his book back up. But Levi's attention hadn't wavered. "I'm sorry to both of you. It started off . . . I wanted to show you that I could make it. So I waited until I was called up to the Show. But by then it had been so long. It got harder every day to call, harder to face you—to come to terms with the man I had become. I wasn't very impressed with me. And I was sure that Mama Potts wouldn't be either."

Oliver chuckled. "She would have told you so too."

"And she'd have been right." Eli grinned, leaning into the pressure of his brother's hand still on his shoulder. "But I shouldn't have let it keep me from coming home, from at least calling you. I'm just—I'm sorry that I missed all these years. That I wasn't here to help you through all the tough times."

Oliver's smile was sad, but there was a touch of hope in it. "We love you, man. I'm just sorry that we weren't there to help you through your stuff. It's not too late though."

Eli shook his head. Hard. "I appreciate it, but I've got to take care of this on my own. But if it's okay . . . I can call and text sometimes."

"Yes."

Eli and Oliver both turned to Levi, who shrugged an unspoken *What?*

"When do you leave?" Oliver asked.

Eli let out a deep breath. "Wednesday morning."

Oliver sucked on his front tooth, his gaze turning a little harder. "What about Violet?"

Blinking rapidly, Eli tried to ignore the shot through his heart at her very name, the simple reminder that he would probably never see her again. "What about her?"

"Maybe I'm wrong, but I thought the two of you were . . ." Oliver gave a double pump of his eyebrows. "I think I warned you about breaking her heart."

Eli fought for a smile, fought for anything but the expression that would reveal just how deep the wound went. He swallowed three times to dislodge the lump in his throat and finally forced the words out around it. "You've seen her with her parents. She'll be fine."

And he knew she would be.

He wasn't so sure about himself.

twenty-two

It took three deep breaths and one mental kick in the pants for Eli to pluck up the courage to knock on the door of the big yellow house. It was just a few doors down from where he'd grown up, from where he'd first met Violet, but the house seemed like a fortress he couldn't possibly face down.

Just get on with it.

This part wasn't nearly as easy as telling Jett he would take the offer. But this wasn't about easy. It was about not making the mistakes that he'd made so many times before. And maybe it was a little bit about proving that he wasn't going to walk in his father's footsteps.

Walking away was his dad's thing. It wouldn't be his any longer.

When the door creaked open, Mable Jean's round face was cocked to the side, the light behind her making her more silhouette than solid.

"Ma'am." If Eli had had a hat, it would have been in his hands. Head bowed, he couldn't meet her gaze.

"Eli Ross? Whatever are you doing here at this time of night?"

He looked over his shoulder, as though the inky sky might tell him the time. He shrugged an apology. "I didn't realize it was so late. But I need to speak with you."

"Me?" The folds of her eyelids danced, a glow of pleasure filling even the shadows of her face. "Well, come on in then. Let me make you some tea. Have you changed your mind about next season?"

"No, ma'am. Thank you though. I won't take much of your time. But—" The lump in his throat jammed any hope of getting out the rest of his words.

"Maybe we better sit down for a bit." She motioned toward the porch swing, its metal chains creaking gently in the breeze.

He shook his head, but Mable Jean didn't seem to notice. She just grabbed his arm and tugged him toward the white swing. The wood had been worn smooth in places, and it molded to his frame in a way that he hadn't expected.

"I suspect that this isn't a friendly call," she said.

"No, ma'am."

"Mm-hmm." She pursed her lips, all but the edges of her lipstick worn off for the day.

"I wanted to thank you for the opportunity to coach. I never expected to enjoy it, but those girls are . . . they're special kids."

"I couldn't agree more." She patted his arm, her skin impossibly soft. "But I don't think you're here to tell me how much you like them."

He stared at where her hand rested on his forearm. "I

made some mistakes when I was playing in New York. And they're coming back to haunt me."

"Well, how bad can they be?"

He finally met her gaze. "Bad."

"Oh." Her mouth hung open, and he knew she understood everything contained in his single word.

"I need to take care of those things."

"All right."

He steeled himself for her response. "I leave in two days. Tomorrow will be my last practice. I'll tell the girls then."

Her mouth opened and closed several times, but no sound escaped.

"I'm so sorry that I won't be able to finish out the season with the Stars. But they're ready for the tournament. They can win it."

"Surely you don't need to leave so soon. The tournament is just a few days away."

He shook his head. "It can't wait."

"But . . . but you're such a good young man."

He bit back a laugh. She had no idea. "No, ma'am. For a long time I turned my back on God and everything I was raised to believe. And it left me a mess."

Mable Jean sat up a little straighter. "You think he can't use all that? You think God is afraid of your past? Let me tell you, he is *not* afraid of your . . . jagged . . . edges." She punctuated her words with three smacks on his arm.

Eli bit his cheek, watching the old woman's red nails curl into his arm. "I turned my back so far—I'm in so deep—that I'm afraid he won't even recognize me. I barely recognize me."

"Oh, he recognizes you. He knows you even better than you know yourself. Jagged edges and all. He knows you, and he loves you anyway. And the good news is that he's not going to ask you to change all those broken pieces."

He snorted in disbelief. "I don't have to change?"

"Oh, you will. It's just that you don't have to do it on your own. All you have to do is ask him for help. Admit that you can't do it on your own. When you do that, well, God moves in and starts smoothing out all those shattered and broken pieces. He's just waiting for you to ask him to fix them."

Could it really be that easy? But asking for help had never been simple for him. Admitting he couldn't handle a situation on his own was hard.

Even if someone like Oliver offered to help.

If they knew him—really knew what he had done, the pride in his heart, all the selfish things he'd done—they'd change their minds and do what they should. They'd walk away.

But he was going to beat them to it.

"I'm sorry, Mrs. Huxley. I can't stay." He pulled an envelope out of his pocket and held it out to her. "Here's everything you paid me."

She shook her head. "You earned it. What you did for those girls—no one else could have done it."

"But I can't make good on our deal. I won't take your money."

"Is it true, then, what they're all saying?"

He looked out over the yard, the darkness seeming to swallow the porch light so that the only evidence of the giant oak tree on the other side of the lawn was the rustling of leaves.

Even a few blocks from the shoreline, he could smell the waves and feel the wind. Fresh and clean.

"What are they saying?" he asked, but he didn't really want to know. He had a sinking feeling that the reports from Latvia had already made it to Victoria by the Sea.

"That you're going to play in Europe. That you need the money."

He pushed himself up, dropping the envelope on the seat. With a quick glance over his shoulder, he tried to smile. "Thank you for giving me a chance to coach. I didn't expect to love it as much as I did."

He stepped off the porch, walked across the lawn, and disappeared into the night.

"You're leaving."

Eli looked up from where he'd stuffed a few hand-me-down shirts into one of Mama Potts's old duffel bags beside his skates. He'd get new pads and a stick when he got to Latvia. He'd figured there was no point dragging them across the Atlantic and most of Europe.

But right about now, he wished he had on all of his gear to face down Violet as she stormed into the living room.

"Shouldn't you be with your parents right now?" he asked.

Apparently, it was not his turn to speak.

"You're leaving, and *I'm* the last to know."

Eli steeled himself against her onslaught. The problem was, he deserved it, without question. He should have told her. But after telling his brothers the truth and his mom that he was leaving, he just hadn't been able to figure out how to say the words, to tell her he hoped she had a wonderful life. His own would never be the same because of her. He was glad he'd known her, even though he hated himself for falling in love.

He'd known it couldn't last. Someone always left.

But he'd let down his guard and let her know him. And this was how it would end—with her yelling and him taking it. He had no defense.

She marched across the room, her eyes glowing like amber flames, every feature of her face taut and fierce. Her ponytail swung, dark hair swishing over her shoulder, but her neck and shoulders never moved. She was a hunter, he her prey.

When she was close enough that he could feel her warmth and could have reached out and pulled her into his arms, she stopped. Then she hissed through tight lips, "How dare you." She poked his chest, punctuating each word.

He rubbed at the spot, but he couldn't tell if the pain was external or from somewhere much deeper inside. "Vi, I'm sorry. You know why I have to go."

"And you thought you were just not going to tell me?"

He rubbed the back of his neck, his head falling forward. "No, that's not—" He sighed.

"You said you were going to protect me." She jabbed her finger at the same spot on his chest. Not that it hurt. He was starting to go numb all over.

"I am. I'm taking care of the situation with Tony so that no one ever has to worry about it again." He could barely swallow around the lump in his throat. "And I'm making your decision easy. You should be with your parents. They love you so much, and you shouldn't miss out on more time with them."

"You said you respected me. But you're just trying to make this decision for me. I didn't ask for your help."

"I know, but . . ." He dragged his hand down his face. "Trust me. I know what it's like to miss out on eleven years and try to make up for lost time."

She pumped her clenched fists at her side. "So you're just going to miss out on eleven more?"

"No, it's different this time. I'm not leaving without saying goodbye. I'll stay in touch. Oliver and Levi—they understand."

"And Mama Potts? You've explained it all to her?"

"Come on, Violet. Give me a break." He hadn't told his mom about his dad and the debt and his own stupidity. He couldn't stand to see the disappointment in her eyes. But he'd explained that he had to leave. "I'm doing the best I can."

She scoffed in his face, blatant and bold and wholly unbelieving. "That's not true, and you know it. You're not trying your best. Your best is staying. Your best is figuring out how to make it work *here*. Your best isn't running away."

"Well, I don't see any offers here. It's not like the Stars booster club is going to pay me seventy-five grand."

"Not when you've walked away from the job you did have and the girls who looked up to you." She crossed her arms and bit her lip, but not quite fast enough. For just a split second he saw it tremble, and his stomach matched the motion.

"Violet, I'm sorry. I didn't know how to say goodbye."

"There. You just said it. Not that hard."

It was his turn to sputter. "It's not that easy and you know it."

"It's not like you promised me anything. It's not like I expected there to be a future for us. You're a disgraced NHL player without a penny to your name."

Every single word he'd used to beat himself up over the last year flew through his mind. Every name he'd called himself, every truth he'd known and lie he'd believed. He'd bought into every single one of them.

Until Violet. Until she'd made him believe that his past choices didn't define him.

He knew even she didn't buy what she was peddling in this moment. He had made promises. He'd promised to protect her, and there wasn't a time limit on that. With every embrace, with every kiss, he'd promised her.

"You don't believe I don't care about you." He grabbed her by the shoulders, afraid she'd walk away before he could make her agree.

"Prove it."

There was only one way he knew to do that. He hauled her against him, slipping his arms about her waist as he pressed his lips to hers. Her icy shield melted in the time it took a flame to flicker, and they were consumed by the fire. His whole body simmered with life, tingled with light.

It was Violet. For him it was always Violet. It would only ever be her.

His heart thundered, smashing into his rib cage, threatening to steal his breath. As if something so menial could make him pull away.

Violet's hands laced behind his neck. Pulling him closer, she murmured against his lips. They weren't really words. Her sweetness filled him until he thought he might burst.

Until he wondered how he could ever do life without this infusion of verve and bliss.

He had to stop thinking about the future and memorize the here and now. The way her lips pushed and tugged on his, gentle and impossibly soft. The way she smelled of coconut and glazes and something entirely, sweetly her own. The way she hummed a little tune in the back of her throat when he kissed her. He could almost match it note for note now, his rumble lower but no less satisfied.

Brushing one hand over her cheek, he tried to memorize the shape of her face, the rise of her jaw, and the hook of her ear. She shivered under his touch, and he smiled so hard he broke their contact. He blinked just in time to see her eyes squeeze shut even further, and he pressed a kiss to each eyelid, then to her nose and each cheek.

Finally, he whispered against her lips, "I'm going to miss you most of all."

"Then don't go." It was more breath than words, and they shook him to his core. He'd heard those words before from Oliver. But his decision was the same.

"I'm so sorry that I hurt you. I never meant to. But thank you."

"For what?" She still didn't open her eyes.

"For letting me love you—even for a little while."

With that, he picked up his bag and did what he did best.

"I think we're just about ready."

Violet nodded at her mom, then set a platter featuring a large outline of the island onto a display stand, brushed her hands together, and stepped back. She'd spent nearly every minute of the last thirty-six hours dusting and sweeping and reorganizing until the shop shone.

If she'd thought it would distract her from the hole in her heart, she'd been wrong. Even now, she tried to smile at her mom but found she'd forgotten how to use those muscles.

This ache deep inside was different from loss. She knew that feeling, knew the sharp pain and the slow road to healing. This was different. This was about being left.

"Honey, are you all right?" Her mom reached for her, wrapping an arm about her shoulders.

"I'm fine." That was the story she'd keep telling herself until it was true. Or at least until she could say it without a tremor in her voice.

Her mother's eyes turned knowing, her lips dipping with understanding. "Is this about Eli?"

"No. Nothing like that. We were just—" She choked on the word *friends* and couldn't get it out.

"Violet, I know it's been a lot of years, but I'm still your mom. Tell me what's going on. Maybe I can help."

Violet pulled away and straightened a wide-based mug so that it matched the same angle as the rest of the row. Perhaps she stared at it just a little too hard. But if she let herself focus on anything else, she was going to fall apart.

"Is he someone special?"

Stupid Eli. He wasn't supposed to be. Then he went and ruined her, being all chivalrous and kind and compassionate and true. And kissing her silly.

She knew why he thought he had to leave. She understood why he'd gotten on that bus. But it wasn't the only way to protect them. There had to be another way. There had to be a way that saw them together.

But the more she wished there was, the more her eyes burned and the harder her chest seized on silent sobs.

"Come here, sweetie. Sit with me for a minute." Her mom tugged her toward a small group of folding chairs that Levi had set up in the corner of the room, "for those who need a little rest," Mama Potts had said.

Violet fell into a chair, her mother gently alighting in the one beside her. Her mom adjusted the single string of pearls at her throat, then held perfectly still.

All while Violet flew apart. She thrashed at the tears tumbling down her cheeks and chomped into the lip that insisted on quivering. "I'm so-orry. I'm sorry."

"Oh, honey. Don't be sorry. I hate seeing you like this, but I understand. Your father and I broke up once. We'd been dating for a year, then I went off to uni, and there were all these amazing guys, and I thought maybe I'd tied myself down too young. Then I realized that none of them cared about me—cared for me—the way your dad did. The way he still does. The truth is that life is hard. But it's easier when you have someone willing to walk through the hard times with you."

"But he left," Violet whispered. "He wasn't just my friend—I mean, he was my friend. But he was more."

Her mom reached for her hand, pressing it between both of her own. "I know. After you experience loss—real loss—you begin to recognize it in others. You see the signs and you know the ache. Some people let loss make them bitter—angry at God, angry at the world. For others, loss builds empathy and compassion. But you have to let it. You have to trust that God will get you through. It might not feel like it today, but he will."

Violet took a shaky breath.

"Maybe this isn't the right time, but your dad and I have been talking. We want you to know that you have a home with us. If you want to come back to Montreal, you can stay with us, or we'll help you get a job and your own place."

How sweet that offer—how tempting that choice. She could go. She could leave every painful memory of Eli behind and go.

Only, she'd done that once. And leaving the pain also meant leaving what she loved—Mama Potts and the studio, Oliver and Meg, and sweet Levi. Leaving would mean giving up the girls on the team she'd come to love and the salty sea air and the gentle pace of their little village.

"Can I think about it a little bit?"

"Of course. Whatever you want to do. If you want to stay, great. If you want to come home, we would love that. We just want to be part of your life. Would that be all right?"

Violet threw her arms around her mom's neck and held on for all she was worth. "That's what I was hoping for when I sent that invitation."

twenty-three

Eli felt like warmed-up leftovers that had been sitting on the counter just to grow cold again. His back ached—definitely a by-product of the lack of lumbar support on first one bus, then another, then the train seats—and his brain was foggy from little more than catnaps for a day and a half. He felt every one of his thirty years—and another fifty for good measure. He'd sounded like an old man when he talked to the girls. Today he felt like one too.

But getting on that bus was still the right decision. He'd keep telling himself that until he believed it.

Dragging himself down the aisle, he made his way toward the exit. After more than a full day of travel, he'd forgotten what fresh air smelled like. Except the air outside the train terminal—the air in New York—didn't smell like the sea and sunshine. He'd forgotten so quickly the odor of exhaust and cement and people that permeated the city.

A longing for the island struck him so hard, he missed the last step getting off the train and landed on his hands and knees.

"Hey, dude, you okay?" A passenger yanked on his arm.

Eli scrambled to his feet, brushing the city off his hands. When he turned to thank the other guy, the man squinted.

"You're Eli Ross, aren't you?" He mumbled an oath. "You lost me a lot of money." He called Eli a few choice words and stomped off.

"Welcome to New York," Eli mumbled to himself, hoisting his bag over his shoulder and stumbling toward the train that would take him to JFK. Once there, he fell into an empty seat, and the young woman two down from him wrinkled her nose and glared at him.

Pulling his collar up to his nose, he took a stealthy sniff. All right, it wasn't great. He hadn't had a shower or changed his clothes in almost two days.

Letting his head fall back, he stared at the ceiling, closed his eyes, and tried not to see Violet's face. He tried not to see how she glowed when he held her, when he kissed her. He tried not to think about how all of her broken pieces fit so well with his.

It wasn't like they were made for each other or like she was the only one who would ever understand why he'd done what he had. And it wasn't like she needed him. She was just fine on her own.

But she did know him. She might be the only person who really knew him.

Sure, like Mable Jean had said, God knew him—God knew all of it. Maybe one of his gifts had been providing Eli with someone who wasn't afraid of what he'd done.

Violet was anything but afraid. No matter what he'd told her, she hadn't been scared off. Maybe he'd been trying to scare her a little bit. He'd wanted to see what it would take to make her leave.

Only, she hadn't. He had.

His stomach twisted and his head spun. Leaning forward, he rested his elbows on his knees and pressed his face into his hands.

He was doing this for Violet. It was all for her.

Except he'd gone and broken her heart. She was right. He'd promised to protect her, and instead he'd hurt them both. No matter his motives, the result wasn't what either of them wanted. He didn't want to live half a dozen time zones away from her or—God forbid—never see her again. He didn't want to pretend that he wasn't head over heels for her.

He wanted to see her smile. Every single day. He wanted to hold her and kiss her and—if he was lucky—be the reason for her saucy smile.

The train stopped at a station, and a mom led her six kids on board, their dad bringing up the rear. "Stay together," she chirped, holding the hands of the two littlest. The kids were stair steps—all with their mom's curly hair and their dad's olive coloring. They looked at the train like it was an adventure, inspecting the seats and the railings, gawking at the passengers—both those who ignored them and the ones who stared back.

"All right there?" the dad asked the mom. He pressed a quick kiss to her cheek, and she beamed at him. "All together?"

Eli felt like he was intruding on a private moment, but he couldn't look away. And he couldn't stop wondering which of his features his kids would carry and which ones they'd get from Violet. Because he didn't want kids with anyone else. He wanted her.

Forever. Always.

So what if his dad had walked out on him? That didn't have to be his own story. He could stay. He could fight for what he wanted. He could find another way.

There had to be a way to pay Tony back, an option that he couldn't come up with on his own. Violet had been right. He hadn't asked for help from the one person who knew what it was like to take on his dad's debts. Mama Potts had done it, and she'd thrived.

Maybe leaving wasn't the answer.

Stay together. The mom's words to her children echoed in his ears.

He'd thought leaving was the only way to protect his family, but what if they were stronger together? What if they could protect each other?

He'd tried to solve his dad's problem on his own, and that had turned into an unmitigated disaster. Now he was trying to solve another problem by leaving behind everyone he loved—and saddling himself with an unspoken favor to Jett that could be worse than Tony's threats.

Stay together.

He needed help. And he needed it from people he trusted. From people who wouldn't let him fail again.

The subway doors began to close. There would be more stops. But now that he'd made his decision, he couldn't wait another minute.

Eli skirted the family, nodded to the dad, and leapt onto the platform. Just in time.

By the time the bus stopped along the highway a mile from Victoria's harbor three days later, Eli had exactly one drop left in his tank. And somehow he had to make it last until he could get to the Red Clay Shoppe. Until he could explain to his mom that he'd wasted her bus money just to end up in the same place.

The wind shifted, and he caught a whiff of himself. Five days on public transportation. No shower and no fresh clothes. He needed to get home first. Before the party started. Before he saw Violet. Before he convinced her to stay with him—that he was going to stay with her. For as long as she'd let him.

He ruffled his greasy hair, feeling all kinds of nasty as he picked up speed and tried to run along the shoulder. It was more of a stumbling trot, and he could only sustain it for a few feet before his legs threatened to crumble.

The low rumble of a truck behind him grew louder, and he threw out his thumb even as he kept walking. The truck slowed, and he turned his head to see his youngest brother laughing at him through the open window of the old rust bucket.

"Took you long enough," Levi said.

"Yeah, well." Eli shrugged the shoulder beneath his bag. "The train doesn't run on my schedule. I'd have been here a whole lot sooner if the train to Moncton ran more than once a week."

Levi motioned with his chin for him to get in, so Eli pulled open the creaking door, hopped up, and slammed it closed behind him.

Levi's face twisted in pain. "What are you wearing? Fish bait?"

Eli shrugged. "Can you take me home? I need to get cleaned up before . . ."

"Violet?" Levi's question wasn't in line with the gossips trying to collect all the juicy tidbits. In fact, Eli had a feeling it had very little to do with him and a whole lot to do with Levi's concern for Violet.

"I'm in love with her. And if she'll have me, broke and stupid—"

Levi grunted in agreement.

"I'm never going to leave her again."

Levi turned onto the road that led into Victoria and picked up speed as he flew toward the house, the white church steeple in the distance as the shoreline rushed toward them. He skidded onto the dirt driveway and slammed on the brakes right at the kitchen door.

Eli jumped out of the truck, but before he closed the door, he looked up at his little brother, so quiet, sometimes shy, but always right where he needed to be. "How'd you know I was coming back today?"

"Didn't." Levi shook his head. "But I hoped."

Eli couldn't hold back his grin. "You're a good man, Levi."

"Go take a shower."

He raced inside, tossed his bag on the floor, and loped up the stairs. He was halfway to the bathroom when a shadow stopped him midstride. He looked up into the watery eyes of his mom.

"Are you back? For good?"

"Mom." The word came out on a sigh, and he rushed to

scoop her into a hug. "I'm so sorry I left." He set her back down gently, only then noticing that her wrist brace was gone. "Does the doctor know you took that off?"

"He says to be careful, but I'm back to normal activity. And I can use my wheel again."

His face felt like it might break under the force of his smile, but he couldn't stop. Until he remembered what he still hadn't told her.

"I saw Dad. About a year ago. He came to me—he was so far in debt, and the bookie was threatening his life. And I . . . I took on his debt. It was so stupid. I thought we could be a family again—that if I helped him out, maybe we could be father and son again."

As he spoke, Mama Potts's smile dipped and trembled until it disappeared. "I'm so sorry, honey. I wish that your father was the one you deserve. But he's not. I'm just sorry he hurt you again."

"How'd you know he disappeared again?"

"Because that's what he does." She reached for his hands and squeezed them tight. "It's like he forgot how to fight for the things worth fighting for. But you, Eli—you're worth fighting for. And I hope you're here to fight for what you want."

His ears burned, and he cracked a smile. "Violet. I'm here for Violet. And for you and Oliver and Levi. I want us to be a family."

"We are family."

Would she still want that when she knew about Tony and Bobby and the fifty grand that he could no longer pay back? He'd called Jett and told him to tell Latvia he wasn't coming.

The money that was going to be wired into his account—poof. Gone in an instant. Jett had sworn in a length and volume that Eli had never heard before, but he had no regrets when Jett promised there would be no more favors. Eli didn't need those kinds of favors, even though he'd given the ten grand back to Mable Jean.

Things were going to get sticky real fast. But if he wanted to be part of this family, he was going to have to be real. About all of it.

The words rushed out of his mouth. The games he'd fixed. Getting kicked out of the league. Selling every single thing he owned. What he still owed Tony. The threats. How he worried that Tony would take it out on the shop—or worse, the people Eli loved.

When Eli finally stuttered to a halt, Mama Potts's eyes were wide, her hold on his hands somehow stronger. "That's some story."

"I'm sorry I brought this back to you. You've already had to deal with Dad's debts once, and here I am bringing you more to worry about. But I'm going to figure it out. I'll get it taken care of."

She nodded slowly. "It seems like it might be too big for one person to take on. But you're one of us."

"One of who?"

"Well, you're part of this community now whether you meant to be or not. You're a coach and a teacher to those girls. A friend. A son. And I don't mind saying that Mable Jean is hoping you'll marry her niece."

He snorted. "What are you talking about? I've never met her niece." And if he ever married anyone, it was going to be Violet Donaghy. Not tomorrow or next week or even next year. But she was his only. His one.

"Okay, well, Mable Jean's niece notwithstanding, this town loves you. They've always claimed you as their own, and they were all the more eager to when I told them you needed some help."

His stomach dropped. "How did you know?"

Mama Potts offered a Cheshire grin. "Your brother Levi has a big mouth."

Eli laughed. "No, he doesn't."

She shrugged and shook off his argument. "Maybe not. But he is a good listener, and sometimes he reads between the lines and knows when someone's asking for help—even when they're not."

If his brother had been there, Eli would have hugged him.

"He didn't tell me everything, but enough. I knew you needed fifty grand. And if I had that kind of money, I would give it to you, no questions asked. But I don't."

A battle deep in his gut pitted hope against fear. But really, there was only one question to ask.

"How much did you manage to scrape up?"

"All of it."

He nearly swallowed his tongue. "But how?"

She shrugged. "I asked."

"Who? The bank?"

She laughed off his remark, as though he didn't need to know who he owed his freedom to. "I went to some friends—and wouldn't you know that just about everyone wanted to chip in to make sure you stayed in town? I mean, with you around, the Stars might actually have a winning season next year."

But there weren't enough people, even with the surrounding communities. There just weren't enough people to raise fifty thousand dollars in five days.

"Mom." His voice had been grated, but the urgency remained intact.

With a quick glance around his shoulder toward the bottom of the stairs, she pressed her hands to her mouth as the seconds dragged by. Then with a decisive nod, she said, "This family has enough secrets. We don't need another one." Grabbing his hands in hers, she squeezed them with more strength than he'd thought she was capable of.

He was an idiot. Of course she was strong. She had held their fractured family together when first her husband, then her oldest son, walked out. She had waited for Eli to reach out—for eleven years. Then she'd welcomed him back into her fold. Those weren't the actions of the weak or bruised.

That was love. Tested. Tried. Unfailing.

"They didn't want me to say anything. But before Levi even told me about your father's debts, he and Oliver were pooling their money."

"But . . ." They weren't rich. In fact, no one in town was. Victoria by the Sea was a modest community of fishermen, artists, and actors.

"Oliver's been saving for years to buy Whitaker fishing, but now that he and Meg are engaged . . . well, Walt signed over the business to him last month. Even after he replaced his truck, there was some money left. And Levi . . ." Her voice trailed off, her smile flickering.

The truth washed over him, stealing his breath. "No. Not

his house," he wheezed. The backs of his eyes stung, and he blinked hard against the sudden tears.

"There'll be other houses." The deep voice snuck up from behind him.

Eli spun to find Levi standing at the bottom of the stairs, his hands on his hips and a crooked smile across his face.

"Only got one—well, oldest—brother."

Eli bounded down the stairs two at a time, devouring the distance between them, and tackled Levi with a hug that threatened to knock them both to the ground.

Levi's dry cough clearly covered a laugh. Eli thumped his back with a full fist.

"Why would you do that?" Eli whispered, his arms still locked around his little brother.

"I wanted you to choose us." There was something more there that didn't find a voice. Levi didn't just want Eli to come back. He wanted him to stay.

The lump in Eli's throat refused to budge after several swallows, and finally he forced his words around it. "I did." *I will.*

Levi pushed back, shoving his shoulder. A dictionary's worth of words worked their way across his features, but finally he just shrugged. "'Bout time."

A soft sniff reminded Eli that they weren't alone and Mama Potts had followed him.

"You okay, Mom?" He didn't turn around.

"Hmm? Yes. I'm fine. Perfect, really." Her hand squeezed his shoulder. "You're home. And I have a surprise for you."

Levi took an exaggerated sniff. "But you should take a shower first."

twenty-four

When the shop door opened that bright Sunday afternoon, Violet turned to tell the arrivals they were early for the party but she'd be happy to put them to work hanging paper lanterns from the ceiling.

Her words were lost as she saw the silhouette of the man in the doorframe. All she could hear was the hammering of her pulse deep in her ears. Every thought vanished except one.

You came back.

For her.

She flew across the store, dodging the shelves, and launched herself into his arms. His whole body was quaking—with laughter or relief, she didn't know. But his smile was wide enough to span the Confederation Bridge. Then he disappeared as she closed her eyes and pressed her face into his neck, letting him spin her in a quick circle.

He didn't say anything—at least nothing she could hear—until he stopped and set her back on her feet. He simply stared at her for a long while, and she understood. She needed to soak up the sight of him, to fill that gap where she'd missed him for days, weeks, millennia.

Finally, he cupped her cheeks in his hands, his fingers combing through her hair. She didn't even care that she'd just washed and styled it and he was probably messing it up. He could mess away anytime he liked.

"What are you doing back? You left."

"I'm sorry. I'm so sorry. I feel like I keep saying that, but I promise, I'm never going to leave you again. I got to New York, and it was like this drum in my heart kept beating, telling me to come back here. Well, mostly it was telling me how stupid I was—am. Everything I want is right here in Victoria—the family I'd hoped to have again, the job that I never knew I wanted, and . . . you. You're here. What was I doing thinking I could solve my problems by leaving again?" He swallowed thickly. "There will always be reasons to leave, but there are so many more to stay. And all I ever needed was one. Just you."

He had a knack for melting her like a popsicle on a hot summer day, and she sank into him, holding on to his shoulders to stay standing. Only when her hands rested against the soft cotton of the blue button-down that perfectly matched his eyes did she realize the shoulders of his shirt weren't too tight, and the buttons closed perfectly. It fit like it had been sewn just for him.

"Where'd you get this?"

He grinned like a schoolboy. "You like it?"

"Yeah, you look great. Whose is it?"

His eyes flashed with humor. "Mine. Just mine."

She laughed, wanting to press her face into his shoulder but hating to spoil his fresh shirt with her makeup.

"Mama Potts figured I'd come to my senses, and she thought I might need something to wear for the party. So she got me a little something yesterday. The pants too." He did a little jig, and her joy bubbled out, unstoppable.

"She has good taste. You look amazing—or maybe it's that I haven't seen you in a little while."

His smile dimmed, slowly at first, then all at once. He reached for her, his thumb tracing the outline of her lips. "Being without you—even for four days—was . . . I can't do that again." He licked his lips slowly. "Please don't move back to Montreal."

She grabbed on to his wrists to steady herself. "How did you know?"

"What?"

"That my parents invited me to come home?"

"How could they not?" His voice was all gravel, hope crushed by fear. "They love you. I met them for three minutes and I could tell. They've been writing you for more than ten years. They weren't doing it for their own sakes. They were doing it for you. No matter what you do or where you go, you'll always be their girl."

She blinked against a gush of tears. "Eli, you can't say things like that. Not when I just put eye makeup on."

His thumb left her lip and brushed away a drop at the corner of her eye. "All right, here's the deal. If you want to go, I'll go with you. If you'll have me. I'll make a life in Montreal. I don't speak French, but I'll learn." He chuckled. "I could join your dad's hockey team."

She threw her head back, her shoulders shaking at the very picture of Eli playing with a bunch of middle-aged men who had never done more than enjoy the game. "I don't want you to move to Montreal. I want you to stay here. *I* want to stay here. My mom and dad are going to be part of my life now. But they can be part of it while I'm still in Victoria. I'm not giving up the shop or my art. And I'm not going to leave Mama Potts or your brothers. They're my family. I already made the mistake of leaving my family once."

"So . . . you're staying?"

"That's what I said."

His face broke with pure joy, his eyes turning glassy as he tried to bite back a smile that was too big to be contained. "Just to be clear—you're going to stay here and I'm going to stay here? And we're going to be together?"

"Yes. I'm going to stay in my apartment. You're going to find someplace to live—preferably someplace where your feet don't hang off the end of the sofa. And we're going to see where this"—she motioned between them—"goes."

He paused for a brief second. "Good. Because I'm in love with you."

Her heart felt too small to contain the joy bubbling inside her. "That works out well." She gave him a wink. "Because I'm in love with you too."

The look in his eyes told her he was going to kiss her, and she could already feel it to the tips of her toes.

Until the door crashed open behind him.

"We heard there was a party and we weren't invited. Bobby was pretty upset."

Eli jumped back, dropping his hold on her face but grabbing her hand to pull her to the safety of his side as he scooted out of the entryway. She tugged on his arm, a thousand questions flying through her mind. If he was here, how was he going to pay back Tony? The bookie's scowl didn't look like he was in a mood to offer another grace period. He had blood in his eyes and the man she loved in his sights.

Well, he was going to have to go through her first. Violet stomped forward no matter how hard Eli pulled on her arm. "You're right. You were—" Her throat turned to cotton as Bobby Moynahan ducked to enter the door behind his brother. The man was a grizzly with a teddy bear's face. His smile was as warm as his brother's scowl was stern. Violet couldn't find her voice in the face of him though.

When Eli whispered in her ear that it was all going to be all right, she took him at his word, sidling back into the cocoon of his protection.

"Tony," Eli said by way of greeting.

"Elijah, Elijah, Elijah." Tony shook his head. "We had an agreement, you and me."

"Yes. We did."

"But the word around town is that you turned down the Latvian job. How you gonna pay me back now?"

Eli opened his mouth, but it was Mama Potts's voice that split the air, sharp and unrelenting. "It's not his debt any longer. I'll be taking it over." Her even steps carried her slowly from the studio door, and she held herself like a queen, neck of steel, chin high.

Tony gave her a hard once-over. "And why would I allow that?"

"Because you can either make an example of my son—which probably isn't going to make you any more money—or you can have your payment. In full. Right now."

Violet's stomach flipped, her face probably reflecting the same surprise that flickered across Tony's. But his expression quickly turned cool. "You've got fifty thousand dollars? Fifty thousand American dollars?"

"In cash." Mama Potts held out an envelope so full that it was about to split its seams. "And it's yours. On two conditions."

Eli's grip on Violet's hand turned fierce.

With a sneer colder than ice, Tony said, "I don't think you're in any position to be making stipulations."

Mama Potts didn't even blink. "When I pay you back, you won't bother anyone in this family ever again. We're fully paid up, and you have no more business on this island."

His eye twitched. "And the second?"

"You'll never take a bet from Jason Ross again."

Tony tried to snatch the envelope from Mama Potts's hand, but she yanked it back. "I want your word."

"You hear that, Bobby?" Tony said in a dandy voice. "She thinks I'm a gentleman."

Bobby's laugh was unexpectedly high-pitched, but Mama Potts cut them both off.

"No, I do not. But you're not the first thug my husband had dealings with. I know there's a code among thieves—rules you live by. And without them, you'll lose the respect of every addict, shark, and ruffian who has the misfortune of running into you."

Violet couldn't breathe. Where had all that gall come from? This wasn't the Mama Potts who had adopted her, who had welcomed her prodigal back into the fold. This was a roaring lion, a mama bear. Tony Moynahan had messed with the wrong family.

"It's all there. Paid in full. Now let's be done with this."

Tony closed one eye, smacking his lips together. Finally he nodded. "Done."

"Antony, wait." Bobby tugged on his brother's sleeve. "I like that plate." His chin pointed toward a slate-blue platter intricately shaped to match the outline of the island, long and slim.

"It's yours." Violet nearly clapped a hand over her own mouth. She'd spent days on that piece, but for the chance to be rid of the Moynahans forever, she'd gladly give it away.

Bobby picked up the platter and petted it like a bunny while Tony took the envelope. He glanced inside. "Good doing business with you."

They left as they'd arrived, loud and conspicuous. When they were gone, Violet could finally breathe again, and Eli's hand around hers began to relax.

"How did you—?" She had only a gaping mouth for Mama Potts, who smiled and patted her shoulder.

"Like I told Eli, he's part of this community whether he wanted to be or not. The people here love him, and it didn't take long to fill up the collection plate—especially with Oliver and Levi chipping in."

Violet shot a look at him. "But they don't know about . . ."

He shook his head. "I told them and Mama Potts all of it."

Violet slid her arms about his waist and held on tight. It had been too much to wish for, too much to set her heart on. Yet God had provided a way for her to have him. Right where she wanted him.

"You came in right on time there, Mom," Eli said.

Mama Potts shrugged. "I guess I did."

"I don't suppose you were listening in." There was a hint of scolding mingled with the laughter in his tone.

"Just making sure you got things worked out," she said.

Violet giggled, and Eli rolled his eyes. "I'm definitely going to need to get a place of my own."

When Mama Potts opened the front door a little later that afternoon, the whole town streamed in. Carson and his wife, Jenny and Dylan, Pastor and Mrs. Dell. Even Sandra Whitaker, who was mostly homebound, was on Walt's arm, a gentle smile in place.

Mr. Huxley escorted Mable Jean, but she unhooked her arm from his as soon as she saw Eli. She marched right across the room, acknowledging Violet with only the briefest nod.

"So you've decided to stay. I put in everything I said I'd pay you when your mother came asking for money. I hope that's earned us at least a few more seasons, Coach."

Eli shook her hand. "Yes, ma'am. Thank you. It's earned you a winning season."

"A winning season?" She practically beamed. "Good. Good. Well then." She bowed away, probably off to find Ellen and the other boosters to tell them.

"That's a big promise," Violet whispered into his shoulder.

"I'll be around long enough to make sure the girls get it."

At that moment, a squeal broke through the chattering voices, and a herd of thirteen- and fourteen-year-old girls charged across the room, weaving between pockets of guests until they stood before Eli.

Madison blinked once, hope shining from every pore. "Coach?" Then she turned to Violet. "Ms. Coach?"

"What do you say, Vi? Want to stay on as Ms. Coach?"

She nodded, and the girls broke every rule in his book, crushing him and Violet in a group hug that left no question about whether he'd made the right choice.

The party could be called nothing but a success, with nearly half the inventory sold—enough to cover the electrician's bill—and requests for many more personalized gifts. Mama Potts reigned over it all, mingling and chatting and bestowing her brightest smile on everyone.

After several hours, Eli itched for a moment of privacy with Violet, a moment where his mom wasn't listening at the door and the rest of the town wasn't pressing into them. Snagging her hand, he tugged her toward the studio door. He slipped through it and closed it quickly behind them before pulling her into his arms.

"Hi," she whispered, her fingers running through his hair, her smile just for him. No complaints about taking her away from her guests. No arguments about sneaking away when they might be needed. She just sighed into him.

"I've been dying to see you."

She tapped his chest. "I've been right beside you the whole afternoon."

"I know, but there were so many people, and I just wanted you."

Her cheeks turned red. "I wanted you too."

Moving toward the nearest worktable, he pulled her with him and sat on the edge, nearly knocking over something he hadn't noticed before. Jumping up, he looked down, trying to make sense of what he was seeing.

Violet pressed a hand to her mouth, her eyes filled with wonder. "Oh my word. Your mom did this."

Suddenly the pieces made sense. All the ruins—the remnants of the fire—had been stacked together, the largest on the bottom to the smallest on the top. A carpet of pebbles fit between each layer of clay, just sparse enough to let each shard's original color peek through. In the center, water bubbled from a vertical pipe, rippling down from layer to layer. A fountain. Never ending.

This was the project Mama Potts had been working on. Something brand-new.

In a hushed voice, Violet said, "Maybe God doesn't always fix what's shattered. But he can make something new and beautiful out of what's been broken."

Eli squeezed her hand, knowing those words were true. "Something like you and me?" He tugged her back into his embrace.

"Something like that."

"The thing is, I know your past. I know what's been broken. But I want to know your future too. What are your dreams? How can I help you make them come true?"

"Right now?"

"Whenever you're ready. I'm not going anywhere."

Fisting her hands into his brand-new shirt, she pressed up on her tiptoes and whispered against his lips, "Prove it."

So he set about doing just that.

one

Meteorologists could not be trusted. At least as far as Levi Ross was concerned. Last winter the guy on the news in Charlottetown had forecasted a light dusting of snow. The snow had reached his knees.

So Levi could be forgiven if he didn't believe the perky blond weather girl who warned Prince Edward Island that an especially early hurricane was on its way. He seemed to be the only person on the south shore who hadn't heeded the advice, ransacked grocery store shelves, and burrowed in at home. Most evenings he saw—and successfully avoided—at least one or two teachers lingering over a test to be graded or a lesson plan to be finalized. Tonight the halls of the county high school were empty, nothing but shadows to keep him company. Just as he liked it.

He usually shared this time with the big orange sun, but the overcast day had given way to a gray sunset. The wide windows of the school's front hallway lacked their typical glow as he pushed a round blue trash bin across the white-tiled hallway.

One of the wheels squeaked, and he made a mental note to fix it for Amos, the usual janitor. Amos, who had called to say he was staying home because of the hurricane.

Levi didn't mind picking up a few extra hours—or the reflection of that on his paycheck. The house he'd dreamed of, the one he'd put an offer on, was gone. Sold to another buyer. Then again, the down payment he'd saved for was gone too. It had been used to rescue his eldest brother, Eli.

Levi barely missed the money. Especially since his brother was back in town to stay. Besides, he could always make more money. And there would be other houses—like the pretty gray two-story Victorian outside of town and right on the water's edge that had just sprouted a For Sale sign in the yard. So, no, he didn't mind putting in some overtime.

He glanced out the window again. Through the dim light he could just make out the trees lining the entrance, their arms bending and swaying to a song he couldn't hear.

Maybe it was better he was at the school anyway. Just in case there was trouble.

At least if he got stuck at the school, he'd be stuck on his own. Eli would be with their mom and Violet. He was always with Violet these days. And Oliver and Meg would be hunkered down in front of the fire in their bungalow.

Levi smirked to himself as he flung open the door to the first classroom on his left. Crooked rows of desks greeted him, crumpled papers a littered path weaving between the metal legs. He stooped to pick up the trash before shooting it across the room into the bin he'd parked at the far wall.

"Three points for the win."

Levi froze, his hand still suspended above his head, his

fingers following the arc the paper had taken. He'd recognize that sweet voice anywhere. He'd heard her perform every single summer at the community theater. From Maria in *The Sound of Music* to Beatrice in *Much Ado about Nothing*, she'd starred in them all. Shone in them all.

Even in the shadow of the doorway—a mile from center stage—Kelsey Ahern very nearly glowed.

He couldn't be any more awkward if he tried as he lowered his hands and offered a shrug and a half smile by way of greeting.

"I thought I had the place to myself," she said and flashed him her straight white teeth. She'd had braces for all of junior high and most of high school, and they had been worth every minute.

With a nod to the waste bin by Mr. Sullivan's desk, he shrugged again.

Brilliant. He sounded like an imbecile. Or, rather, *didn't* sound like a well-read individual with an operational tongue.

Ms. Ahern nodded as though he'd managed to get out a full thought. "Just ignore me," she chirped as she slipped toward the metal cabinet at the back of the room. "Mike said he had some extra copies of *The Count*." After flinging open the double doors, she practically disappeared into the closet, rummaged around, and reappeared with a short stack of paperbacks. Waving the top one at him, she smiled.

The Count of Monte Cristo. Sword fights and duels. Lost treasure and prison escapes. Betrayal and revenge. Levi had read it at least half a dozen times, and it only got better. Her class was in for a treat.

She glanced down at the stack of books now tucked under

her arm, her eyebrows pinching together. "I was going to have them read *The Three Musketeers* over the summer, but the tenth years will be studying Napoleon in their history class. It's the perfect tie-in, but I don't have enough books for everyone in my class. I'm having to change all my lesson plans, but I think it's worth it. Do you think so?" She looked up, hope in her eyes.

Levi blinked at her, not sure if she was looking for confirmation or for someone to tell her to go back to her original plan. He wanted to tell her that he thought it was a great idea. That he'd read a biography of Napoleon after reading *The Count* for the first time, when he was just a few years older than her students would be when they started back in September.

He wanted to tell her that she couldn't go wrong. That all she had to do was show her students she cared about them.

He wanted to tell her that her smile lit the hallways—long after the students went home for the day. That he actually looked forward to seeing her, hoped every evening that he'd stumble upon her singing to herself in the drama room.

But since he'd managed to say exactly five words to her since the start of the school year almost ten months before, he settled for lifting a single shoulder and picking up the trash can he'd come to empty.

"I'm sorry." She shook her head but didn't make a move toward the door. "I'm sure you have better things to think about than my lesson plans. It's just that I doubt Mrs. Davis ever second-guessed herself when we were in school. I don't want to fail these kids—I mean, do the wrong thing for them. I don't want any of them to fail my class either." Her cheeks turned a pretty shade of pink, and she rolled her eyes—likely at herself. "I know, I know. I'm sure it's just second-year jitters." As she readjusted the books in her arms, her shoulders rose and fell like she was letting out a deep sigh.

But the sound was drowned out by a rush of wind that shrieked past the building. The windows rattled and the floor shook. In that instant, rain hammered against the roof, angry and sullen.

Ms. Ahern's eyes flashed wide, and she hugged her books to her chest. "I guess maybe the weather girl was right," she whispered, as though raising her voice might incite the wind again. "Should have gone home early today."

Levi nodded, tearing his gaze from her and watching the torrent against the windows. The sky had been merely gray only a few minutes before. Now it was black, sinister. He couldn't see to the parking lot beyond. He couldn't even see to the trees he'd planted a few meters from the building three years ago.

A gust rattled the windows again like the storm wanted to be inside too.

His gut twisted. He took three cautious steps backward.

Ms. Ahern let out a little peep, a sound of uncertainty mingled with something like fear. But when he turned to look at her, she was wrestling her features into something that he called "teacher face." No nonsense. In charge. Unflappable.

Every teacher at the school had one. Hers just happened to make his skin tingle and his breath catch.

"Well . . ." She nodded toward the hallway and her classroom beyond. "I guess I better—"

"You're not leaving." He blurted it out like a command, not

the question he'd intended. He didn't know which of them was more surprised that he'd spoken.

Ms. Ahern blinked quickly, her mouth opening and closing, but nothing came out.

He wanted to clarify. It wasn't safe. She could be injured. The roads could be flooding, her car swept away. The best thing they could do was wait out the storm. Right here. Together.

Well, together-ish.

Now that he'd actually spoken—and so poorly at that—he wanted to disappear into his work and pretend she'd never walked into this classroom.

She blinked those big brown eyes again—slowly, thoughtfully, as though trying to pick from the glut of words she could unleash on him. Finally she said, "No." She paused. "I won't. I'm going to go back to my classroom now."

She left him to his trash bins and litter and enough self-chastising to rival the downpour outside.

Kelsey had read the same paragraph four times, and the sentences still didn't make sense. Probably because the letters quivered and ran together, blurring words and sentences into a collage of lines that made absolutely no sense.

She rubbed the heels of her hands against her eyes and then blinked hard. It didn't help.

Maybe the rain was too distracting. It had bypassed a simple pitter-patter and instead snapped and popped like an angry fire. Just when she'd thought it might let up, the wind had whipped through the courtyard on the other side of the windows, roaring its displeasure.

She looked behind her into the darkness beyond. There wasn't much to see except the reflection of the classroom lights in the window, nothing but midnight blue on the other side. She pulled her sweater tighter around her shoulders, a shiver snaking its way down her spine.

But it wasn't really the weather keeping her from the book in her hands. This was perfect reading weather—even if she wasn't curled up in front of a fire with her favorite Shakespearean-insults mug filled to the brim with hot cocoa. She couldn't blame her lack of concentration on the time either, although a quick glance at the clock above the whiteboard confirmed that it was well past her pajama hour.

The words on the page weren't making any sense because every time she tried to read them, three little words echoed louder in her mind.

"You're not leaving."

Levi Ross hadn't said so many words to her in a row since they were kids. And certainly never with such conviction. His voice was deeper than she'd remembered, more resonant.

If only he could teach a few guys in her drama class to project so well. Of course, that would require him to speak. Publicly.

Maybe he did speak privately. But that begged the whole "if a tree falls in the forest" question.

She was supposed to be working on vocab and comprehension questions from *The Count* for next term's tenth years. She was not supposed to be daydreaming about Levi and his soft smile and deep dimples and rich voice.

She had more important—

Her world exploded with a crash of shattering glass. There was no time to investigate before something shoved her to the floor, pressing her face against the icy tiles and pinning her arms beneath her. She gasped for air and only managed to choke on the water pelting her. Whatever had pinned her snagged her cotton sweater as she tried to wiggle free. But she stopped on a scream as something cold and sharp sliced into her back.

"Help." She gasped and sputtered and tried again. "Help me." She couldn't make her voice any louder. Not without air.

Breathe. Just catch her breath. That's all she needed. Then she'd be able to get up.

She tried to capture a full breath, but an elephant had taken a seat on her back.

All right. She'd get up. Then she'd breathe.

Pressing her palms flat against the floor, she pushed with everything inside her. Every muscle, every cell in her body trembled. Hopeless.

The classroom lights flickered high above. Once. Twice. Then everything went black.

There was nothing except the unending pinpricks of rain as they bit into her legs and the painful shriek of the wind rustling leaves. Right next to her ear.

All the pieces rushed together then. The tree outside her window had come down. It had crashed through her window. That was what was pinning her down.

She was in a fight with a tree.

She was pretty sure one of her drama professors had made her act out this exact scenario in an improv class. The tree had definitely not weighed this much. And her legs hadn't gone numb, which they most definitely were at the moment. Probably from the cold. Maybe from paralysis.

That was ridiculous. She was not paralyzed. She was—as her mom liked to say—imaginative.

A sudden rush of footfalls echoed down the hall outside her classroom, and she tried to call out.

"Ms. Ahern? Are you still here?"

Six words. In a row.

She'd never heard anything sweeter.

"Help." It wasn't more than a strangled whisper, but a beam of light broke the darkness, sweeping across the floor. Blinking against its brilliance, she tried to wave at him but couldn't get her arm free.

It didn't matter. He was there in a moment, coaxing the elephant off her back until she could gather a whole breath. Sweet oxygen. Sweet air. Sweet breath.

Levi grunted, and she twisted just enough to see that he was still holding the tree above her. She should crawl free. As long as she wasn't paralyzed.

A few quick scoots confirmed that she had full use of her chilled extremities as she untangled herself from the twigs and branches.

The tree collapsed behind her, and then she was scooped up, held against his chest, surrounded by his warmth. Levi Ross was better than a heater, and she shivered as she curled beneath his chin.

In a blink she was being set down on the sofa in the teachers' lounge, carefully deposited in an upright position. Two electric lanterns magically appeared, bathing them in a soft glow. Levi flipped his wet hair out of his face as he squatted before her, his blue eyes filled with worry.

"Blank-ket?" She couldn't keep her teeth from chattering.

He nodded quickly and disappeared outside the circle of light, then returned moments later with a throw that looked scratchy but warm. When he squatted again to tuck it around her legs, she stopped him with a hand on his forearm.

"I want to wrap up in it."

The muscles of his face twitched, and he shook his head slowly, pressing a hand to the outside of her left shoulder. Maybe it was his heat that made pain shoot down her back, but she wasn't holding out hope. A twist and a glance confirmed her doubts. A jagged piece of glass jutted out from her shoulder, a red smear slashed across it.

So, she was impaled and bleeding. And she was probably going to pass out. Perfect.

A tree with a nefarious agenda? She'd survived.

Possible paralysis? She'd figure it out.

A single drop of blood? Nope. Just nope.

She squeezed her eyes closed and sagged into Levi's shoulder. His flannel shirt was soft against her forehead and smelled like rain and wood shavings.

"Ms. Ahern?" He spoke in a quiet tone, his voice flush with concern but still calm, as he slipped an arm around her side to hold her up.

Her head spun, her stomach on a roller coaster without end.

This was going to get embarrassing. Fast.

Acknowledgments

Some books feel like they write themselves. Some are birthed kicking and screaming. This book was definitely one of the latter. It seemed the longer I thought about it, the less I knew what to write. But in his faithfulness, God made a way. And he provided many wonderful people to help me find these words.

Rachel Kent and Books & Such Literary Management, thank you for believing in my stories. Thank you for believing in me. Thank you for your steady guidance and calm assurance for more than a decade.

The amazing team at Revell makes every one of my books better and helps each one find readers like you. I am eternally grateful to Vicki, Jessica, Michele, Karen, and the rest of the team. Thank you for helping me tell my stories well.

For the Panera ladies, my fellow writers, who walk this journey with me. Thank you, Lindsay Harrel, Sara Carrington, Jennifer Deibel, Sarah Popovich, and Erin McFarland, for your brainstorming and your input, your kindness and your encouragement. This group is even sweeter than a Panera cookie.

To the Circle Chicks, whose prayers and support sustained me in the dash to finish this book on time. Dawn, Jennifer, Beth, Kathy, Neicy, and Rhonda, may God continue to answer your prayers in miraculous ways.

A special thanks to Jennifer Zarifeh Major, who often answered my questions about hockey and Canada. All mistakes are entirely my own.

A word to the ungrateful little boy who goosed me during a public skate while he tried to stay on his feet: you're welcome. Thanks for giving me the idea to put it in this book. And a huge thank-you to all the lovely staff and handsome hockey players at AZ Ice Peoria, where I spent several hours almost every weekend while brainstorming and writing this book.

For my family, who loves me enough to lace up skates of their own and join me on the ice. God gave me an extra blessing when he made me a Johnson. Being a part of this family is the best.

Finally, I owe all my gratitude to the One who knows the depths of my heart and loves me anyway.

Liz Johnson is the author of more than a dozen novels, including *Beyond the Tides*, *The Red Door Inn*, and the Georgia Coast Romance series, as well as a *New York Times* bestselling novella and a handful of short stories. She works in marketing and makes her home in Phoenix, Arizona. But she wishes she could live on Prince Edward Island—at least during the summer.

Escape to
PRINCE EDWARD ISLAND . . .

"A charming inn in need of restoration, Prince Edward Island, and a love story? Yes, please! I thoroughly enjoyed the vicarious visit to the Canadian Maritime Province of Prince Edward Island. I could almost feel the sea breeze!"

—BECKY WADE,
ECPA bestselling author of the Porter Family series

Revell
a division of Baker Publishing Group
www.RevellBooks.com

Available wherever books and ebooks are sold.

Meet LIZ JOHNSON

LizJohnsonBooks.com

Read her BLOG

Follow her SPEAKING SCHEDULE

Connect with her on SOCIAL MEDIA

- Share or mention the book on your social media platforms. Use the hashtag **#TheLastWayHome**
- Write a book review on your blog or on a retailer site.
- Pick up a copy for friends, family, or anyone who you think would enjoy and be challenged by its message!
- Share this message on Twitter, Facebook, or Instagram: **I loved #TheLastWayHome by @LizJohnsonBooks // @RevellBooks**
- Recommend this book for your church, workplace, book club, or small group.
- Follow Revell on social media and tell us what you like.

RevellBooks

RevellBooks

RevellBooks

pinterest.com/RevellBooks